Selim Özdoğan was born in Germany in 1971 and has been publishing his prose since 1995. He has won numerous prizes and grants and taught creative writing at the University of Michigan.

Ayça Türkoğlu is a writer and literary translator based in North London. Her translation interests include the literature of the Turkish diaspora in Germany and minority literatures in Turkey.

Katy Derbyshire translates contemporary German writers including Olga Grjasnowa, Clemens Meyer and Heike Geissler. She teaches literary translation and also heads the V&Q Books imprint.

52 Factory Lane

Selim Özdoğan

*Translated from the German
by Ayça Türkoğlu and Katy Derbyshire*

**V&Q
BOOKS**

Creative Europe Co-funded by the Creative Europe
programme of the European Union

V&Q Books, Berlin 2022
An imprint of Verlag Voland & Quist GmbH
First published in the German language as:
Selim Özdoğan, *Heimstraße 52*

© Aufbau Verlage GmbH & Co. KG, Berlin 2011

Translation © Ayça Türkoğlu and Katy Derbyshire
Editing: Isabel Adey
Copy editing: Angela Hirons
Cover photo: Unsplash
Cover design: Pingundpong*Gestaltungsbüro
Typesetting: Fred Uhde
Printing and binding: PBtisk, Příbram, Czech Republic

ISBN: 978-3-86391-328-1

www.vq-books.eu

I

It's quiet.

Much quieter than Gül had imagined.

You can get everything there, they'd said – her mother-in-law, her stepmother, the neighbours – *and it's all much better than here*. That's why Gül had only brought her cardboard suitcase with her.

She'd boarded the train in Istanbul, a noisy city where everyone seemed to have something to do, where the voices of street vendors mingled with screeching train brakes, the braying of a donkey with the rattle of a carriage overtaken by a car.

This must be what it's like in Germany, Gül had thought, *just not as many animals, and even more people.*

At the stations where she'd had to change, she'd been afraid of not finding the right train and getting lost in some unfamiliar place. This last station is so small that Fuat, standing on the platform, looks taller than she remembers him, though he's lost weight – there's nothing left of the belly he put on in the army. In fact, it's the opposite: his cheeks are sunken and even his hair seems thinner now.

Gül clutches at him, relieved that someone is there to hold her, someone who knows the way. As she feels his body, her mind wanders back to the image of Ceren crying as she said goodbye at the foot of the stairs in her in-laws' house.

Fuat's mother Berrin was holding her, a child of almost three kicking and screaming as her tears flowed and she scratched at her face and grabbed at her head, tugging out tufts of hair while Berrin tried to get a grip on her little arms. Ceyda, who will soon be six, stood next to her grandmother, seeming to grasp less than her sister the meaning of that goodbye. *Ceyda is a good girl, obedient and hard-working*, Gül thought, as she stood there at the foot of the stairs. *She's a clever girl, she'll make the best of the separation.* But Ceren is still so little, and even though Gül makes no distinction in her love for her children, part of her heart stayed right there, forever tied to Ceren's screaming, scratching and writhing, things she's too old for now. That's how she will remember Ceren over the next 18 months.

But right then on the platform, the image vanishes when she frees herself from Fuat's arms. He takes her suitcase, and they walk together along empty-looking streets. Gül can't imagine any people inside the houses, even though there are lights behind the curtains.

They hear the faint buzz of a flickering streetlamp.

Fuat asks how the journey was, but Gül doesn't want to tell him how scared she was at the stations. Not this man, who could hardly wait to come to Germany, who left behind his wife and daughters without a backward glance, for longer than the year they'd planned. She doesn't want to tell him she hadn't been able to do her business in that stinking, cold train toilet for the past three days, nor how much joy and relief she felt when she saw him on the platform.

'The journey was long,' Gül says, 'like the journeys in fairy tales.'

'Oh yes, it's a long way by train. We'll fly back, God willing. It's quicker than taking the bus to Ankara, you'll see.'

He was right, Gül thinks when she sees the flat. It's a single room with a big bed, a bedside table, a single wardrobe and a chest of drawers; there'd be no space for anything else. There's a small kitchen with a table and two stools, and a tiny hall.

'The toilet's in the stairwell,' Fuat says once Gül has put her suitcase on the bed. 'Come on, I'll show you.'

Her in-laws had an outside toilet and there was no flush like there is here, but she's never seen such a tiny flat. She thought

Fuat was exaggerating as usual when he said there was no room for children here, even if they slept standing up in the wardrobe.

'I've got to go, time for work,' he says. 'I'll be back in the morning.'

Gül closes the door behind her husband, sits down on the bed and opens her suitcase. A pair of shoes, a pressure cooker, two dresses, underwear, two skirts, a cardigan and very little else.

Why lug along cheap tat from here, they said, *when you can buy nice things there?*

Gül wants to put her clothes away, but when she sees the mess the drawers are in, she simply tips them out onto the bed and starts sorting the contents. Once she's finished with the drawers and the wardrobe, she makes her way into the kitchen and lights a cigarette, a Samsun. She smoked almost two packs on the journey, and there's only one last cigarette left after this one. She pulls her feet up on the stool and leans against the wall; there's a small mirror above the sink. Gül gets up to look at herself. She still looks exactly like she did in Turkey, but she doesn't feel the same.

The feeling inside her is bigger than the image in the mirror. Perhaps that's why she feels like such a stranger.

She wakes up the instant she hears the key in the door, and she immediately knows where she is. She leaps up, greets her husband in her nightshirt and puts the kettle on in the kitchen. Fuat's eyes are small and red; he doesn't talk much over breakfast, only nodding at the stories Gül tells of home. When he's finished eating, he takes a bottle of whisky out of the fridge and pours three fingers into a tumbler. Gül stares in amazement.

'Oh yes, that's how it is,' he says. 'Whisky, real whisky like in the films. You can make real money here – and look what you can buy for it!'

'But so early in the morning…'

'So what? I've been on my feet all night long – I deserve a little drink after work.'

And he tops up his glass, as if in defiance.

Fuat sips silently at his drink while Gül washes up. She's still in her nightshirt and hasn't been to the toilet yet.

'Aah,' a satisfied sigh escapes Fuat's lips after he takes his last determined slug of whisky. 'Come,' he says, leading the way to the bedroom.

Once Fuat falls asleep, Gül washes his glass, dries the dishes, puts the kettle on for another tea, and lights her last remaining cigarette. She takes out the newspaper clippings she collected over the past few weeks and puts them on the table.

She's been using these clippings to learn the German words for door, day, week, time, street, apple, house, key, breakfast, lunch, bed, chair, table, trousers and skirt. Words she found difficult to remember, and which were of no help with the German customs officers.

Back home they'd told her she would have to go through Customs, but the word had sounded strange to Gül, even in Turkish, and was linked in her mind with the image of a brightly lit corridor dotted with men in uniforms, guns heavy by their sides.

She hadn't imagined the man with a black moustache, who took a pack of cigarettes out of her coat pocket, then put her suitcase on a table, opened it and searched inside. He seemed to be asking questions too, but Gül simply shrugged and stared back at him. The words *Tür, Haus, Tag, Woche, Apfel* she might have recognised, but the only one she guessed was *Zigarette*, which sounded similar to the Turkish word.

None of the words Gül knew helped her to say: *I don't have any more cigarettes. The ones in my coat pocket are my last pack.*

She could probably just have said, *Nein, Zigarette*.

But eyes and real life helped where language was not enough.

Gül goes over all the lessons she's learned from the newspaper, then she writes a letter to her father and one to her mother -in-law, has another glass of tea and smokes another cigarette, which she's pinched from Fuat's pack and which tastes completely different to the ones she's used to. She looks out of the window, cleans the two rings on the electric hob, empties the cupboards and wipes them down before filling them up again. She smokes another cigarette and gazes out of the window a while. The streets still seem empty, but they look clean, as if they're swept every hour.

Fuat wakes up around two that day, wanting his breakfast. At about four, Gül goes outside with him, to Germany.

The two Greek men who live opposite work alternating shifts and share the flat because it's cheaper that way. Above them live a Greek couple, and a Spanish couple and their child. There's only one apartment on the ground floor, and it's home to an old German couple who hardly ever go out.

The Spanish couple's son's name is Rafa, as far as Gül can tell. He looks around eight years old, and he has to stay home alone when he gets in from school because both of his parents work. Gül watches from the kitchen window as he walks home with his satchel on his back. It won't be long before he's back outside the door to the flats, peering upwards. Every day they play beştaş, a game with five pebbles, which Gül has taught him. They sit on the step outside the front door, and Rafa teaches her German words. The words for stick and stone, for skin and bone, for head and heart, for pen and paper, and many more. After five days or so, Gül realises Rafa has passed on all the words he knows. When she points to a motorbike, the nameplates by the doorbell or her shoelaces, the boy simply shrugs.

For several weeks, they sit outside the front door in the afternoons playing beştaş together – a schoolboy and a woman in her early twenties, mother to two daughters. Sometimes Gül talks at him in Turkish, and sometimes Rafa speaks Spanish to her. She enjoys this hour or two before she heads back inside to prepare Fuat's breakfast.

At the weekends, Fuat often leaves the house at the same time as he would for work. 'What else am I supposed to do?' he says. 'It's not like I can sleep.'

And he comes home about the same time his shift would usually end. Sometimes he's so drunk that he throws himself on the bed fully dressed and seems to find sleep of some sort instantly. But mostly he's so drunk that he pulls Gül out of the kitchen into the bedroom or tugs up her nightdress if she's still in bed. He never comes home sober.

While he sleeps, Gül sits in the kitchen without any book, radio or newspaper to speak of; the days don't quite know how to pass. At the weekends, she can't even reckon on Rafa standing outside the front door and looking up at her kitchen window.

But Fuat and Gül do go out on Saturdays and Sundays, to meet up with others who have come from Turkey. There aren't any Turks living on their street, but there are a good fifty of them in the area. They're often young men, like Fuat; some are unmarried, others have left their wives and children behind in Turkey.

Ozan lives nearby with his wife Nadiye and their son Ergün, and both Fuat and Gül like visiting them. Fuat, because Ozan likes a drink as much as he does, as they put it, and because the two of them are keen gamblers, bound by their love of making a quick buck. And Gül, because Nadiye seems like a woman with a good head on her shoulders, someone who knows exactly what she wants, though she's even younger than Gül. Sometimes Gül finds her a bit cold, like when she talks about her older sister's first son.

'He was almost two years old,' she says, 'and he was often sickly, but they thought he'd pull through. But then he had a bout of diarrhoea that had him in the ground in the space of a week. Maybe it was better that way. May the Lord keep others from suffering the same pain, but the child just wasn't tough enough for this life. He wouldn't have made it much further. You can't expect to be rubbed down with rose water every day in this world.'

Maybe that's just how people are in that part of the world, Gül says to herself. Nadiye and Ozan come from the Black Sea region, and Gül sometimes has trouble understanding them at first.

'I got to know Turkey when I was in the army,' Fuat says. 'Kurds, Circassians, Alevis, Georgians, the ones from the mountains, blond chaps from the Aegean, fancy Istanbulites, men from the Black Sea coast with big noses, all the people of our country. And you're getting to know them here in Germany. This is your military service,' he says, laughing.

Neither of them suspects that this period of service will last well over fifteen years.

Nadiye's son isn't one yet, but already she's heavily pregnant again. Gül wonders what will become of these children.

Gül has been in Germany for almost two months when she realises her period is late. She spends the first few days fretting and hoping, but one morning Fuat comes home and finds her crying in the kitchen.

'What's happened?'

'I think I'm pregnant again.'

Fuat just looks at her. Gül can't say whether it's the hope of a son she sees in his eyes, or happiness, or even disappointment.

'I came here to work,' she says. 'What are we supposed to do with another child? Am I supposed to leave it with strangers, like we did the girls? Will this one have to grow up without a mother, without a father?'

'Are you sure?' Fuat asks.

'No,' Gül says, knowing full well that her period's been late before and her husband has almost always been careful, no matter how drunk he's been.

'We'll talk to a doctor, then.'

Nadiye has to see the doctor too, because it's only a matter of days before the baby is due. The doctor explains to her and her husband, by drawing on a piece of paper, that the baby hasn't turned around and they're going to have to perform a caesarean. Nadiye will need to spend a few days in hospital.

The doctor who examines Gül doesn't use drawings to help her understand. Gül is shy around this grey-haired old man, who seems a little doddery and is constantly groping in his shirt pocket for his glasses, which are propped on his head. She doesn't understand a word he's saying.

When they're out of the surgery, she asks Fuat: 'Yes or no?'

'You heard what he said.'

'And how was I supposed to understand what he meant?'

'He said *baby*, didn't he? Surely you've heard that word before? What's not to understand?'

Gül holds back the tears until she gets home, and then a little longer, until Fuat has left for work.

'What am I going to do with this little one?' Nadiye says. 'I can't exactly take him into hospital with me. Would they give Ozan time off, do you think? But what's the poor man supposed to do with a child all day? Oh Gül, life's so much harder when you haven't got your people around you, looking out for you.'

'I can look after Ergün,' Gül says. She can tell from Nadiye's eyes that she hadn't reckoned on her offering to help, or even wondered if she might. Nadiye's look of surprise makes Gül want to give her a hug. Hers is a pure heart.

'You're mad,' Nadiye says. 'You don't want to be lumbering yourself with a kid at the moment.'

Gül hasn't told her about her pregnancy. Has Nadiye sensed something's not right?

'Don't be silly!' Gül says. 'Just give Ergün to me, you know I've got two children of my own and you can't go leaving a baby with your husband; he's here to work. He wouldn't like it and you know it.'

'What's all this in aid of? What are we supposed to do with an infant?' Fuat scolds. 'You know I need my sleep. As if it weren't enough that I work nights and you're always making noise, now you want to bring a child into the house, is that it? You and your ideas. It beggars belief.'

While her husband sleeps, Gül sits quietly on her stool in the kitchen or plays with Rafa. She can't do anything about the fact that her husband wakes up when a plane flies past overhead. She even tries to light her cigarettes quietly.

'We won't disturb you,' she says now. 'You won't even hear him; we'll be in the kitchen the whole time and you won't hear a peep.'

He's your friend's son, she could say. *Why are you acting like it's nothing to do with you? It's our duty to take care of this child.* She could say that, but then he'd get even more wound up.

'Not a peep, you say? He's a baby! You don't know when he'll scream and when he won't, are you having a laugh? *Not a peep.*'

He sticks a cigarette between his lips and sucks the smoke in angrily.

Where do I get these ideas? Gül thinks. *I wait in the kitchen all day long for my husband to get up, there's no space at all here, my own children are far away, I'm pregnant again, and I get it into my head to look after someone else's child. But what else was I to do?*

Gül is lucky. As it turns out, Ergün is quiet during the day. Every morning, once Fuat's gone to bed and she's finished washing the dishes, she carries the little boy in her arms to visit his mother. The hospital is about ten minutes away, and Gül is still scared of getting lost when she goes out on her own, but she only needs take two turns before she reaches Nadiye.

Ergün is quiet during the day thank God, but at night, at night while Fuat's at work the child cries. He stirs, and at first, only makes enough noise to wake Gül. But as soon as Ergün sees her face, the face of a stranger and not his mother, he starts wailing and almost nothing calms him down.

Which is probably why Gül starts to cry soon after him.

'See,' she tells the baby. 'That's life for you, we can't change it. My children and I have been separated, too, and I'm not happy about it either.'

She cuddles the little boy, hugs him to her chest, and they cry together through part of the night until Ergün falls asleep, exhausted.

'That's life for you,' Gül says. 'Soon I'll have another child and there'll be many more things I never would have wished for.'

The first time Gül drank alcohol, it was liqueur that she drank in her mother-in-law's kitchen, liqueur that the many guests who visited during Eid had turned down, and which tasted better with every sip. Eventually, she grew queasy and threw up. The following morning, she threw up again and thought it was the after-effects of the alcohol, until her friend Suzan explained that she was probably pregnant.

With her second daughter, Ceren, she had only felt sick in the mornings two or three times, and now in the mornings with Ergün, before Fuat gets home, she doesn't feel great – her eyes are swollen, she hasn't slept enough, her mind is on her daughters – but she doesn't feel bad.

After four nights she takes Ergün back to his mother, and at home, in the toilet in the stairwell, she discovers a big dark-red stain in her white knickers.

'I came here to work,' Gül says. 'That was the reason. Not to spend all my time sitting here in the kitchen, so far away from my children. We wanted to earn money.'

'You didn't want any money,' says Fuat. 'You always refuse when you're offered it.'

He's replaced the stools in the kitchen with chairs now, and he even managed to get hold of an old armchair that just fits next to the door, where he's sipping whisky and Coke.

'I didn't do it for money,' Gül says, 'I did it to please God. It's not right to earn your bread from other people's need. We're in a foreign country, we have to stick together.'

'Money's money,' Fuat says. 'You'll never be rich until you understand that.'

'Well, I can't exactly go to Nadiye now and say I do want it after all,' Gül says.

'We'll never get enough saved if you keep working for everyone for free.'

'I want a proper job,' Gül says.

Fuat twists the glass in his hand and takes another sip.

'Look,' he says, 'everything in this country has to be done just right. You need a permit for everything. They let you come here because you're my wife. And they have a rule that you have to have been here for six months before they'll give you a work permit. Without a work permit, you can only work off the books, and that's not easy. I'll see what I can do, alright?'

Fuat knows his wife is a hard worker. Back in Turkey, she asked him to buy her a sewing machine so she could contribute to the family's income. He was sceptical at the time, but the investment soon paid off.

He already has an idea of what Gül could do. It may seem like the rules in Germany are different to Turkey, but Fuat knows you've still got to be smart if you want to make it. People who follow the rules don't get far. Wherever you are, you have to keep an eye out for opportunities and people who can level your path.

Two days later, Gül finds herself at the conveyor belt of a chicken factory, plucking chickens for eight hours a day. She has a fifteen-minute break for lunch, and she's allowed one visit to the toilet on each side of the break.

The first night, Gül dreams of those naked and half-naked chickens, pink flesh as far as the eye can see. Flesh, flesh and more flesh; the smell of blood, and the faces of the men whose job it is to pull the heads off the slaughtered birds. Half-formed eggs removed from the meat, feathers floating on the air. In her dream, the seas fill up with naked, dead chickens and threaten to flood the land.

The second night, her dream is much worse.

Ceren has got into trouble and Gül has to rescue her, get her out of somewhere, free her. She has to be there for her daughter; she has to reach out her hand and help, but Ceren keeps slipping away and every attempt is in vain. Gül kicks and struggles and tries, she toils and travails, but Ceren slips away from her in a maelstrom of fear and angst; Gül simply can't get a grip on her.

It's four thirty in the morning when Gül wakes up, more than an hour to go before Fuat comes home from work. She gets up, the images pale but the feeling of the dream painted in such stark colours that her hands tremble as she sits down at the kitchen table with pen and paper. She writes a letter to her mother-in-law: *Is something the matter with Ceren? Is my daughter healthy? Has something happened to her? Write back, please write quickly. Don't leave me wondering.*

She makes breakfast for herself and Fuat, but the dream has her trapped beneath a bell jar of anxiety. No matter where she goes, no matter how she moves around the kitchen, something is cutting her off from the world. Something is behind her, above her, inside her, and even when she doesn't think about it, she can feel that it's there.

She sticks a stamp on the letter, one of the many Fuat bought for her, along with paper and envelopes. 'What are you planning to do,' he asked, 'write a letter a day? What do you want with twenty stamps at once?'

'Yes,' she told him. 'Every day or every other day, perhaps every third day, but I want to keep writing – it's the only way we can stay close to each other.'

Gül posts the letter on her way to work, and the bell jar around her grows a little thinner; a little air gets through to her anxiety and one or two clear thoughts form in her mind, but then she's back at the conveyor belt plucking chickens, with scraps of last night's images in her head and the weight of the dream still pressing down on her.

People say light as a feather, she thinks as she rips out the down, *light as a feather – they must have come up with that one long before they had chicken factories.*

Just before lunchtime, the man who showed Gül the ropes two days earlier comes rushing in. Herr Mehl is a skinny man with glasses, whose upper body always looks like he's leaning forward, and whose wrinkled neck reminds Gül of a turkey. Behind him are two women and one of the men who pulls the heads off the chickens.

'Quick, quick, quick, an inspection!' Herr Mehl says, dragging Gül away.

She works out what's going on.

In Istanbul, Gül had seen street hawkers running away from the police with big trays covered in simit. She'd felt sorry for the traders; they earned their money by the sweat of their brow, but if the police caught them, their sesame rings ended up trampled in the dirt.

Herr Mehl runs into the walk-in refrigerator with the four workers. Gül has to hide in a big box that she only fits into if she draws her knees up to her chin. She's curled up so tightly that she can't even see how many hands are covering her with plucked chickens.

If anyone looks in the box they'll see me, with or without the chickens, Gül thinks as she waits there, feeling the weight of the meat. And: *At least the simit sellers were outside in the fresh air.* And: *I did forget the dream for a moment, though.*

Two hours, she could have said, *two hours I spent in that box in the walk-in refrigerator. It was so cold that it froze the marrow in my bones, I had no feeling in my fingers or in my toes. Two hours I spent there with those cold, dead chickens on top of me. It's not like being in a house where you've run out of coal. It's not just the cold; there's the fear too. How was I to know what would happen if they found me? For all I knew, they might take me to the police station, put me on a train and send me home. I can't speak the language, can't even tell left from right in German; what would I have done, trembling at a police station, exposed, fished out of a box of dead chickens?*

Two hours. The idea of exaggerating a little only occurs to Gül later. Doesn't Fuat always say you've got to be smart in this world, so you don't go under, so you don't lose out?

'About twenty minutes,' she says. 'About twenty minutes I spent there, hardly daring to breathe, worrying they might see the steam coming out of my mouth. I don't want to go back there.'

'You can't choose where to work if you haven't got a work permit. You can't even choose *with* a work permit.'

'I don't want to go back there,' Gül says. 'Who knows when the next raid will be, and I don't want to get pushed around police stations and courtrooms half-frozen to death. I'm not going back there!'

To her surprise, Fuat nods. Perhaps her last words sounded determined enough, perhaps what she says makes sense to him, perhaps he has an inkling of what it feels like to lie in a box of dead animals.

'I'll keep an ear out,' he says, and it sounds like all he has to do to find her another job is listen out for a minute.

At the end of the orchard at Fuat's parents' house is a little swimming pond, about fifteen feet long and four feet wide. When Fuat stands in it, the water comes all the way up to the thick hair on his chest. The pond is somewhere pleasant to cool off on hot summer days, though it's an effort to fill it with water from the well and it's two days before the water is warm enough to get in. In the space of two weeks, the pond's cement walls are covered with algae and the water is full of duckweed.

Ceren had been sitting at the edge of the pond, dipping her hand into the water and playing with the streaks of green, when Meryem called over from the next garden. Ceren's grandmother, Berrin, who was sitting by her side shelling walnuts, stood up to have a natter with her neighbour over the wall, which only came up to her waist and ran between the two gardens.

While the two women were talking, Ceren fell into the water. She thrashed, gasped, cried out, gulped water; the three-year-old girl who, just weeks ago, had scratched her face because her mother had left her.

Once, Gül fell through the floor of the cellar in her mother-in-law's house, into a covered hole that had been forgotten for some time. Back then, Berrin had ignored Gül's cries, not realising what had happened.

This time, she realised right away and ran over to the pond. The duckweed repulsed her, she had never been in the little pond before and was no better a swimmer than Ceren. It took a moment for her to conquer her fears and step into the water.

Meryem had climbed over the little wall and was peering into the pond, watching as Berrin attempted to grab hold of her floundering granddaughter. Three or four times Ceren slipped away from her and then, when Berrin thought she'd finally got a hold of her and lifted her out, Ceren hit out in her panic, slipped on the duckweed, and fell back into the water, wriggling about more panicked than before.

Now Meryem jumped into the pond too. She was a little bolder than Berrin, and together the two women managed to heave the little girl up onto the edge, where she coughed and cried and kept on kicking.

So that's what had happened.

You've got a very good inner voice, Berrin writes. *Even in a foreign country you sensed that something wasn't right. You should be proud of your mother's intuition; it binds you to your child.*

Gül will often ask herself whether she was a good mother to her daughters. And Ceren, unlike her mother and her grandmother, will learn to swim.

Gül's first day at the dressmaking factory is behind her when she receives the letter from her mother-in-law. That morning, she turned up for work an hour late.

First they had to get the bus, then board a tram. 'Keep your wits about you,' Fuat had impressed upon Gül on their way into the factory in Bremen. 'Remember the route. And don't be surprised: places aren't as far apart here as they are at home. You can travel from one town to the next in half an hour.'

Gül tried to concentrate when they got off the tram, paying attention to all the landmarks she saw along the way. *Turn right at the building with the sign that starts with an A*, she murmured to herself a few times over. *Oh, it's an Apotheke, a pharmacy – so, right at the pharmacy, then keep straight, then go left at the big crossing.* The crossings here were all bigger than she was used to, but she had never seen one quite as big as this before. *Keep straight until you get to the end of the wooden fence, then go right.*

The building, when they eventually went in, was huge, a world away from the chicken factory. They even had a Turkish interpreter on site, Nermin, and Gül had thought she'd be more relaxed here. This was somewhere she could work; there was a translator, and she wouldn't be in a fix just because she couldn't speak the language.

She hadn't been daunted when she saw the room full of dressmakers sitting at electric sewing machines, all the piles of bras. She hadn't even wondered if she'd be up to the task of using an electric sewing machine – she thought it had to be easier than having to pedal all the time.

It's just getting there that's the tricky bit, she said to herself. And as if he wanted to prove precisely that, Fuat had got lost in the building's corridors.

'It beggars belief,' he grumbled. 'It's as if they build these factories just to confuse us. These rich men, they don't want us to see what's really going on. What sort of corridor is this? Where does it even lead? There's not so much as a sign – I expect they charge extra for that.'

All weekend, Gül walked the route to work in her mind over and over; *Get the bus first, then the tram with the number 6 on it. Get off at the street with the long name made up of two words, the first one beginning with F, the second with M. Walk back in the direction the tram came from, then turn right at the chemist's …*

I'll manage it, she kept telling herself, but she felt uneasy all weekend and started awake again and again on Sunday night. As if it wasn't enough that she was worried about Ceren, as if the horror of the dream wasn't still creeping into her waking hours.

But it seemed the more she traced the route in her mind, the less she was able to remember it. It was a big city, Bremen. What would she do if she got lost? She had been scared enough in Istanbul, and everyone spoke her language there.

On Monday morning, she sat on the very edge of her seat on the bus counting the stations, deep in concentration as she looked out of the window. She got on the right tram, couldn't find a seat, but she kept looking out, constantly, and counted backwards: *four more stops to go, three more stops, two more, one more.*

She walked back in the direction the tram had come from and turned right at the pharmacy, then took the left turn at the big crossing. She walked and walked and walked, but the wooden fence never appeared. She had been on the right street; she'd recognised everything up to this point and had taken the correct turning both times. Something told her she should have passed the wooden fence by now, but it was nowhere to be seen.

Just to the next turning, she'd said to herself. *Just one more, or perhaps it's the one after that, or the one up ahead, might that be it?* She had been walking along the same road for twenty minutes before she decided to turn back. She felt hot and her breathing was going faster than she was.

She was confused; she couldn't explain what had happened. *Fuat got lost too, in the factory*, she tried to reassure herself, but she simply couldn't understand where she'd gone wrong.

Until she came to the point where the wooden fence must have been before. *Oh, what a fool I am*, she scolded. *What a clod!* A building stood there, so new it almost gleamed; the fence had been hiding the building site.

Building sites and construction pits aren't fenced off in in Turkey, that's why I was so foolish, she thought. But it was obvious that this was where the fence had been. *If we had fences like these in Turkey, Orhan Veli wouldn't have stumbled into that hole and died*, she thought. *He'd still be alive and could have given us more poems.*

She got to work almost an hour late. Her forewoman, a tall, well-built woman who reminded Gül a little of a horse, simply shook her head and pointed at a vacant sewing machine.

Sonja – that was the woman's name – sat down at the machine herself and showed Gül what to do. Gül nodded, then she sat down and took Sonja's place.

She trod carefully on the pedal, and the needle rattled away. The machines Gül had used before were mechanical; she'd had to use her feet to keep them running.

Gül thought of her first ever time at a sewing machine. She was thirteen years old and had left school early, and her father had sent her to Esra the dressmaker to help out. Back then her short legs barely reached the pedal, and she hadn't many other skills, either.

Bit by bit, though, she had learned to sew, and now, after spending a few minutes getting used to the electric machine, the work seemed like child's play.

Her movements were always the same, so she hardly needed to think, and after the first hour her hands did the work automatically. The needle ran smoothly, she didn't have to coordinate her hands and feet, and if it weren't for the noise of over a hundred machines, if it weren't for her worrying dream, if it weren't for her shame at arriving late, her fear of perhaps not finding her way home – it might almost have been pleasant.

During the break, Gül saw the other women on the machines take something out of their ears. Toilet paper. It was a good idea, so she decided to go to the toilet and get some for herself. She didn't want to go on her own; she might not find her way back to the hall or she might get lost on the way there. She looked around but none of the other women looked Turkish. *That one over there might be Spanish or Italian, that one definitely looks Greek. And that one.* And a few other faces stood out to Gül. *It's funny how quickly I've learned to tell the Germans and the non-Germans apart*, she thought. *If only there were a few more Turkish people around.*

Sonja came up to Gül, who was standing stiffly in the corridor, looking unsure. She put a hand on Gül's shoulder and said something Gül didn't understand, but because she smiled, Gül smiled back. It was as simple as that.

'Tuvalet?' Gül asked.

The German word was so similar that Gül just couldn't remember it. She regretted saying it as soon as the word left her mouth. She'd have to find her way back as well.

'Komm,' Sonja said.

Standing outside the toilet stalls, Sonja made two sounds at once: a low *Aaah* from her mouth and a loud *Pfff* from her guts.

Gül stared at her in shock. She'd never heard an adult fart with such lack of inhibition. It was one of those things that simply weren't done. You weren't supposed to cross your legs in the presence of elders, smoke in front of them, or return borrowed plates and bowls empty to friends and neighbours. Women weren't to curse, at least in mixed company, or go out in the street half-naked, and you weren't supposed to break wind in public.

Sonja laughed when she saw the face Gül was pulling.

'Luft,' she said, slapping her abdomen, 'It's just air, you have to let it out.'

Gül hurried on the toilet to make sure she finished before Sonja. She tore off two sheets of toilet paper and put them in her pocket.

The rough paper in her ears made the noise easier to bear, and Gül worked and thought about farts, this strange country, Ceren, the way home. She thought about how much money Fuat had probably lost at cards over the weekend, what she would earn here, whether they had raids in this huge factory, and where they'd hide her if they did.

Sonja kept popping over, taking a quick look over Gül's shoulder, nodding and taking the finished bras away. When the shift ended, she beckoned Gül over, and Gül recognised the interpreter with the Istanbul accent, alongside the forewoman.

Oh dear, she thought, *they're unhappy with me – I did turn up late on my very first day. And I bet I didn't work fast enough – I've been lost in my thoughts for the last few hours. Or maybe I didn't do the sewing how they wanted it. That'll be 200 bras that need throwing away now. Oh dear.*

'Good afternoon,' Nermin said. 'How are you?'

'I'm well, thanks be to God. And yourself?'

'Fine, fine. Did you have any problems today?'

'No. Yes. Well… I couldn't find the way. It won't happen again.'

'Don't worry about that,' Nermin said. 'What did you do in Turkey?'

'I was a housewife.'

Just because she'd had a sewing machine at home, that didn't make her a dressmaker.

'A housewife,' Nermin repeated with a smile. 'Do you know how many bras you sewed today?'

Gül shook her head. *Oh dear.*

'312. And do you know how many the others manage?'

I bet it's over 500, Gül thought.

'I'll tell you. The fastest workers manage about 380. And you were almost an hour late. We do piecework here, which means you can earn a lot of money. Sonja's very pleased with you, she told me to say so. We can always use good workers like you.'

Then Nermin said something to Sonja in German. She had a proud, almost arrogant air about her, this Nermin; she looked like a rich young lady from the upper classes with her nylon stockings and bouffant hairdo, with her skirt that barely grazed her knees. No doubt she had a good life in Istanbul. Gül couldn't imagine what she was doing here, so far away from home. Or what she was looking for.

Gül would have liked to be glad that they were pleased with her, but she was worried about the journey home and troubled by her thoughts of Ceren, which had grown less frequent but lost none of their urgency.

It was only when she got home, when she saw the opened letter on the kitchen table and read it, that something warm and gentle flowed through her body, making her heart grow light. For the first time since she'd come to Germany, so it seemed.

'Hats for the fat twins,' Fuat said. 'So that's how we'll earn our money. You'll be on time tomorrow, I bet.'

Hats for the fat twins was what the street hawkers shouted when they were selling bras in Istanbul.

'And as soon as we've got enough money, we'll get a bigger flat and bring the girls over.'

'God willing,' Fuat said, but it sounded more like: *We'll see.*

Certain that Ceren is alright, that nothing has happened to her daughter, and with the prospect of living here with her children, Gül is no longer worried about travelling to work the next day.

Future happiness is always the simplest kind, she'll say one day. But no one would lift a finger were it not for that postponed happiness.

Fuat believes in future good fortune, in winning the lottery or having a long lucky streak at cards. He believes in dividend payouts and interest. He often sits at the kitchen table, adding things up out loud. 'If I won this or that amount at the weekend, then invested part of the money, bought a car, a plot of land in Turkey, laid foundations for a house, got on the property ladder… I could get whisky delivered by the crate. I could charter planes and arrange flights to Turkey – no trouble at all with a bit of capital – and in the summer holidays I could multiply that money by investing such-and-such an amount, budget in this or that much for expenses, such-and-such a percentage as a profit margin…'

Perhaps he could have been a mathematician, Gul thinks. *His head's always full of numbers.*

Friday is payday and the women line up to receive their pay packets. Gül hasn't got lost on her way to work all week and has turned up on time every morning. In the evenings, her head drones with the sound of the machines. The toilet paper isn't much help after all, nor are the cotton plugs she made from a pair of Fuat's old underpants.

Once they've been paid, the women stand around chatting and counting their pay.

'There are four other Turkish women working in this hall,' Nermin had explained to her.

Now Gül compares her wages with theirs. And though she thought she would get the most money because she'd sewn the most bras, it turns out she has the least.

Her head's full of numbers now, too. She tries to work it out, to find some explanation. *I did only finish my basic schooling*, she thinks, *but something's not quite right here. Nermin said I broke the record yesterday: 391 bras. Surely that means I should get more money – more than anyone else, if it's the record.* 'Piecework,' they'd said, explaining to her what that meant, and then…

'Ask them, something's not right here,' the other Turkish women urge her. Gül goes to the man who hands out the pay packets.

Maybe I've miscounted, she tells herself, even though she's counted three times. *Perhaps you need to have worked here for longer first, or perhaps there's something else I've missed.*

'Little,' she says to the man, showing him her pay packet.

She feels uneasy, like she's demanding something that's not rightfully hers. If the other four weren't standing there watching her curiously, just a few metres away, she would probably just make a gesture as if to say, *Oh, forget it.*

The man counts her money, then he nods.

'It's all there,' he says.

'Piecework,' Gül says, 'I many piecework.'

She feels hot, like she's done something wrong, but she can hardly back down now.

The man nods again and beckons Nermin over. He speaks to her briefly but emphatically, and for a moment Gül thinks she sees a glimmer of delight in the interpreter's face. Then Nermin turns to her with her big-city accent and her painted lips.

'You're working here off the books. You don't have a contract like the others, you don't have a work permit. He says they can't pay you like they do the other workers. They're taking a risk by having you work here.'

Gül looks at Nermin and then back at the man, who nods in agreement as though he's understood every word. Then she looks at Nermin again. *Something about her bothered me right from the start*, Gül thinks, *I might not be a student, but I'm no fool either.*

'You told me yourself just this Monday gone that I'd earn more if I sewed so many bras.'

'But… at that point I didn't know that you were working illegally.'

Gül nods.

'Next week, then…?'

'I'll see what I can do, but you're bound to make more next week if you keep working the way you have been.'

On the tram home, Gül thinks about the times when Melike would bully her into following her into the furthermost corner of the garden while she smoked. If Gül was there with her, she wouldn't be able to tell on her sister for smoking. And later,

Melike would always let her have a drag. *A little sweetener*, they called it. The words keep running through her head. They were children then. And they were sisters.

Once she's put her pay packet on the table, she says to Fuat, 'I don't want to work there any more. They're paying me less because I don't have a work permit. I spent four days sewing more bras than anyone else in the factory, and I got the least money. I'm not a mug.'

'But that's good money,' says Fuat, counting the notes and coins, then slipping them in his pocket.

'They're just using me, I don't want to go back.'

'Oh I see, using you, are they? What else are they supposed to do with you? Night after night I work at that factory, I never get any proper sleep, all of us here are grinding away like oxen. It's not like it is in Turkey, where you can coast along and have a natter and a glass of tea. It's not a funfair here – you have to work.'

'I've got nothing against work, but they're shafting me,' Gül insists.

'So I'm supposed to trot off and find a job that's more to your liking, am I? Sure, I've got nothing else to do! Why don't I spend the whole day searching for a job that really takes your fancy?'

He pushes his plate away.

'This slop, every day,' he says. 'Can't even get a decent meal in this country, and now my wife's being fussy about her work. It beggars belief, it does.'

He can be short-tempered, unfair and cruel, and sometimes he's unpredictable, but he rarely swears. Where other men would curse, he always says, *It beggars belief.*

'You're dreaming,' he tells his wife, 'You're dreaming. You've got a husband who's slaving away every night, but you still haven't woken up.'

He gets up, slams the door and leaves.

Gül can't help that Fuat doesn't like the food, but she feels guilty all the same. She's not that keen on it either, but she doesn't know what to do about it. She came here with a cardboard suitcase because they have everything here, and yet there are lots of things she can't buy. Where they live, there's not a single butcher who sells lamb, let alone garlic sausage like sucuk. She seldom finds garlic anyway, and she gets the feeling it's sold by the clove, not the kilo. She rarely finds fresh chillies, and the grocer has weights as small as 100 grammes by his scales. There's no pepper paste, but they do have tomato paste in the kind of tubes used for shaving cream or toothpaste in Turkey.

'They like to tease newcomers with that tomato paste,' Fuat explained. 'Tomatoes in a tube, no one would believe it; tubes are for things that belong in the bathroom. So they hand the new chaps a tube and say, "The Germans have this shaving cream that gives you a proper shave. Your face'll be as smooth as a baby's bum, you won't look a day over twelve." And when I say it, as a former barber, then there's real weight to it,' Fuat brags. 'So these poor lads smear the tomato paste over their faces, and the prats are none the wiser, so they take a razor to it. It beggars belief. And you're standing there, egging them on: "Go ahead, go on – don't be surprised by the colour. It's got an ingredient in it that stops the blood, that's why it looks the way it does." As if that makes any kind of sense.'

He laughs as if he's known the score since his first days on this earth.

They don't always find things they're familiar with here, but some of them find fruits with names they've never heard before. A man from Kars, who can't read or write, gives Fuat a banana.

'You can't eat the seeds,' he warns him. 'They're poisonous.'

And the fool chews away on the peel and says, 'Doesn't taste all that great if I'm honest.'

They'll still be laughing about it years later.

'Ozan had a moped before you came,' Fuat explains. 'But he crashed it, and all because of some aubergines.'

'It's market day and he's driving along on his moped, then suddenly he sees a stand on the other side of the road, and he thinks he's dreaming. It's full of aubergines, the first he's seen since he's been in Germany, big and plump, deep, dark, almost glowing purple. Ozan slams on his brakes, ready to turn around and buy ten kilos of the aubergines. Then the car behind goes into the back of him. God saved his life, but the moped was a write-off. That evening, Nadiye made karnıyarık with the aubergines. It was the most expensive karnıyarık anyone's ever eaten; it cost a whole moped.'

Fuat laughs when he tells these kinds of stories, but when he sits down to eat, he moans. No decent white cheese, no good olives, no rose jam; you can't buy anything here and the canteen is the worst; the Germans only seem to know two spices, salt and pepper; and there's never any bread to go with the food. The bread you can buy does seem to be made of dough, but that's the only thing it has in common with the bread in Turkey.

'What do they actually do in there? How come the bread never tastes any good?' he asks Gül, who has started working at a bread factory in Bremen.

She never went back to the dressmaking factory. A few years later she'll sit at one of those machines again, for two weeks, working off the books again because she has a permanent job elsewhere. At least this next time she'll be paid well – so well that it'll be worth taking two weeks' sick leave from her usual job. She'll use the company's production shortage for her own ends, and it will give her great satisfaction. Sonja will recognise Gül and laugh and pat her belly as she farts, and Gül will say, 'Yes, I know – you have to let it out.'

But right now she's working at the bread factory, and she can't tell Fuat what they do to the bread there.

'I'm at a different station almost every day,' she says. 'Sometimes I'm here, sometimes I'm there; I just go wherever they need someone. It's not a bakery; it's a factory. I don't even understand everything that goes on there, how am I supposed to know how they make the dough? And they're just used to different things here – they have lots of kinds of bread, but they don't recognise the sort we have. They don't know flatbread, or village bread, or winter bread, or thin bread. But their bread rolls taste a bit like our bread, don't you think?'

'Bring some of those home with you next time, then.'

'There aren't any where I work.'

'There must be some, it's a massive factory,' Fuat says. 'As usual, you haven't a clue.'

'That's what I'm saying. It's a factory; it's bakeries that make bread rolls, isn't it?'

'You're talking nonsense. Bakery, factory, wherever – there's just no decent bread here.'

Fuat pushes his plate away and lights a cigarette.

'At least these taste better than they do at home,' he says. 'They're still looking for people to work at the factory, and there's this woman, Saniye, who's looking for work. I told her to get to the bus stop in good time tomorrow. You'll spot each other easily enough. Take her along with you.'

Gül looks at him. Couldn't he have phrased it differently? Couldn't he have asked her? It's not like she'd have said no. At least this Saniye woman won't have to worry about finding her way.

Gül doesn't find the factory work difficult. Once you've learnt the ropes, everything else is easy. She doesn't even struggle when she has to do lots of different kinds of tasks, which she's only briefly shown how to do. Gül can tell they're happy with her work. Her head doesn't drone with the noise of the machines in the evenings, and she earns more than she ever did at the dressmaking factory. And the words *a little sweetener* no longer flit through her mind.

She's happy for this Saniye, even though she's never met her.

The next morning Gül instantly spots Saniye, though she looks very different to how she had imagined her. Saniye has red hair and is slightly shorter than Gül but much thinner. Gül hasn't lost the weight she put on when she was pregnant with Ceyda; she has grown rounder and fuller. Saniye is so slim she looks almost fragile, but somehow her hips seem wider than Gül's. Her face is covered in freckles and something in her eyes catches Gül's attention. They look sad and stubborn at the same time – but then all of a sudden, those same eyes are laughing and Gül wonders whether she might have been wrong about them.

'Thank you, sister,' Saniye says. 'Thank you for taking me with you. May I pay all my debts to you.'

'How long have you been here?' Saniye asks on the bus.

'Not quite four months. You?'

'Oh, don't get me started! I've been here for two months. I went to Hamburg first, but I didn't like it. I was always afraid there for some reason, maybe because it's by the sea. How did you picture Germany? Did you think it would be like this?'

She gestures out of the window.

'I didn't picture much at all. I thought it'd be like Istanbul, only a bit more modern.'

'And I imagined it would be like in the movies, you know, where they come home and throw themselves on the bed with their shoes on, in their big tidy houses. Don't ask me why, but I've always wanted to walk in with my shoes on and then lie down on the bed, light a cigarette, and fold my arms behind my head. That's how I imagined Germany. And then you end up in a hostel where the beds are even worse than back home, and you don't feel like leaving your shoes on!'

Saniye laughs, and Gül can't say whether it's a sad or a happy laugh.

'So you came here from Hamburg, just like that, because you were scared there?'

'Yes. And because I'd heard there were people here from Malatya, like me.'

'What did your husband say?'

Saniye looks out the window and shakes her head.

'I haven't got a husband,' she says.

Gül wonders what a woman on her own might want here.

'Where in Malatya are you from?'

Saniye says the name of a village Gül has never heard of.

'What are you doing?' Saniye asks.

'I'm stamping my ticket.'

'But that's this morning's ticket.'

'So?'

Saniye laughs.

'We need a new ticket – we can't go back on the same one.'

'But then I'd have to pay twice as…' Gül begins, before a feeling tells her Saniye is right. A feeling that makes her cheeks burn.

Saniye hasn't been here as long as she has, but already she seems to know her way around better. She doesn't seem to be afraid, either.

'Where's Hamburg?' Gül asks Fuat that evening, while he's putting his shoes on to go to work.

'Hamburg, why are you asking about Hamburg all of a sudden?' Fuat snaps, with no apparent reason for his vehemence. Gül is shocked but tries not to let it show.

'Saniye was there before she came here. She said it's by the sea. How far is it from here?'

'Just over an hour.'

'Is there really a sea in Germany?'

'Hamburg's not by the sea,' Fuat says. 'It's just got a port, that's all.'

'But there is a sea?'

'Yes of course there's a sea. Where else would the ships go? Any more questions, or can I get to work on time?'

In Gül's imagination, Hamburg is now a city a bit like Istanbul. *Would I be scared to live so close to the water?* she wonders.

It's not just water Saniye is scared of.

'Come on, let's have another ciggie,' Gül says on their way home a few days later, glad to have a companion by her side. They turn down a side street. Gül will never drop her habit of smoking in secret, her whole life long. She's never smoked a cigarette in front of Fuat, though he might not mind. And she's never smoked in broad daylight before, like German women do.

The two of them stop by a low wall with bars along the top at chest level. A front garden is visible through the bars. They put their bags down on the wall, take out their cigarettes and are about to light them when an Alsatian comes hurtling their way, barking loudly.

Gül and Saniye take a few shocked steps away as the dog barks at them through the bars, its front paws on the wall. Gül's heart is beating so fast she can barely breathe.

'Are you scared of dogs?' Saniye asks.

Gül nods. She can't speak; there's a wild thudding in her throat.

'Me too. Especially big ones like that.'

Their bags are still on the wall.

'What should we do?' Gül asks after a pause, her own voice sounding unfamiliar in her ears.

'Just wait until he calms down. Come on, let's have a quick smoke.'

'I dropped my matches.'

They stand there, cigarettes between their fingers, and they take a few more steps back as the dog goes on barking at them. After a while, the dog calms down and backs off from the wall. But as soon as Saniye or Gül get anywhere near, he leaps back up on the ledge and bellows.

The game plays out over and over. It doesn't make a difference whether the women creep up slowly or try to move faster than the dog, whether they wait a long time or sneak up on him in quick succession: no matter what they do, they can't get near their bags.

'I threw my ticket away this morning because of you,' Gül says.

'You wouldn't be allowed to use it again anyway,' Saniye replies.

'How are we supposed to get home? My money's in my bag.'
'Mine too.'

By this point, a German woman has come out onto the balcony of her house by the wall and is watching them.

'We'll have to beckon her down,' says Saniye. 'There must be something she can do to help.'

'What makes you think she can help us?'

'Maybe it's her dog.'

'If it was her dog, she'd have done something about it, wouldn't she? What kind of country is this, where people who aren't even shepherds own dogs?'

'We need money to get home,' Saniye says. 'We can borrow some money from her. I'll wave her down. You're better at German, you speak to her.'

And just like that, Saniye starts waving. Once again, Gül's heart is beating far too hard. She's better at German.

The woman has vanished from her balcony now. When Gül looks up she notices there are more people staring down from their balconies. *Since I've known Saniye, I keep getting in hot water*, she thinks.

The woman appears in the building's doorway with a cigarette between her fingers, and then strolls slowly towards the two of them.

'Guten Tag,' Gül says when she gets close enough.

'Guten Tag,' the woman replies, and Saniye puts on a friendly face and says the same words back to her.

'Dog,' Gül says. 'Bag. We want home. No money.'

She pulls a golden bangle off her wrist and holds it out to the woman.

'Until Monday. Money. Ticket. Pick up Monday.'

The woman takes a drag on her cigarette and looks at Gül, thoughtful. Then she asks a question, but Gül doesn't understand, so she simply shrugs and widens her eyes.

The woman smiles; her cigarette has a bright print from her lipstick around it.

'I thought you were playing with the dog,' she says. 'Playing? No?'

She walks up to the wall. The dog comes running and barks at her, but she doesn't let it bother her. Perhaps it *is* her dog?

She inserts the cigarette between her lips and grabs the dog beneath its muzzle with one hand, stroking it between the ears with the other. Then she simply takes both bags and hands them to the women, who stare at her with unbelieving eyes.

'Danke,' Saniye says.

'Danke,' Gül repeats.

'They're not bad people, the Germans,' Saniye says later, on the bus. 'She could have taken your bracelet and run off with it. We couldn't have done a thing about it. I'm going to learn their language.'

Gül thinks she's right, but still she can't help but wonder why all the others just looked on from their balconies and did nothing.

'Cry,' the man at the office tells Gül. 'You see, there's always a way. You have to cry at the labour exchange and say you need this work permit. Tell them you need it now. If you don't cry, they won't budge, I know them. Understand? Cry.'

The man presses this on her again and again and even shows her how, until he's sure she has understood. Gül's a good worker but he can't keep her on any longer: it's already an effort to keep her work off the books. It would have been sorted soon enough: Gül's already been in Germany for over six months but now the law has changed, and he'd have to wangle something for another seven months. She needs a permit.

Labour exchange: that's another term Gül won't learn in Turkish until much later. She knows what it is and why people go there, but just like health insurance, sick notes, holiday pay, Christmas, and Easter, she doesn't know the Turkish word for it.

She knows just enough German to relay the situation to the man at the employment office. Her boss at work has also given her a letter to take along. And even though her boss repeatedly insisted that she should cry, she can't do it.

'We had a Greek woman working here,' her boss said. 'She was in the same situation as you, and she sat there and cried bitter tears, otherwise they wouldn't have made an exception for her. They're just people, they have hearts too.'

But Gül sits there with her hands in her lap and wonders if she's finding the work harder than she'd like to admit. Or if she feels ashamed in front of this strange man. What will Fuat say if she has to leave yet another job? How can a person suddenly cease to qualify for a work permit after six months? Saniye got a work permit straight away because she came here to work and didn't come to join her husband like Gül.

Gül still doesn't know what Saniye is doing all by herself in Germany, but when she does find out, she's glad not to have insisted on asking.

'You couldn't cry?' Saniye asks the next day. 'Oh, if it were me, I'd have bawled my eyes out. I'd have blubbed so much I'd have drowned the man.'

It's their last trip home together; Saniye will stay on at the bread factory, and Gül will go back to sitting in the kitchen.

'It's not easy,' Gül says, 'crying on cue like that.'

'Isn't it?' Saniye asks and looks at Gül with glassy eyes. What shocks Gül is not the tears that have slowly gathered at the rims of her eyes, it's the sorrow that is suddenly there. As if it had been lurking there in the background the whole time. As if Gül had been right, that first morning at the bus stop.

'I lost everything in a single day,' Saniye says. 'My father, my husband, my son. No matter how much I cry, it'll never be enough.'

Gül looks at her, helpless, and wishes she knew what to say.

'That's right,' Saniye says, 'a single day.'

An hour later, they're sitting in Gül's kitchen. Fuat has left for work already, and Saniye smokes cigarette after cigarette as she tells her story. In the years to come, Gül will often wonder why people confide in her, why she gets to hear all these stories they rarely tell. Why so many choose her, of all people, to share their suffering with. Why they believe that the words they say to her might help somehow.

'Alper had been drinking, and when he drank, he would hit me. He wasn't a bad man; it's just that the drink always seems harmless when it's still in the bottle. But you know what they say: give a mouse a sip, and it'll march over to a cat and grab him by the scruff.

'If it weren't for the damn drink, we could have got along just fine. But alcohol is such a bitter temptress.

'There was always a fight when he'd been drinking – he'd beat me black and blue. The next morning he'd be sorry, but come the evening, he'd be off his head drunk again. So I packed my bags and went to my dad's. My mum had been dead for three years by then. She died of blood poisoning. Who'd have thought when she fell over that death was knocking at the door? It just looked like a grazed knee.'

Gül thinks of when her mother died, much earlier, from an illness that her father survived.

'I went to my dad's because things weren't easy with Alper. He was a good man with a soft heart, room in it for everyone, but the drink made it small. When a week had gone by, he came to my dad's house one evening and got down on his knees, really on his knees, begging me to come back; he lay his hands on my feet, and my dad just got up and left the room.

'"I'll be your slave," Alper said, and swore he'd stop drinking. Ufuk, our son, was only six months old at the time, and why should a child grow up without a father? I didn't want to be a burden on my dad either. And the first time he promised, I really believed him.

'He stopped drinking for four weeks, then after that, I put up with it for four more. I was black and blue all over; my ribs hurt, maybe a couple of them were broken. Alper knew no mercy when he was drunk. Two days later he was back at my dad's again, begging and pleading for us to take pity on him.

'After that, he stopped drinking for two months. And the third time he came to my dad's house to take me back, my dad knew I wouldn't say no to him, so he collared him as soon as he stepped over the threshold. He told him: "Son, it can't go on like this, you've got to decide. She's my daughter and she's free to stay here or go back with you, but her heart's as soft as bread dough – you talk her round every time. But me, I won't stand by and watch any more. It's breaking my heart. You've got to learn your lesson; this isn't how it works. Saniye's not a toy, she's a person like you and me. So, listen here: if you ever, if you ever come knocking at my door again wanting to take her back, I will shoot you. Upon my name, I'll do it. So think good and hard about whether you want to drive my daughter to the point where she comes running back here. And if it does get to that point, think even harder about whether you want to be coming knocking on my door, trapping her with your tears and promises. I'm an old man, I've got nothing left to lose. If you turn up here again trying to get Saniye back, I'll shoot you."

'"Got it?" he yelled, and Alper nodded.

'I stayed with Alper for over a year, even though he started drinking again and hitting me; I put up with it all for a year, to keep things from getting worse. It was my last try. It wasn't until he broke my nose for the second time and I spent all night coughing up blood that I went back to my dad. I begged Alper not to come after me – for his sake, not for mine. But there was nothing the man overestimated more than his own will. Alper came to my father's house that same evening. And my dad took his gun down from the wall and took aim at him. Alper thought he just wanted to scare him, but my dad said, "I warned you," and he pulled the trigger.

'He went to prison, and my mother-in-law took my son because I couldn't provide for him on my own; my husband was dead.

'And so I came to Germany,' Saniye says. 'I could cry for two whole lifetimes and still it would never be enough.'

II

Gül props her elbows on the fence and looks down the road, watching out for the postman. Perhaps he'll have a letter from Ceyda, her mother-in-law, or her friend Suzan, her old neighbour from Turkey who left for Germany long before she did. Suzan was originally living in Duisburg, wherever that was. Gül had thought it was nearby, but Fuat says you can't just go there. Suzan had her children with her, at least, but they liked the country as little as she did. *The Germans are so cold*, Suzan had written from Duisburg back when Gül was still in Turkey, *and they talk so little it's hardly worth learning the language.* She had learned Italian from the Italians in her neighbourhood, and now her letters come from Naples, where the family lives.

Gül's new neighbours are Spanish, Greek and Turkish, and there's a handful of Germans too. Factory Lane, where they now live, isn't tarmacked and has no pavement or paving stones. The water pools into brown puddles when it rains, and then even the Germans take their muddy shoes off outside their front doors.

Every house on the estate has a little front garden and a bigger garden round the back, where they can grow fruit and vegetables. There's also a coop – Fuat wants to buy chickens to put in it. The house has a big kitchen and a living room downstairs, and two bedrooms upstairs. The toilet is inside, at the end of the hallway that leads from the kitchen to the back garden.

It's a bit like back home, Gül thinks: *there's room to breathe, space to feel the earth under your feet and hands, and most importantly, there's room for the girls.* Soon she won't have to prop herself up on the fence and wait full of yearning for the postman, like so many times in the past few months after working the late shift in the nearby wool factory.

Four weeks after leaving her job at the bread factory, she had managed to get a work permit from a different labour exchange.

'Why is it suddenly alright? I don't get it,' she said to Fuat.

'Bremen is a different province; they have different laws,' Fuat answered, and Gül just frowned. What a strange country, with a new town, district town or village every few yards. People didn't seem to need much space, but living closer together didn't mean they felt any closer to one another.

Once she got her work permit, she'd started at the factory where Fuat worked. The two of them saw even less of each other when Gül worked the late shift, as Fuat was still only working nights. And even though he was still gambling and drinking and being unnecessarily generous towards his friends, the money mounted up.

Fuat has a moped now; he drives it home at the weekends with no difficulty and no major swerving, but as soon as he gets off it, he feels like he has round feet on swaying ground.

'Once the girls are here,' he says, 'I won't work so many nights.' And he does the maths for Gül over and over, telling her how many bonuses he gets just because the sun's not shining outside.

'What do I need sun for?' he brags. 'It doesn't shine on the factory floor anyway. Whether the wool gets washed at night or in the daytime doesn't make any difference to the wool or to me, but it does make a difference to my pay packet.'

Gül stands at the fence with both feet on the ground, but her heart takes flight with joy every time the postman brings her a letter from Ceyda.

My little darling, she thinks, *barely started school and she can write already – faster than the others, too, because her mother's left her alone and it's the only way she can keep in touch.*

She must take after her Auntie Sibel, Gül's younger sister, who started school a year early because she wept every day at the end of the holidays for the children who had been her playmates all summer long and who now left her alone every morning to go to school. And although she joined them six weeks after term had started, she was near the top of the class by the end of the school year.

May my children get a good education like their aunties, and not have to catch up on school by distance learning after they're married like I did, Gül prays. She failed her exams in the fifth and last year of her basic schooling and had to resit them. But instead of trying again after the summer holidays, she simply never went back, and soon enough her father sent her to Esra the dressmaker to learn a trade.

Today the postman shrugs at her.

'Nothing for you this time, sorry,' he says.

Gül doesn't wait for the responses to her letters; she writes a new one every few days, so she hopes almost daily that she might get post. The postman sees her at the fence every day of the week; only when it's raining hard does Gül wait by the window in the living room, looking out on the road.

Words, she tells herself, *we only have words to soothe our longing. If you don't have someone to hug and embrace, you seek solace in words.*

The calendar on the wall also seems to alleviate her yearning. She tears off another sheet of their separation every day.

Five months to go, just five more months, then they'll fly to Turkey, and she'll see and hear her daughters, taste them and feel them – at last she'll have the scent of her children all around her.

She's been in Germany for over a year now. Looking back, that time seems long and hard, especially in the tiny flat. Moving to Factory Lane seems to have made everything easier.

She'll never forget the jobs she worked in before she started at the wool factory, all those hours in the kitchen, the visit to the doctor, Fuat's face when he said: 'He said *baby*, didn't he? Surely you've heard that word before? What's not to understand?'

The relief she felt when she saw the blood, the dream that stayed with her for days, those long minutes buried under chickens.

It seems as though she's lived and aged so much in that year. She hopes her daughters are still exactly as they were when she left them, even though Ceyda can write now; even though the image of Ceren scratching her face still weighs as heavy on her heart as if it were an anvil in her father's forge.

'"Come on, just five more minutes" mine's always saying,' complains Ela, one of Gül's colleagues. 'He wakes up after his nightshift when I'm supposed to be getting up and off to work, and he's grabbing me here there and everywhere, begging me to stay in bed with him.'

'Mine's just the same,' Huri says. 'He's always after a few more minutes when I'm supposed to be leaving for work.'

'Men! They're all the same,' Işık says. 'Do you think mine's any different? If it were up to him, I'd be late every day.'

Gül bites into her bread and says nothing. She still can't get used to the taste either.

She likes working at the combing factory. It's not too big and the work isn't too hard. It's barely a ten-minute walk, the route is easy enough, and quite a few other young Turkish women work there, as well as Greek, Spanish and Yugoslavian women. But this conversation stirs something up in Gül, something she doesn't like at all. She pretends she's savouring every bite of her bread.

Gül married Fuat because she wanted to. Other men had asked her father for her hand, but she said no. She married Fuat because she wanted to. She wanted to leave her father's house to make it easier for her sisters, so that there would be one less mouth to feed. Fuat is her stepmother's younger brother. She knew him and thought it would be easier for her to be with someone who wasn't a stranger.

Fuat was good-looking; he was one of the most attractive men in town – even the other women said so. He still had all his hair in those days, shiny with brilliantine, and he liked to dress well. He had learned a trade and seemed to be up to the job of feeding a family.

Back then Gül didn't know how much Fuat drank and gambled, but lots of men – especially the younger ones – had these vices, commonly known as 'bad habits', so Gül never thought she would fare any differently to other women.

Gül's husband never begs her to stay in bed with him for just a few more minutes. On the contrary, he always says, 'Up, up, off to work with you. This is Germany, you can't just turn up late here – there's an order and a time for everything. You know what the Germans say: Work is work, schnapps is schnapps. Come on, off you go,' and he shoos her out the door.

Gül hardly speaks to her new friends for the rest of the day. She does her work and makes it look like it requires more concentration than it really does.

The next day, she's almost forgotten all about it when Fuat starts haranguing her again: 'Up, up you get!'

She's never late. As a child, she often dawdled and lost track of time, but those days are gone now. Even if Fuat never said anything, she'd still always be on time. It offends her that Fuat doesn't seem to know that. She butters herself two more slices of bread than usual.

'Same story today,' Huri says later on, during their break. 'He grabs me by my coattails and tries to pull me back into bed!'

Gül listens to these stories for two whole weeks. She can't even bring herself to be happy about the two chickens Fuat brings home with him. Her glimmers of light are those moments at the fence when the postman smiles at her from a distance and gives her a nod. After that, nothing else matters; after that, she feels like Fuat when he's drunk. But in these two weeks, she finds herself looking at her husband more often, trying to understand why he might be different to the other women's husbands. He never hesitates to wake her up when he's in the mood, but he's never asked her to stay in bed with him.

When two weeks have passed, Gül says to her friends: 'Yes, but if they keep asking over and over, why don't you just stay in bed? Do them a favour. What's the worst that can happen if you turn up late once or twice? Look at Rocío, nothing's happened to her.'

Rocío is scrawny, feisty, and talks a lot. When her German fails her, she switches to Spanish. She seems to think if she just speaks forcefully and quickly enough, if she gesticulates enough while she's talking, then the others are bound to understand her.

Rocío also lives on Factory Lane with her husband and children. Gül has never seen Rocío walking; the woman always seems to be in a hurry. She moves around at speed and smokes in haste, but she often turns up once work has already begun. The only thing faster than her feet is her mouth.

'It would be nice, wouldn't it?' Gül says. 'Give it a go.'

Gül has no hidden agenda, she's just curious. She wants to see what it is that makes Fuat different from the others.

She hadn't remotely reckoned on Huri and Ela coming into work the next day not just on time, but visibly disgruntled. Gül hopes she hasn't been looking that same way for the last few days, even though that's how she's felt.

'What happened?' Gül asks, genuinely surprised.

'Oh,' Ela says, 'I went back to bed, and two minutes later he goes, "Best not be late, though."'

'Mine was the same,' Huri says. 'He gave me a pat on the backside and said, "Ah well, work's calling."'

'Mine didn't even ask today,' Işık says. 'But I can guess how it'll go.'

Gül feels bad that she's landed her friends in this situation.

'Forgive me,' she says, 'I had no idea…'

'Relax,' Huri says. 'It's not your fault, is it?'

They're the same, Gül thinks. *They're all the same. The only difference is that Fuat can't do sweet-talk. At least he's not been putting it on.*

And though she feels brighter all of a sudden, she feels guilty too, and regrets ever suggesting such a thing to the three women.

Huri, Işık, Ela and a few other women from the estate regularly get together in one of their big kitchens at the weekends. They gather at one house one week, then at another the next, but never at the same house so often that it becomes a burden. The men sit smoking and playing cards in the living room, which is smaller than the kitchen. Sometimes the radio, a reel-to-reel tape or even a cassette recorder will be playing, and there'll be tea and, once it gets dark at the latest, alcohol.

Weather permitting, they sit in one of their gardens and Gül is reminded of the times at her father's summer house, though his garden is fifty times bigger. They used to sit out on the front steps in the evenings, knitting or crocheting, chit-chatting, nibbling sunflower seeds and listening to the radio that belonged to Gül's father. For a long time he was the only person in the street who owned one, and he ended up attaching a loudspeaker to the roof of his house because he grew so tired of the constant visits.

On Factory Lane, they're all together like they were back then in Turkey. Gül can walk out of her front door and pay a friend a visit. It's not like it was for Suzan and Murat, who had hardly any other Turks living nearby. Suzan wrote to Gül about it. Murat made a few friends on the train to Germany, friendships that endured even when they had been living in Naples for some time.

For as long as they were living in Germany, Suzan and Murat would send a postcard to their friends in nearby regions every Wednesday to say they were planning to visit on Saturday. And when the day came, if they hadn't been turned down, they knew it'd be worth making the journey.

It's at the gatherings on Factory Lane that Gül first really grasps what Fuat meant when he said her time here was her version of military service. She meets women from different regions in Turkey and hears about their unfamiliar customs, which astound and sometimes even horrify her. She becomes well versed in telling the different accents apart, and it's here that she learns to properly recognise envy and resentment, treachery and deceit.

In the beginning, the women guess where each of them comes from. Havva, an Istanbulite, says to Mevlüde, a woman from Kayseri: 'Your accent's so broad and lively, and a little rough – you must be from Anatolia, am I right?'

'Yes,' Mevlüde says. 'And what about Gül, can you tell where she's from?'

'She always speaks in whole sentences and never makes any grammatical mistakes. She doesn't sound it, but I reckon she's most likely to be from Istanbul, like me.'

'What? Istanbul?' Mevlüde flies off the handle. 'She's from a town two hours from us. Where are you getting Istanbul from? It's the arse end of the world! You haven't got a clue. You come here from your fancy Istanbul, but the minute you open your mouth a load of drivel comes out, a whole river of drivel!'

Everyone is shocked by her reaction, and Gül tries to pacify Mevlüde: 'Mevlüde, my love, it's nothing to get het up about, is it? Havva said it herself; I don't sound it.'

'Oh, you and your strange guesses,' says Mevlüde. 'It doesn't really matter where any of us comes from, does it?'

'Of course not,' says Gül. 'We're all Turks, we all speak the same language. But more importantly, we're all people. There's no reason for us to be so harsh to one another. We're all in the same boat.'

They may well all be in the same boat, and one day they may all sink in the same sea, but what's true for one of the women will be just another story for the next woman; while one of them might have eaten fish for breakfast every day, the others will only have seen fish in schoolbooks.

As Gül gets to know Mevlüde better, she thinks she can understand why this young woman from Kayseri is so quick to get in a lather. Her husband is losing his mind. Whether it's to do with Germany, with his wife, his genes, his history, no one can quite say.

'You've been putting chilli in my underpants,' Serter says to Mevlüde. 'You've put a hex on my mother, that's why she's stopped writing to me. You've cursed me with constant constipation.' Every day he accuses her of something new.

'His mother can't read or write,' Mevlüde says. 'She's never written a thing in her life, not even her own name, let alone a letter. The man's getting more deranged by the day. We'll have to split up; it can't go on like this.'

Serter gets on with his work just fine, but he has delusions and is convinced his wife wants to kill him. Mevlüde cooks their dinner in the mornings before she goes in for the late shift, and by the time she gets home at night, Serter has thrown the whole meal away without even tasting it, certain he saw his wife adding poison.

'He was in bed when I was cooking,' Mevlüde says. 'Bedbugs could have danced on his backside, he was sleeping so soundly. He's got to go! I want him out of my flat.'

As it happens, Serter has already started looking for a new flat.

'I don't want to live with her any more,' he says. 'One morning I just won't wake up again – that witch is bent on killing me.'

At work, the wheels on the wool carts often get blocked because all the fluff floating in the air gets wrapped around them. Rocío is always kicking the carts and saying things in Spanish – swearing, presumably. Some of the women lean forward and put all their weight into pushing the carts. They keep trying until there's nothing else for it and they have to sort out the fluff-clogged rollers. The first thing Gül does when she starts her shift is to unblock all the carts.

'I want to work with these carts,' she says. 'I don't want to get annoyed with them. They're here to move things around, and that's what they ought to do.'

'You're a fool,' Mevlüde tells her. 'The others get the rollers all tangled up and then you come and unblock them – you're doing other people's work.'

'I'm making my work easier,' Gül replies.

One day, once Serter has started looking for a new place, Gül catches Mevlüde bracing herself against a blocked cart, her face bright red and her teeth clenched. It's just before the end of the shift and Mevlüde seems to want to leave the unblocking to the next shift. She's pushing her weight up against it in one last attempt, when one foot slips and her face slams against the edge of the cart.

At first, she looks from side to side, then she turns around to check behind her. Gül quickly focuses on her work. She doesn't want Mevlüde to think she's glad about her mishap; she isn't, she really isn't. And Mevlüde seems embarrassed about it. Why else would she look around and not make a sound if she's hurt herself?

The next day, Mevlüde comes in with a swollen cheek and a slight bruise under her eye.

'As if it weren't enough that he throws my cooking in the bin and tries to drive me crazy with his constant accusations,' she complains. 'As if it weren't enough that he's moving out, now he's started hitting me as well!'

Some of the women take pity on her, telling her she can never be safe with that madman: who knows, he might slit her throat while she's sleeping one night, they've heard all sorts of stories.

Only Gül says: 'Mevlüde, your husband is looking for a new flat and that takes a while here – I found out the hard way. Be a bit patient with him. One more fortnight or so won't make any difference now. Then he'll move out and leave you in peace.'

'If I'm still alive by then,' Mevlüde barks.

On their way home, when no one else is there, Gül says to Mevlüde: 'Look, sister, we have to be honest. Truthfulness brings us peace. We'll be old one day, and we don't want to be tormented by our consciences. We want to go in peace when the angel of death comes to fetch us. He ought to find us with a smile on our faces. And that will only happen if we try hard to be good people. There's no escaping truthfulness. Our religion commands it – humanity commands it. It's not always easy, but we have to be honest.'

Mevlüde looks at her, her face a picture of astonished innocence. 'Perhaps you should write a book if you're so clever,' she says. 'And thank the Lord that he didn't punish you with a husband like Serter. You wouldn't be talking so clever then, I'm sure. Look at what he did to me.'

Fuat sits at the kitchen table with paper and pencil, adding, subtracting, writing down and crossing out numbers, and eventually he puts the pencil aside, lights a cigarette, tosses the pack onto the table and leans back in his chair.

'It beggars belief. You run around pulling out all the stops and getting your people a flight home to the loved ones they're missing, you work your fingers to the bone so they don't have to take the train or drive all the way, and at the end of the day you're still miles away from being rich. Miles and miles away. I feel like I'm running some kind of charity. Buying and selling plane tickets isn't all it's cracked up to be. We'll only just get our own flights out of it, after all that running around.'

He grabs a biro while Gül kneads dough for lahmacun, then he fills in a lottery slip.

'Another one?' Gül asks.

'Yes, another one. All this drudgery's not worth the bother.'

'That's your fourth one today.'

'I'm going to do a fifth one as well. It improves our odds. The more you play, the better your chances of winning big. It's as simple as that. It's not like poker. And money – money's not something you can keep on hoarding, hoarding, hoarding; it doesn't multiply like that. How do you think this country got so rich?'

Because people work hard, Gül could say. *Because they don't spend their time gambling, drinking whisky and Coke, and getting their moped fixed after crashing into the chicken coop and stopping the chickens from laying for four days in a row now.*

She could speak, but if she's that clever she might as well write a book. Or keep her mouth shut.

But why get upset? There are two plane tickets on the table next to the lottery slips and the pencil and paper. They both have the same date and time on them, but one says Fuat's name on it and the other has hers. They'll board the plane in Hannover and three hours later they'll touch down in Istanbul. Then they'll take a taxi from the airport to the coach station and get a coach home.

With that to look forward to, she can cope with the longing. Let Fuat play the lottery as much as he wants. Soon Gül will be reunited with her daughters, God willing, and she won't leave them alone again, not ever, not until they're big enough to go their own way one day.

Lord, you let me live as I asked you, but I didn't want this life for myself. What kind of life would it be if I only lived it for myself? she thinks.

Ever since she fell down the hole in her mother-in-law's cellar and feared for her life, Gül has never forgotten how short a life can be.

Lord, reunite me with my daughters, and grant me this borrowed life until I can go without a backward glance. Lord, if it is your will, I'll see my daughters soon.

'What are you smiling at?' Fuat asks.

Gül takes her eyes off the plane tickets. 'I was just thinking,' she says.

The browns of the plains soothe her tired eyes. *Oh, how I've missed this*, she thinks. *Germany's brightest green isn't as warm as the dullest brown here.*

There's a young couple behind them on the coach. Judging by their conversations, they've spent time in Germany too – longer than Gül, almost twenty-two months – and they have two daughters, who stayed behind with the woman's oldest sister. The little one was just six months, and the older girl was two when they left.

'Our little one will be bigger now than her sister was then,' the wife says.

The further they get, the more she talks, and the more she talks, the less she has to talk about. For over an hour, she's been picturing in technicolour how much the girls will have grown and what it will be like to see them at last.

Fuat is in the window seat, dozing. Gül is glad of the woman's words, partly because they're distracting her from her own thoughts, and partly because the woman is in the same boat as her.

Not feeling alone, knowing there are others forced to see the world from the same standpoint as you: that's what makes you feel alive.

Decades later, Gül will say: 'This internet thing is a good invention. You can always find fellow sufferers.' But right now, she's perfectly happy to listen to the woman in the seat behind her.

A car overtakes the coach with a flurry of beeps when they're still about an hour from their town. Moments later the coach pulls over behind the car, which Gül can see through the big front window.

'They said they'd be at the coach station,' the woman behind Gül says.

'No,' she almost squeals, her voice suddenly high and trembling, and in an instant, she's running down the aisle to the sound of the coach door opening at the front.

A man and a woman have stepped out of the car, along with two girls in shiny blue dresses with red bows in their hair.

Gül cranes her neck to get a better view.

The woman stumbles on the coach steps and almost falls flat on the ground. Her husband, following her, just manages to grab her by the arm.

Suddenly the whole coach is buzzing, everyone eager to see what will happen next.

Gül doesn't stand up like some of the others, but she can see from her seat as the woman drops to her knees and embraces both her daughters at once. She can see the woman's back shuddering with sobs, and tears prick her own eyes.

'What's going on?' Fuat asks, sleepy.

Will I hug my girls like that too? Will I cry like that? Will they have got Ceyda and Ceren all dressed up like that? Will I overflow and forget where my body ends and theirs begin?

'What are you blubbing for?'

Gül wipes the tears from her eyes.

'They surprised them. The couple behind us. They brought their daughters in the car; they didn't wait at the coach station.'

That's no reason to start snivelling, Fuat could say. Gül wouldn't be surprised if he did. He gives a slow nod.

'That's life,' he says. 'You do all your sums at home, and then out there the numbers are all different. You never know what God has in store for you.'

Gül looks at him. *It's making him go soft*, she thinks. *He'd never admit it, but coming home is making him go soft.*

Who could ever guess that in a few years' time, the opposite will happen when he comes to Turkey.

When Gül's father learned of his wife's death one morning at breakfast, he threw the spoon he was holding at the wall. Gül was six years old. She was listening by the door when she heard that her mother was dead, but not until she saw her father react, not until she heard the spoon, did she realise how unthinkable what had happened must be. She'll never forget the sound of that spoon hitting the wall, as long as she lives.

It was a sound that wrenched the ground from under her feet. But she didn't float; she fell and never landed.

Nor will she forget the sound of Ceyda shouting *Mummy* at the coach station before she ran into her arms.

Mummy.

'Perhaps you should write a book if you're so clever,' Mevlüde had said to her, but words in books have less power because they lack that sound.

Mummy.

Five letters; Gül can hear eighteen months in those five letters.

Mummy.

In a voice that doesn't seem to be Ceyda's. *Mummy.*

It's a sound that tells Gül more than she wants to hear right now. *Mummy.*

I've been here all alone, please don't ever leave me behind again, I need you, they don't look after me well enough here, I'm scared, Mummy. What did I do to make you go away? Mummy, please never go away again.

Mummy.

Gül hears all this, and it's not like it was back then with the spoon; this time she's quicker to grasp what's happened.

And yet it's exactly the same: the world opens up, and she can't find her footing. *Mummy.*

Gül couldn't tell what was wrong from her daughter's letters. She had delighted in those short little sentences as Ceyda described what she'd been doing and how much she missed her.

There are so many kinds of longing. How could Gül tell which kind was in her little girl's handwriting?

There are so many kinds of longing. How could Gül not have heard which kind was in her daughter's voice?

Gül cries, but she doesn't cry like the woman at the side of the road. She also cries when she wraps Ceren in her arms and finds that this little girl has almost nothing in common with the toddler who once sat at the foot of the stairs and scratched her face. *She seems to have had an easier time of it*, Gül thinks.

And when she hugs her father, Gül cries again.

Gül's father went to see her every morning when she got married and moved into her in-laws' house. When Fuat was away for eighteen months on military service, she only saw him when he was on leave, but she saw her father every day. When Fuat went abroad to work, she didn't see him for almost a whole year. She had never been away from her father until she joined Fuat in Germany.

Now she hasn't seen her father for a year and a half.

Her mother has been dead for so long – she's the eldest of the siblings, and she feels that her father is the only one now who can soften life's blows for her and help her find her footing. If he were to suddenly die one day, she'd be even more defenceless, at the mercy of this life; there'd be no one left to support her. She suspects this and dwells on the thought as she breathes deeply, taking in her father's scent: the smell of sour sweat, fertile soil, the cheap fabric of his suit, iron, smoke and soot from the fire. Her father is a blacksmith, after all; only he can provide the warmth that goes all the way to her bones.

Everyone asks Gül what life's like over there and whether it suits her. Gül doesn't lie. She tells them what she's seen and experienced, but she leaves out the hours spent in the kitchen and the many tears she's cried; the pain and homesickness are all but forgotten now.

'It's all a bit confusing,' she says. 'The money, the prices of things. When they sell pears, there's a sign that says how much they cost. And then you buy a kilo, but you pay double that. In time, I realised they were weighing them in half kilos, and they put the price for half a kilo on the sign.'

People love hearing these kinds of stories, and the stories about how clean the streets are. They like to picture tarmac and tidiness when they think of Germany.

Gül neglects to mention the state of Factory Lane, and a few other things too, and even Fuat doesn't warn them: *Folks, stay here! They'll have you bent over 'til your back's crooked; they time your breaks to the minute, and they've no time for excuses or leisurely chit-chat.*

He doesn't tell them the joke that's doing the rounds among the migrants in Germany, where a worker goes to his boss to complain: 'Boss, the wheelbarrow's always going squeak... squeak... squeak.' And the boss replies, 'No, no, this is Germany: wheelbarrows must go squeaksqueaksqueak.'

Fuat much prefers to take his old friends along to look for a plot of land, enthusing about all the creature comforts he'll have in his new home.

Melike, the oldest of Gül's sisters, is the only one who really asks for the details this summer. 'What's shift work like? What are the hours? How much do you make? How much is the rent? How much for a loaf of bread?'

'The money Dad sends me, it hardly touches the sides,' she says. 'I even have to ration my cigarettes. But I want to finish my course. Would you be able to chip in a little?'

'Of course,' Gül says, wondering how she'll pull it off. Fuat manages the money and he'll say, 'Don't we have enough to worry about without funding your sister's slovenly student lifestyle in Istanbul? She probably spends her time cavorting in the streets, getting into fights with the police, that charming little sister of yours. That's what you get with these left-wing ideas: they make people lazy. And you're expecting us to support that, are you? You want us to encourage these people, do you?'

Melike has never been to a single demonstration, but in Fuat's eyes she's been corrupted: because she once sat in a train carriage with men she didn't know and smoked cigarettes in front of them, because she lives in a student dorm, because there are so many wanton women in that rotten city and so many ideas that threaten the system.

Fuat doesn't yet know that Melike has fallen in love with a sports student who she will marry next year. Last summer, she brought him home and introduced him to her father, who gave them his blessing. Fuat isn't as progressive as the blacksmith. Bringing a man home from Istanbul, it beggars belief.

'Of course,' Gül says. 'Of course I can support you. Don't you worry about that.'

The swimming pond was filled up over four weeks ago and already the water is streaked with green. The water level has dropped so low in the heat that it's not even waist-high.

'Mummy, can we go for a swim?' Ceren asks.

'A swim? *A swim?* Wasn't it enough that you nearly drowned in that pond? Or have you forgotten about that already?'

'Like you'd care,' Ceyda says. She's standing behind her little sister and wants to swim too.

Feelings are like invisible people. The guilt is heavy and hot; it sits on top of Gül, like it's trying to crush her. It wasn't just guilt she felt when Ceyda cried *Mummy* at the coach station, there were other feelings too. But now as she sits here, looking at her elder daughter, she can't respond. What should she have done?

'Come,' her husband had urged her. 'Come to Germany and leave the children with my mum; they'll be well looked after there. Come, we'll work and earn money so our children will be better off than we were.' What else could she have done? Did her heart not bleed that year and a half in Germany? Did it not bleed all the more when she heard those words? Did she do something no other mother would have done?

'Come here,' she says, pulling Ceyda and then Ceren onto her lap. 'You two are my life, you're all I have. I'd sacrifice everything for you, understand? We'll go to Germany together soon, and I'll never, ever leave you on your own again.'

Gül has yet to learn not to make such promises.

'We went to that country for you, for your futures,' she says. 'We didn't want you to suffer. We didn't want to suffer either.'

She doesn't want to cry; she just wants to hold her daughters, tight enough for them to understand.

Later on she's sitting at the edge of the pond, watching Ceyda and Ceren splashing around. If the pond were full, she'd be scared. Where was she supposed to learn how to swim in this town?

When she was little, there was no swimming pond; instead they played in the stream, which only came up to their knees if they dammed it.

There are swimming pools in Germany, she's seen them. But why learn to swim if you don't live by the water?

To protect my daughters, she thinks. *That's reason enough to learn. Is that why there are so many swimming pools in Germany, because the people there love their kids so much?*

She thinks of Fuat, who knows how to swim. He learnt during his military service, in a lake. He can swim, but would he have learnt just for his children's sake?

In almost thirty years' time, Gül and Fuat will have a house by the sea, and Gül still won't be able to swim.

Sitting on the edge of the pool, Gül eats walnuts and köfter, chewy treats made from thickened grape juice. She can't get enough: she eats and eats from morning to night, all the things she's been missing for so long.

She had lost a little weight since starting work at the woollen mill, but in the five weeks she spends in Turkey this year, she puts it all back on and more – so much so that by the end of the holiday, all her relatives are commenting on it.

Fuat has filled out too, spending every evening after dinner sitting with a lavish platter of cold dishes, treating himself to several rakıs and happily waxing lyrical about whisky and Coke, never tiring of mentioning that he'd usually be at work in Germany at this hour.

This time, Gül won't fly back with a cardboard suitcase, having let those around her cluelessly insist that they'll have everything she needs in Germany. She'll take back some köfter, pepper paste, red lentils, bulgur, and some tarhana – a seasoned, dried dough used to make soup. She'll be twenty kilos over the baggage limit, and Fuat will make a fuss. 'Isn't it enough that we have to work 'til our backs are crooked in Germany? Do we have to lug great tonnes of baggage with us too?' he'll say. But he'll be pleased with himself when, after endless discussions and a little pocket money for the official, he won't technically have to pay any extra.

You've got to be smart, and his happiness at having bypassed the rules will outweigh his anger at his wife, who seems to want to hoard things away just in case.

Back in Germany, Fuat and Gül try to coordinate their shifts so there's always someone at home to look after the girls. But after spending only a few mornings with Ceren, Fuat says: 'This isn't going to work; we need another solution. I can't look after such a small child. She doesn't listen to a word I say; she doesn't do what I tell her and she's constantly asking for things. I'm a grown man, I can't spend half my day playing with her.'

Nadiye and Ozan live not far away, and it's Nadiye who offers to take care of Ceren.

'I've got two toddlers at home anyway; one more won't make a difference. She's a big girl, she can help me out and keep a bit of an eye on the boys.'

Should we give them money for it? Gül could ask Fuat now, but she accepts the offer gratefully and often brings Nadiye a treat: a few strips of köfter – a novelty for people from the Black Sea – or a plate of her stuffed vine leaves or börek.

'What are those, by the way?' Gül asks one day when she sees Nadiye's washing drying on her balcony.

'Bloomers,' Nadiye says.

Gül looks at her.

'We have a lot of rough terrain on the coast; you're bound to stumble and fall now and then. We wear these so men don't get aroused if they catch a glimpse under our skirts.'

Gül looks at the big, black pants.

'Do any of your neighbours have underwear like that?'

'No, they all have white ones on their washing lines, much smaller.'

'How long have you been here now?'

'It'll be two and a half years next month.'

'And you've still got these pants, even though there are pavements everywhere here? If you ask me, it's not right to hang them up on the balcony in front of so many German neighbours. Who knows what they'll think?'

The next day, Gül brings Nadiye a pack of a dozen white towelling knickers. They weren't expensive, but Gül bought them out of her housekeeping money. She's sticking to a tight budget to make sure there's a bit left over for Melike at the end of the month.

She and Fuat have spent hours discussing how much money she needs for food, clothes, two children, school things for Ceyda, washing-up liquid, cleaning cloths, and all the other things she reeled off to persuade her husband to give her more. Most he dismissed with a wave of his hand: 'Those odds and ends don't cost anything.'

But everything costs something, especially in a country where you can hardly get anything on tick, let alone haggle for it. If something costs ten marks and Gül only has nine left or even nine marks eighty, she can't buy it.

Asking Fuat for twenty pfennigs might start a row, which Gül finds pointless because Fuat would happily drink or gamble away twenty pfennigs faster than Gül could say 'Just twenty pfennigs.' Pointless because Fuat insists on Gül getting by with the amount they've agreed. Though he's constantly treating his friends and had nothing better to do in Turkey than draw attention to himself with generous rounds of food and drink, he's a real scrooge inside his own four walls.

Nadiye will never know what those twelve pairs of towelling knickers cost Gül.

Ceyda comes home from school every day, sits down at the kitchen table, and looks out at the garden. There's a pen in her hand but she doesn't do any writing.

'What am I supposed to do?' she asks her mother. 'They write their letters differently, I don't understand a word, I sit there bored all day long.'

Gül remembers what it was like for her when she moved from the village to the town, from a one-room school where all the primary classes were taught by the same teacher, to a huge building with so many classrooms and corridors that she kept getting lost.

Of course Ceyda is disappointed. She has gone from being one of the first to learn to read and write, writing her own letters to her mother, to the bottom of her class. She can't even remember the teacher's name. But all the same, she has to go to school every morning.

At least she's no longer living with her nene, who always gave her so much housework to do. She never got her the winter coat Gül sent the money for either. 'It's good money – we can buy a fur for that,' her nene said to her dede.

'It's for Ceyda, not for you,' Faruk answered.

'I know it is,' Berrin replied. 'We'll get the dressmaker to alter my old coat so that she has a new one. She's just a child – she'll have grown out of it in a year's time, but I could really use a new fur.'

And that was what they did.

Ceyda spends half her days at school, but at least she can be with her mother the rest of the time. Still, she can't help but worry that her mother might send her back at any moment.

After a few weeks, Ceyda makes some friends in the neighbourhood who speak more German than she does. They help her, and before long she too can say *Frau Schafenstein* when she wants to get her teacher's attention. But she'll be in her fifth year at school before she realises that Factory Lane is a world away from Elm Gardens or Poplar Road.

Gül is always missing something. Even though she's finally been reunited with her daughters; even though the postman is glad she doesn't feel such pain when she doesn't get a letter; even though she has a job; even though the houses in their road belong to the woollen mill, which means the rent is low and they can save plenty of money; even though her father sometimes goes to the petition-writers outside the town hall to dictate long letters to her; and even though her father's typed words fill Gül's heart with joy, she's always missing something.

She's missing those eighteen months with Ceyda and Ceren. And though she senses it's impossible, she tries her best to fill that gap. 'That's life,' she'll say later on. 'They send you to fetch water but all they give you is a basket. There's no bucket for you to fill.'

It's not just time and attention Gül wants to lavish on her daughters; she wants something tangible, even if it's just something other than a bucket. She stands in front of the department store shelves, baffled by all the toys in their brightly coloured packaging. She used to play with pebbles when she was a child, and even in her early days in Germany with Rafa, who she hasn't seen for a long time now. She made things out of clay, she played hopscotch and they jumped rope, but Ceyda and Ceren can do all that too.

The most precious toy Gül and her sisters had was a plastic ball. Their father brought it back from Istanbul, and their stepmother kept it locked up in a trunk, only handing it over to them for a few hours at a time.

That's why we're here, isn't it? Gül thinks, standing in the toy department. *So we can buy more things, so we can have our own bit of this world.* There are dolls and cars; jigsaw puzzles and cuddly toys; little plastic figures packaged in cardboard; and a miniature shop complete with tiny food boxes, all of which are empty.

Gül looks at the prices, the packaging, and the money in her purse. Finally she picks out a cardboard box of square cards with different pictures on them, which appeal to her, and a doll. Melike will get a bit less money this month.

At home, she sits on the kitchen floor with Ceren and takes the game out of the box. The cards have pictures of oranges and lemons on them, apples and chestnuts, feathers and eggs, just right for a girl like Ceren, Gül thinks, but she doesn't understand why there are two of each. She gets Ceren to tell her the names of the things, while she tries to make sense of the German instructions. There are instructions in Spanish – Rafa could have read those – and in Italian – for Suzan to read – but none in Turkish.

The German is too complicated for Gül, and she thinks: *It's for children – can't they write it in a way that children will understand?* But it's probably her fault; she still can't speak enough German to understand a simple game. Or perhaps they didn't check it properly in the factory and that's why there are two of each card.

Gül starts sharing out the pictures. 'One apple for Ceren, one apple for Mummy, one shell for Ceren, and what does Mummy get?'

Ceyda is playing outside, and Fuat is having a lie-down before he starts his late shift. Gül jumps when he comes down to the kitchen.

'What time is it?' he asks, and before Gül can say anything, he snaps at her. 'What did I tell you? You're supposed to wake me! And what are you doing? Pretending to be not much older than your daughter. Is it too much to ask for you to keep your eye on the clock for five minutes?'

Ceren sits frozen on the floor, intimidated by her yelling father, while Gül gets up and doesn't seem to know where to put her hands. He's right, he's absolutely right, so she says: 'I'm sorry, I got so carried away. I shouldn't have lost track of time. Forgive me, it won't happen again.'

Fuat gets even louder, as if that only made matters worse. 'Got carried away! How old are you, eh? It beggars belief. Carried away with children's games. How old are you? Can you even tell the time yet?'

'You're right, I'm sorry,' Gül murmurs, looking at the ground.

'What am I supposed to tell my foreman now if I'm late? That my stupid wife was playing with my daughter and lost track of time? He'll think I've got a screw loose on my moped. Any man would go mad in a house like this; no man could stay normal. You wanted the children here, and now they're here you go and forget your husband. What's next, eh? Are you going to throw me out, poison me? What's next?'

He slams the kitchen door behind him, grabs his coat and leaves for work.

Gül remembers the time he almost hit her, years ago now. And she remembers the time her father asked her: 'Did I send you out to play? Tell me, did I send you out to play? I went and fetched the water myself!'

That was even longer ago. Back then she'd been so busy playing, she'd forgotten her place in the queue for the public water tap.

I don't seem to have learned much since then, she thinks. Ceren, no longer fearing her father's rage, starts crying.

When Ceyda comes home from playing outside, Gül says: 'There's something on the table for you, look.'

Ceyda lifts up the box, which Gül has wrapped for her.

'This?'

'Yes, that.'

'What is it?'

'Open it and see.'

'What's in there?' Ceyda asks, her tone bored.

'Everything you want, my little lamb,' Gül says. 'If you don't like what's in there today, there'll be something else in there tomorrow.'

She hasn't got the money to buy more toys; she hopes her daughter will like the doll.

Ceyda rips off the wrapping paper with some reluctance, but Gül can tell she's trying to hide her joy when she sees the doll. The tiny moment when her daughter's face beams with delight doesn't escape her.

'If you don't like it, we'll find you another one,' Gül says, and just like her daughter, she conceals her joy out of fear Ceyda might mistake it for triumph.

Now she has her daughters with her, Gül's feelings of longing take a new direction. Almost all of their neighbours have framed black and white photographs in their sitting rooms, family photos of everyone together, looking serious at the camera: the children standing in order of height; the boys with short hair and slingshots peeking boldly out of their pockets; the girls in their best dresses with their hair neatly plaited; the men in suits and white trousers, their hats set straight like when they were in the army; the women with perfectly pressed headscarves, their legs hidden from view beneath their long skirts but probably freshly epilated. If only Gül had a photo, just one, of all her siblings together.

On the far left: Melike, who's younger than Gül but was already taller at twelve than her sister was at fourteen. Melike, who shares their mother's dark complexion, though that's hardly clear from the photo. Melike, who never listened to her father or to Gül when she was younger, whose will always seemed stronger than anything it came up against. Melike, the only one with a glimmer of a smile in the corner of her mouth, like she's going to run off as soon as the photographer has finally finished. Next to her, a hand's width away: Gül with a bow in her hair, the way she wanted it for the photo for her school leaving certificate. On the right next to Gül stands Sibel, who was often ill as a child but completed her schooling before she came of age, which meant she hadn't been allowed to work as a student teacher until the blacksmith had her date of birth changed by a couple of months in front of a false witness in court. Next to skinny Sibel stands Nalan, the first child the blacksmith had with his second wife, Arzu – another girl, but what a girl. Nalan, the pretty one; the men started leering at her early on. As her breasts grew, few of the men managed to keep their eyes off Nalan's ample cleavage, and so she got used to rounding her shoulders and hunching her back. And next to Nalan is Emin. He has inherited his father's fair hair and his eyes change from blue to green and back again. The baby of the family, somewhat pampered, he took eight years to finish his five years of basic schooling but is no fool. One day, he'll be the only member of the family to strike it rich.

A photo of the five of them, standing in order of height, in front of the big mulberry tree in the summer house garden. If only Gül had a photo like that, a photo like the ones other families have, a photo like a wide gateway onto all their memories, so she could believe she might once have lived in paradise.

Had all five of them ever stood by the mulberry tree at the same time? Hadn't Gül always looked out for Melike and Sibel, hoping to replace their dead mother? Hadn't she tried just as hard with Nalan and Emin? Had she ever been filled with calm and contentment because she felt she'd done everything she could? Didn't she always feel overwhelmed, if only by what she expected of herself?

But who else can you feel so connected to but your own siblings? Who else have you shared your life with so intimately that your hearts can do little but touch?

If only Gül had a photo, though one was never taken – just one photo, maybe that would quench the longing in her eyes.

Years from now, a photo of their mother will turn up in a trunk, and Gül, Melike, their children and Sibel will each have a copy made, and then the picture of this woman, who even Melike can hardly remember now, will hang in seven different homes. They have all come to feel close to her through Gül's words.

Meanwhile, Serter has moved out, and now Mevlüde is living alone in their big house on Factory Lane. She doesn't even speak to him any more; instead she looks away whenever she encounters the man – who is still her husband – at work or on the street.

Serter's paranoia is no longer reserved for his wife. He keeps talking, just as before, about how she wants to poison him, how she's an old witch, that her mother was well known for visiting disaster upon whole families by cursing them, but he also believes that his landlady, an old German woman who has rented him her spare room, comes to him at night and steals the vigour from his loins.

'I wake up in the mornings feeling completely weak,' he complains. 'I can hardly get up and go to work; my knees can barely hold my legs up. I'm close to toppling over on the way to the bathroom.'

His Turkish colleagues enjoy listening to him and laughing behind his back. If they're looking for a laugh, they go over to Serter and get him talking.

Havva, the Istanbulite, has been on her own for the past two weeks because her husband had to make a last-minute trip to Turkey. Though the two women live not fifty metres apart and have plenty of time to talk about their absent husbands now, they don't meet up once. Even though it was Mevlüde, in part, who made it possible for Havva's husband Yunus to fly to Turkey in the first place.

Yunus got a telegram saying his mother was on her deathbed and he should get there as soon as possible if he wanted to see her alive one last time. Yunus and Havva didn't have enough money for a plane ticket – their savings had all gone on his mother's treatment – so the Turks from their street all had a whip-round. Everyone knew what it was for, so it was only natural to chip in, to give a small amount not as a loan but as a gift. In the space of six hours, they had raised enough for a plane ticket.

Gül put some money in too. *My husband's turned me into a calculator*, she thought to herself. *He's so stingy at home that I have to go back and forth over the numbers in my head, just like he does.* But once she's contributed her little sum, she discovers that Fuat handed over 100 marks without a moment's hesitation.

As soon as Yunus was on his way, the gossip in the street started up. *There are lots of different customs and traditions, but that gossip, that tittle-tattle, seems to be the same all over Turkey,* Gül thinks. That fear of being the laughing stock of the town.

Now, behind Havva's back, the women have started discussing how much they gave the couple, saying that it was enough for more than one ticket and that no doubt that snooty, shameless woman will be buying herself makeup and even shorter skirts now, flaunting her beauty all the more.

No one forced them to give them any money, Gül thinks, annoyed, *and it's not like Havva didn't wear makeup before – what do they expect her to do, throw away her lipsticks because she didn't have the money for a plane ticket? What a bunch of hypocrites.*

But who can she say this to? Who can she talk to about all this? People prove themselves through what they do, not what they say.

The box is enormous; Fuat and his colleagues pant and wheeze as they carry it into the living room. Fuat is beaming. Gül looks at him and is glad to see he's happy, but she can't work out what could be in the box.

'Well now,' Fuat says. 'How's this for creature comforts, how's this for luxury? In Turkey only really rich folks get them, but here on Factory Lane we'll all have them soon enough, you'll see.'

He seems to grow a little taller as he says the next words.

'We're one of the first families to get one of these. Quality German craftsmanship from Nordmende.'

Gül has seen the factory in Bremen. It's one of those huge buildings she's a little scared of because she knows if she went in, she'd struggle to find her way back out.

'It's as heavy as a donkey,' Fuat says. 'But a television like this will take you further than a packhorse, much further. It'll you take you all round the world, and you don't even have to get up – you can just sit back in your seat and relax.'

Which is something he does his fair share of in the days that follow. At one time they would have all sat together in the kitchen, but nowadays they only really linger in the living room when the TV is on. Fuat, Gül, Ceren and Ceyda sit in front of the screen, and in the weeks that follow, they learn more German than they did in all the months before then.

They watch it all, from Daliah Lavi to *Zum Blauen Bock*, which alienates and bores them in equal measure, to *Star Trek* and Ilja Richter, *Die Sendung mit der Maus* and *Sportschau*, *Tatort* and *Spiel ohne Grenzen*, and most important of all, as far as Fuat's concerned, the lottery draw.

Before this, they had been a little trapped in their world, in the little sections of Germany that they'd come to know, but this big, heavy TV set opens a window onto an entire language and culture, right from their very own living room, albeit in black and white.

The newsreaders tell them all about what's happening across the country. And though they don't always understand it all, sitting in the living room and watching TV takes them deeper into Germany than simply going out and participating in everyday public life.

For now, Fuat will still consider it a luxury to be able to kick back in his armchair with a whisky and Coke in front of the Nordmende set, feeling like he's made it. But twenty years later, it will seem like he's being dealt an almighty punishment when his satellite dish breaks, and all of a sudden, he's forced to watch German programmes again, even though he hardly understands them any more. But, of course, no one suspects this at a time when you still have to adjust the antenna to get a clearer picture.

'I don't like fat women. I like the look of slim women, like the ones who tell you what's up next on TV. Modern women, a little bit sporty, nice and slender like your sister Melike; her skin would be too dark for me, though.'

Fuat doesn't usually have a good word to say about Melike, and there's no way he would have supported his sister-in-law just for her figure, the way Gül has been helping her out behind his back.

Gül is offended, but she doesn't point out that Melike used to play volleyball on the school team and could always run the fastest and jump the furthest, that it's no wonder she never puts on much weight, with all the running around she does. She doesn't say that her sister is often unfair and always puts herself first, and what use is a nice figure when the heart underneath it is hard? Gül would never talk like that about her family; she'd rather keep quiet.

It's not just that Fuat doesn't know how to flatter people, she thinks. *He doesn't find me attractive either. Why did he ask for my hand in the first place? Just because I weighed less back then?*

They're in Turkey for the summer; she goes to her father's kitchen, where there's baklava in the green cupboard with the wire mesh doors. She hasn't had baklava for a good year. Where would she get it in Germany? And what's wrong with baklava? It tastes good, as sweet as comfort would taste, and sweeter than revenge can ever be.

Life only comes into us because we have mouths. God breathed our life into them; we use them to draw in the strength to go on breathing.

At least she doesn't go pouring alcohol down her throat, forgetting who she is or which way the world spins; she doesn't swallow poison that makes her breath stink and turns her into a beast that can't think beyond what's between its legs, forgetting what it likes the look of and what it doesn't.

But Fuat doesn't just use the holidays to drink more than usual. This year, he buys land, a bare plot in the town with enough space for a house bigger than the one on Factory Lane, but with no garden. None of the houses in the town have a garden; that's why people have their summer houses just outside town, summer houses with huge orchards.

Fuat can't pay off the plot straight away, so he tells the owner he'll give him half in cash now and get the rest to him as soon as he can. Gül hopes Fuat doesn't lose too much by gambling while they're here, or at least if he does, she hopes the man selling the land won't find out. How can a man with debts gamble? That's like betting someone else's money. A man can only indulge in gambling if it's his own hard-earned money he's throwing away, Gül's father used to say.

He shouldn't drink on tick either; only if he's earned it by the sweat of his brow. But Fuat has a mind of his own; he drinks the whisky he bought at duty free, four bottles more than he's allowed, but the customs men are happy to take a bit of pocket money home with them. He's just as generous to his friends, he bets on the cards, and he gets his kicks without consequences. A weight has fallen from his shoulders since he brought home the contraceptive pill for Gül. Now if only the weight would fall from her hips...

Fuat might be happy these days; things are moving in a positive direction, and it looks like good fortune is coming his way. A man keeps moving forwards, and where would good fortune be if not up ahead?

For Gül, happiness is here right now, not somewhere up ahead. She spends time with her sisters and brother, chatting away; she can talk to her father every day again like she did as a newlywed; and her daughters are close by, roaming through the gardens of the summer houses all day with other children. Her life feels rich. The neighbours listen to her when she talks about Germany, and it sounds better in her stories than what she sees when she's really there, but she doesn't know how else to tell the stories.

Ceyda sees her old friends, guarding her doll jealously all the while, and on the way to the summer houses Ceren keeps asking which road leads home, as if all unsurfaced roads were linked together. Her older sister laughs at her, but at night Ceyda dreams of a short-cut from Factory Lane straight to her dede's summer house. She's so thrilled to discover it that she wakes up every time. Night after night, all summer long, she has the dream – at least that's how it seems – and night after night, she wakes to a disappointing reality.

Two years have passed since those dreams, dreams like nightmares in reverse: instead of waking up relieved, Ceyda would open her eyes to the crushing weight of reality. During the next-but-one summer holidays, she spends a night in the house of an Istanbul policeman, not getting a minute's sleep, while Gül is in Germany, wondering in the darkness whether she'd feel better if she strangled Fuat, sleeping beside her.

Everything went so fast. The six weeks they spent in Turkey that year passed quicker than a blink, as did their time in the airport. But from then on, everything moved slowly, torturously slowly, time dragging as if someone had blocked God's clockwork.

That summer, Gül put on the pounds she'd starved off in Germany, Ceren worked out how long the road was from there to Factory Lane, and Fuat finally paid off the plot of land, though he didn't have the money to start building the house yet. Ceren was surprised by how much she missed her friends from Factory Lane. It felt strange that most of them were in Turkey too, but further away than they could ever be in Germany.

The family took a coach to Istanbul together and a taxi from the coach station to the airport, something that seems perfectly normal to them by now.

The man at the airline desk looks long and hard at their papers. He keeps looking at Ceyda, and then he says to Fuat: 'Your daughter can't go on the flight; her residence permit's expired.'

'Beg your pardon?' Fuat says, as if he hasn't understood.

'The residence permit for Ceyda Yolcu has expired. She can't go to Germany.'

While the man speaks, Gül notices his words growing ever more distant, as though they were suddenly coming from somewhere far away. As though she couldn't hear properly. But she feels no panic yet. You've got to be smart, Fuat's always saying. He'll get his daughter through, like he did the bottles of whisky.

'Can't we just take her with us and sort it out at the other end? She's only a child.'

'Brother,' the young man says respectfully now, 'you live there, you ought to know how it works. Everything goes by the book. You can't just wait and see what happens. I'm not allowed to issue a boarding pass for her.'

'But what if you did? You could have just overlooked something, couldn't you?'

'Then the customs officers would notice it.'

'I'm sure we can find a solution, don't you think?'

The man shakes his head in a regretful, final gesture.

Fuat looks over at Gül. If only he'd show as much concern when he's too drunk to see straight. 'You stay here with her.'

'It's none of my business,' the friendly man at the counter says, 'but if you do that then you'll lose three flights. Little –' he checks the documents in front of him – 'Ceren. Ceren is on her mother's passport. She'd have to stay here too.'

'What are you looking at me like that for?' Fuat says to Gül. 'Can I help it if you didn't check when her residency permit runs out?'

Although the sound of her voice seems to come from far away, Gül hears how firm and determined she sounds when she leans in close to Fuat's ear so the man can't hear her.

'You're staying here with Ceyda, even if it costs you your job,' she says. 'You're staying here with her. We won't leave her alone again. I promised her that and I'm keeping that promise.'

To Gül's surprise, Fuat nods.

'We'll find a way,' he says.

Gül and Ceren pick up their boarding cards and go through passport control to the waiting room. 'I'll take care of everything,' Fuat promises.

Searching through her mind in the waiting room, Gül can't find a single thought in her head. Ceren sits next to her obediently, asking no questions. But perhaps Gül would prefer it if she talked, if she wanted to know something. That way, Gül would have to dress up the emptiness in words and she'd understand for herself what's just happened. Perhaps she'd find a reason for it, something or someone to blame and a little time to grasp why they don't give you more time for a decision like that.

Moments later, or so it seems to Gül in her frozen state, they're on the plane. Gül doesn't know where the time has gone. Ceren has the window seat, with Gül next to her, whose eyes are fixed absent-mindedly on the aisle, not looking at anything. All of a sudden, she sees Fuat. He's on his own.

She flushes as if someone had put a hot blanket over her, a blanket of lead pressing her into her seat. She feels like she's falling, and now panic arrives too, a guest that was missing from the party. Now something is happening to lend weight to the emptiness of before.

'Where's Ceyda?' Gül asks.

Her voice is weak now and she's dizzy. She feels like she might fall out of her seat.

'I've taken care of everything,' Fuat says. 'It's all fine. She's staying the night with Havva's family. They're coming back later than us this year. What are neighbours for, eh?'

'Who's taking her there?'

'A policeman. A servant of the state, a reliable man who saw what a situation we were in. Not like that airline employee.'

'Where did you get the address?'

Gül is surprised at how practically she's thinking under the circumstances.

'They live in Bakırköy, right near the airport. As if Yunus hasn't told us a thousand times.'

The hot blanket and the panic are joined by a dark shadow of foreboding.

'If anything happens to that girl, I won't let you off alive,' Gül says. And she means it.

They don't say a word to each other for the next ten hours.

'Don't make my husband a murderer,' Gül's real mother is supposed to have said to a man who tried to kidnap her. *Perhaps I get it from her*, Gül thinks. *Here I am, my mother twenty years dead, and just like her I'm threatening someone with murder. But it's true: I'd kill this man with my bare hands.*

The thought is a comfort to her.

Meanwhile, Ceyda is on her way to Bakırköy with the ever-so-friendly policeman. He's memorised Fuat's description well enough, but he simply can't find the house belonging to the family from Germany.

'What does it look like, your friends' house?' the policeman wants to know, once he's asked a few passers-by. Ceyda shrugs.

'You've got to help me out a little bit here.'

'I don't know,' she says. 'I've never been there. I've only ever been to their house on Factory Lane, in Germany.'

The policeman looks round, looks out of the car window and then turns back to Ceyda.

'Not to worry,' he says.

But once he's asked the district chief and left Ceyda waiting in the car outside various coffeehouses, he doesn't know what else he can do.

'Bakırköy is big,' he says. 'We could be searching for their house 'til we're blue in the face. How about this: I'll take you home with me, we can all have dinner together there. My wife will make you up a bed, and tomorrow morning I'll put you on the bus and you can go back to your hometown. Shall we do that, poppet?'

Ceyda nods timidly. What other choice does she have?

Her mother once told her the story of how she got lost when she was a little girl. A strange man took her back to her family, and her grandmother didn't smack Gül until the strange man had left.

If only Mum could smack me like that, Ceyda thinks. *She could smack me once at the end of all this, or twice, or ten times. If only I could get a smack from my mum. Then nothing else would really matter.*

When she gets out of the car, her knees feel like they could give way at any second; as if they're not made up of bones and joints, but young green branches that can't take her weight. But Ceyda doesn't want anyone to see that she's scared. She bravely puts one foot in front of the other.

Never go off with strangers, that's what her mother taught her. That's why she told her the story of the smacking; never go off with strangers. But what is she supposed to do, all alone in this city?

The policeman does have a wife and two little children, younger than Ceyda, and his mother also lives with the young family in their flat, which is little more than a big kitchen and two tiny rooms.

Ceyda is slightly relieved, but she hardly speaks and hardly eats, and when she's tucked up in bed in one of the rooms with the other children, she doesn't sleep. She waits. She waits to see if the strange man will come in and try to do something to her. She waits for the trembling to stop. She waits and she daren't even cry.

The next morning, she doesn't eat much at breakfast, though the policeman's wife chats away to her cheerily and keeps stroking her hair with her soft, warm hands, trying to put her fears to rest. She makes Ceyda up another couple of pieces of bread, packs her some fruit and something to drink, and then the policeman takes her to the coach station, buys her a ticket and puts her on the bus. Ceyda will never forget this image of him standing by the bus, giving her one last wave goodbye, with a smile on his lips that's probably supposed to be encouraging.

'Why haven't we heard anything?' Gül asks. 'How did you give the man directions to the house if you don't have the exact address? An address we could send a telegram to? If anything happens to that girl, I won't let you off alive.'

They're in Germany, it's a Friday and they've got work on Monday. That night, Gül sleeps as little as Ceyda does at the policeman's house.

'Gül and Fuat have had an accident!' Gül's stepmother cries, distressed. 'God forbid, but I think they're dead. Ceren, too!'

'What?' says Timur. 'What are you talking about? What kind of accident?'

The blacksmith is a picture of fear. Everything feels numb, like he's been plunged into ice-cold water.

'How do you know? Tell me, tell me!'

'Look, look outside. Ceyda's come back all on her own.'

'So you come to me, woman, instead of running over to her?' Timur says, pushing his wife aside and running out of the door. His heart is beating faster from the fear, but it doesn't seem able to pump the cold blood around his body. Even before he sees Ceyda, there's something inside of him, something that whispers to him that nothing has happened to his daughter: his Gül, his lamb, the light of his eyes. No, if something had happened to her, he would have felt it.

When he sees Ceyda running over to him, he relaxes, crouches down and opens his arms wide.

Ceyda runs over, crying and smiling.

'Come on, come here, treasure.'

Timur strokes Ceyda's hair as he puts an arm round her and picks her up.

'That's it, it's alright. Tell me what happened.'

More than two thousand kilometres away, Gül is wondering what on earth could have happened. Was the policeman really trustworthy? Did they find the flat? She has forced Fuat to find Havva's Istanbul address and send a telegram. *Is Ceyda there? Please reply quickly.*

Four hours later comes the reply: *Ceyda not here. Hope all's well.*

It's Saturday afternoon and Gül is wandering around the garden and the house like a wind-up toy. She doesn't know what she could do to make the time pass quicker. She thinks of the whisky in the cupboard. If it helps Fuat, it might help her too, but she's frightened of losing control. Ceyda might need her. Sober. Clear-headed.

I promised, Gül thinks, *I promised her I'd never leave her alone again. My mother wasn't there for us because she died. That'd be my only excuse: if I were dead.*

It's worse than thinking she might be pregnant again. It's worse than sitting in the kitchen all alone and the days just not seeming to pass. It's worse than breaking her nose, and her stepmother not wanting a doctor in the house. It's worse than hanging over an abyss in the cellar of her mother-in-law's house and fearing that death is at hand.

Lord, let me be reunited with my daughter, Gül prays. *Do as you will, but don't burden me with this separation. Lord, I don't want to complain; I've been blessed with two wonderful daughters and a father you could only dream of. I've been blessed to be able to help my sister to study, I've been blessed not to suffer as much as Saniye. Lord, I know to treasure my place here on Earth, but please, please don't take my daughter from me.*

On Saturday evening, Timur's telegram arrives: *Ceyda here safe and sound. I kiss you all.*

It takes another three weeks to deal with all the formalities, then Fuat and Gül can finally pick Ceyda up from the airport. Three weeks, during which husband and wife speak not a single word to each other, and Fuat wonders why he bothered with the pills when he never gets any. Three weeks, which he deems enough time to buy a car. A car he has lots to say about, all of which Gül simply ignores.

It's barely a ten-minute walk to work, the area they live in isn't all that big, and they've just got back from a holiday they spent a lot of money on. Fuat has spent plenty of time banging on about how much the missed flight, the new passport and the telegrams had cost them. He did the calculations out loud again and again, sitting at the kitchen table, but still he couldn't tell whether Gül was taking it in and whether it distracted her from her anger.

'It's a used car, in good nick. It only cost the same as two plane tickets, and next year it'll take us to Turkey – all four of us, on five or six tanks of petrol. It'll save us money, lots of money – it'll be our best purchase yet! We won't have to lug our shopping home ourselves anymore; we can drive our fruit and veg right up to the front door. This is a proper country: you just hand over a few notes, and you've got yourself a car. There's all sorts on offer – you can buy something real for your money here; you're not stuck looking at empty shelves. And the Germans really don't have a clue about haggling. You've got to be smart. I got it down to nearly half the asking price.'

Gül would very much like to scream at him, tell him to shut his mouth once and for all. Tell him she has no desire to hear about his little sums, and that he can go ahead and buy his damn car; she's not interested in the slightest. But she's not talking to him. She doesn't say a word to him, not once. She doesn't even say, 'Look, your other daughter's just started school. If you've got such a guilty conscience, why not pay her some attention? Don't try to distract yourself and us. Don't spend all day gabbling on about a car; it's just a heap of junk at the end of the day, just like the rubbish that comes out of your mouth.'

When Fuat comes home at the weekend, drunk but not blind drunk as he might normally be, he repeats those words that hurt Gül, words he should really keep to himself instead of swaggering about with his silly little sums: 'I really prefer slim women, if I'm honest.'

Gül pushes him away, takes her blanket and her pillow without a word, and goes down to the kitchen.

But once Ceyda has come back and the family is reunited, Gül's heart softens. And even though she fights it deep down, the words soon start to flow again.

God loves me, she thinks. *He makes me suffer, he torments me and he tests me, but in the end he bathes me in light. I've no cause to complain.*

'Don't cry, my darling, don't cry.'

'But it hurts so much.'

'The clove will make the pain go away. Just keep it in your mouth – soon you'll hardly feel a thing.' Ceren is lying in bed next to her mother, wishing the pain would stop, wishing her mother would press her even more firmly to her bosom, wishing her mouth felt just as soft as her mother's cheek, wishing away the pain, both dull and stabbing at once and barely leaving her room to breathe.

The bedroom door opens.

'What are you doing here?' Fuat asks Gül. 'And you, shouldn't you be at school?'

'Shhhh,' Gül says, urging him to lower his voice a little.

She lays Ceren's head gently on the pillow and gets up. Her daughter whimpers so quietly they can hardly hear it.

'She's got toothache,' Gül says.

'Right,' Fuat says, 'but what are you doing here? Aren't you supposed to be at work?'

Gül closes the bedroom door behind her.

'Yes,' she says. 'I should be, but you can see she…'

'What can I see? It's work, it's a factory – you can't just stroll in and out of there like it's your father's forge.'

'They won't throw me out just like that.'

'No wonder there's never any progress where we come from. Look at you, you've no sense of duty.'

'Yes, I do,' Gül says. 'I do have a sense of duty. But I'm not married to the factory, and I haven't got children with it either.'

I not married to factory, piss off, arsehole! – those were the words Saniye's new husband had hurled in his foreman's face. That was what Saniye told her, and Gül was so impressed that she finds herself repeating the words now.

They sound good when she says them too, she decides. And she likes the part she's added about the children as well.

'There are more important things in life than the factory,' she adds, since Fuat doesn't come up with an answer straight away.

'We're here to work, not to comfort crying children. It's toothache, right? Have you given her a clove?'

Gül nods.

'It's a milk tooth, isn't it? That's easy enough to deal with.'

Gül looks at him. He's just like all other men. Saniye's new husband seems to be the only one who's any different.

Saniye met Yılmaz here. He comes from Malatya like her, but he went to university in Istanbul, where he took to the streets to protest, got expelled and ended up coming to Germany. Not for work, but because he wanted to get out of the country he had come to despise. He talks about the proletariat, about workers' rights, trade unions and comrades and other things that sound new and unfamiliar to Gül.

He married Saniye in Malatya in the summer. Now Saniye is pregnant, and when she felt sick one morning Yılmaz simply stayed at home with her.

When his foreman went to give him a bollocking for not turning up without leave the previous day, Yılmaz barked at him with his few words of German: 'I not married to factory, piss off, arsehole!'

Fuat is not that kind of man, but to Gül's surprise he says, 'I'll take care of her tooth.'

His hand is already on the door handle, when Gül tells him, 'Be gentle with her.'

Fuat pauses and looks at her, shaking his head. 'You seem to think I'm some kind of monster. Come on, get dressed, get to work. Trust me, I'll take care of it.'

Ceren has never been alone with her father in her parents' bedroom. From now on, the scent of cloves will always remind her of this moment, when she didn't know if the pain in her tooth was greater than her fear of what might come next.

Her father smiles in a way Ceren rarely sees, because she's usually asleep when he smiles that way. It's a smile that usually takes two whiskies and Coke to appear.

Fuat sits down on the bed.

'It hurts a lot, doesn't it?' he says.

Ceren nods, wary.

'You poor thing. I was a hairdresser when we were back in Turkey – you know that, don't you?'

'Yes,' Ceren whispers.

Her father doesn't have a bosom where she can seek solace. 'I had a salon. Do you remember where we always bought kebab in the summer?'

What he calls *always*, was three times.

'Yes,' Ceren says, a little louder now. As though her voice might drown out the tooth pain.

'I had my salon around the corner from there, and people used to come to me for a haircut or a shave. But do you know what else hairdressers used to do in the olden days?'

'No,' Ceren says, because shaking her head would bring tears to her eyes.

'They used to pull teeth. They didn't have dentists in those days, so people went to the hairdresser when they had toothache. And he'd help them. Would you like me to help you?'

Ceren shakes her head now, afraid to say no.

'That's fine,' Fuat says. 'We don't have to. But I would like to know which tooth it is that's hurting so much. Will you show me?'

Ceren hesitates.

'I won't do anything, don't worry. Look.'

He puts his hands behind his back. Ceren opens her mouth and points at the place where it hurts.

'Can I come a bit closer?'

Ceren nods open-jawed, and Fuat leans forward and looks into his daughter's mouth.

'Okay,' he says. 'You can close your mouth again. I know all about these things. It won't hurt any more in a minute, believe me. You just have to close your eyes now and clench your teeth together; just keep biting no matter how much it hurts. You've got to bite, bite, bite and keep your eyes closed tight, no matter what happens. That's the only way it'll work. Alright? Close your eyes, then, and bite. Harder. Is it hurting? It'll be all over in a minute. Keep your eyes shut.'

Ceren hears the sound of drawers opening and closing.

'Right,' Fuat says. 'Trust me, I won't touch you. Now I want you to open your mouth nice and wide. Wider. And keep your eyes shut. Shut tight. Right. That's it. Close your mouth, open your eyes.'

Ceren sees her father holding something white between finger and thumb.

'No tooth, no pain,' he says. 'Or does it still hurt?' Ceren is confused; she really can't feel any pain. But that can't be her tooth in her father's hand, can it?

'Here you are,' Fuat says, placing the tooth in the palm of her hand. 'As easy as that. Just a little trick, I'll tell you all about it later. Now give me the tooth back, and get yourself dressed and off to school.'

You've got to be smart; he hasn't spent whole nights at the poker table for nothing – Fuat knows how to bluff.

Once his daughter has left for school, he puts Ceyda's old milk tooth back in the box, then lights a cigarette and smokes it on the bed. He watches the smoke curling its way to the ceiling, and he sighs. For some reason he finds it much easier to relax when there are no women in the house.

'Strange bloke,' Fuat says. 'What's he doing here if money doesn't matter to him? Why did he come?'

'Ask him yourself,' Gül tells him.

Saniye and Yılmaz have just left. It's a dull Saturday evening, and at some point Gül got the feeling Fuat was waiting for the visit to be over so he could go out. Yılmaz drinks and smokes, but he's not a gambler.

'Doesn't want to leave his wife alone with the baby – talk about hen-pecked! No Anatolian man talks like that.'

'Sevgi's only four weeks old,' Gül says.

Fuat was away on military service when Ceyda was born. Two days later, he came home, spent his leave harvesting the apples and getting together with his friends, and was disappointed to learn that he didn't have a son.

'Exactly,' he says, 'that's what I'm saying. She's still tiny – what's he meant to do with a tiny baby like that? It's Saturday night: Saniye and Sevgi could have stayed here, I suggested we head off for a proper lads' night out. I just don't understand what it is the man wants here. He's not into money or pleasure, he's like a plant or something. Just air and water, that suits him down to the ground.'

'You saw yourself that he likes a drink,' Gül says to Fuat. He's standing in front of the mirror, trying to comb his hair to hide his bald spot.

'Yeah, otherwise I would have seriously doubted the man's sanity. Something's not right there, coming here without a dream, just because you don't like it back home. Home's the best, isn't it? That soil gave us our way of life and our strength, that soil soaked up the blood of our forefathers. Here there's nothing but tarmac,' he says, although it will be a good few years until Factory Lane is tarmacked. Like the other residents, Fuat doesn't think of Factory Lane as a real part of Germany.

'You can use the money you earn here to make a better life for yourself at home. Saniye's gone and got herself a real card; she'll be stuck here forever now,' he says, finally putting the comb down.

'See you later.'

Gül likes Yılmaz. He doesn't boast that he'll soon own half of Malatya, and he seems to be a good husband to Saniye. She deserves someone like him after losing her husband, son and father so young. Whenever Gül thinks she's had a hard lot in life, she thinks of Saniye. Gül's husband is still alive, he doesn't hit her, her two daughters are with her, and her father didn't end up a murderer, even though he certainly would have been up to the task.

She's never had to start all over again. How wonderful that Saniye has found a husband like Yılmaz. When he marched through the streets of Istanbul chanting slogans, it must have been for all the right reasons.

Gül doesn't envy Saniye her husband, but sometimes she wishes she could be like her friend: someone who isn't scared of anything except water and dogs, someone who can speak good German because she likes to join in wherever she can, someone who only says good things when she talks about Germany. Someone who can laugh loud and long, even if the darkness in her past sits just in the corner of her eye. Someone who makes filthy jokes when there are no men around, and who has few other inhibitions besides.

But God has laid down a separate path for each of us. And he gave us eyes to observe our neighbours and learn from them. There's no need to be afraid; the path leads us into the light.

'I'm signing you off sick up to and including Wednesday,' the doctor says. 'Take these pills and get some rest. Come back if you're not feeling better on Wednesday.'

Fuat coughs and asks: 'Work Wednesday?'

'No,' the doctor says, 'not before Thursday.'

'Okay,' Fuat says. 'Thank you.'

He has the flu, but that's not what made him go to the doctor. At home he lights a cigarette; it doesn't taste any good, but he smokes it almost down to the filter anyway. 'I'm not so sick that I have to stay in bed and go without a smoke,' he says.

He's been toying with the idea of going to the doctor for some time now, but this is the first time he's done it, because today he really doesn't feel well, and you've got to be smart about these things.

When the doctor signs you off, he's learnt, your insurance pays out the money the factory would have paid you.

He lights another cigarette: this one tastes better than the last. He makes himself a glass of tea with a slice of bread.

It's too easy, he thinks, putting his shoes on fifteen minutes later. *These Germans aren't the brightest sparks, otherwise one of them would have hit upon this ages ago.* On the way to work, he lights a third cigarette. It almost tastes good after a glass of tea. After a few drags, he flicks it into the gutter, content.

But I'm not well, the doctor said it himself, otherwise why would he have signed me off? It's only right that the insurance should pay me. And the factory, too, because I'm still going in to work anyway. You've got to be smart.

When Fuat is called into the staff office two weeks later, he hardly suspects that it hasn't all gone as smoothly as he'd imagined. *It won't take me long to weasel my way out of this*, he thinks, opening the door.

Minutes later, he's still stammering, claiming that he misunderstood the doctor, his German can't be good enough, couldn't they do with getting in an interpreter, it's probably all a misunderstanding.

When he leaves the office, he's pleased that he didn't go bragging about his idea all over the place. But nor does he suspect that he'll be telling this story himself in a few years' time. 'When I was still young and stupid and hadn't been here long,' he'll say, failing to mention how long he'd already been in the country at that point.

'It just goes to show,' he'll conclude, 'There's an order to everything – there's no wheeling and dealing, no cheating and hoodwinking, everyone gets his due. There's a fairness to things here – it's not like it is in Turkey, where everything relies on contacts and favours, where rules only exist to be written in books.'

And people will enjoy listening to him because he has a knack for storytelling, because his words have power and he finds his own ways to express things, because his passion is palpable; that urge to build a world out of words, a world that others can see and almost touch. A world where Fuat is always the good guy. He's quick to believe that the system is fair, but only because he wasn't up to cheating it.

That's how it must have been for my mother, Gül thinks when she sees the men gathering around Fuat as he embarks on a monologue. That's how it must have been when Timur and Fatma moved to the village, and the women there clustered around Gül's mother, who was the only one who knew fairy tales and could tell them well too, as if her words were colours and she had entered the world with a paintbrush in her hand.

Gül doesn't share her talent. When too many people listen to her at once, she grows hesitant. She doesn't like that kind of attention, and she doesn't even notice that she confuses her audience because she rarely sticks to one topic, following whatever associations pop into her mind instead. Observed through her words, the world is like a kaleidoscope – everything is constantly moving, hard to grasp – and just when you think you've understood, along comes a new gem, and the whole pattern changes.

Fuat usually has just one gem. He shows it off at an angle, if only from one side, but still, the gem is there for all to see. And when it comes to telling stories, that's what matters most.

She hears the knock at the door, but she doesn't answer. Dusk is drawing in; she had run up and down the road earlier calling her daughters' names and asking the neighbours whether they'd seen Ceyda and Ceren – but no one had.

Alright, Gül had sent the girls outside because they'd been galumphing around the house, running races up and down the stairs, screaming and jumping, not giving her a moment's peace.

She'd thrown them outside more than sent them; she was glad to see the back of them. If they wouldn't obey their mother, they were welcome to run around the streets and see if they couldn't get on someone's nerves out there. And then she went to look for them, but they were nowhere to be found. Now Gül, sitting in the kitchen, hears the knock at the back door, and thinks: *You knew perfectly well you're not allowed to leave Factory Lane.*

She hears brisk footsteps approaching the front door, then she hears the bell and still doesn't move.

What if nobody's in, eh? I'll show you not to stray so far from home.

More footsteps, and the next knock is at the kitchen window. Gül is sitting by the heater, barely visible from outside. Then she hears Ceyda's voice: 'Mummyyyy.'

She leaps up, sees Ceyda at the window and notices that Ceren isn't with her. All at once the fear is everywhere in her body, like someone has switched on a light. Or switched it off.

That moment when mother and daughter stare at each other through the window and Gül understands more in an instant than could ever be put into words or sounds. That moment when the shock still has no name. That moment when there *are* no names to hold onto.

The fear isn't just in Gül's body; it has taken grip of the whole world. Gül needs something small, tiny crumbs to give names to, pieces she can choke down if she has to; right now the fear is so huge that it might easily swallow her whole.

That moment.

How much fear can fit into a single moment, one so short? One that has to be short if anyone is to survive it.

'Which hospital?'

Ceyda stares at her mother, guilt-ridden, shrugging.

'How do we find out? How far did it send her flying? Come on, tell me.'

'I didn't see it properly.'

Ceyda feels responsible; she should never have missed that moment.

'How far away was she from the car when you saw her?'

'About… about as far as the chicken shed is long.'

'What do I do now? What shall I do, my God, what do I do?' Gül's voice trembles; she's about to start scratching her face like Ceren did that day at the foot of the stairs.

'Ask Auntie Tanja?' Ceyda suggests. Auntie Tanja is an elderly widow, the only German still living on Factory Lane. She speaks in a dialect Gül doesn't understand very well. Only decades later, after the fall of the Berlin Wall, will she recognise it as coming from East Germany.

'Yes, we'll go to Auntie Tanja,' says Gül. 'She's got a telephone. We have to know what hospital she's in.'

On the way there, Gül talks incessantly and Ceyda senses it would be worse if her mother were silent. But it would be even better if Gül were to slap her.

'You know you're supposed to stay here, on our road.'

'But it was so muddy.'

'So? Were you born in a tarmacked country? Have you turned into a little madam here? You're her big sister, you shouldn't have let her out of your sight.'

'She was hiding, between two cars.'

Auntie Tanja sits at the front of the taxi, Gül and Ceyda in the back. Gül looks at her daughter; she seems to get smaller and smaller with every second of silence.

'What happened, happened,' Gül says. 'Ceren's alive, and there's no solution for the past; that's what your dede always says. It could have happened anywhere, even on our road. No one can escape their fate.'

Gül strokes Ceyda's head.

'You have to do everything you can, you have to use all your strength and do everything as well as possible, but once things have happened, you have to let them go. Things aren't up to us.'

She remembers Mevlüde's words: *Write a book if you're so clever.*

She has no lack of faith, but letting go is so much harder than it sounds. How can she say such wise words while she's sitting there as if perched on the glowing coals of a blacksmith's fire, not on soft leather? How can she act so wise when it feels like forty foxes are stalking around inside her? How can she give advice when all she wants to do is cry, weep, clamour, and hope the day has no more surprises in store, hope they can take Ceren straight home, hope there's nothing broken, no bleeding or wounds that might never heal?

She was born healthy, Lord. Don't make her live the rest of her life disabled.

When the two of them fall silent in the back and Ceyda feels her mother's bosom against the top of her head, Tanja does something to stop the fear. She divides up time with words.

'It's not that bad, Mrs Yolcu,' she says. 'They said on the phone that her life's not in danger. Ceren will be home soon. There's always a bit of a shock after a tumble like this, but everything's going to be fine, you'll see.'

Auntie Tanja has turned around, and Gül looks into her slim, wrinkled face, angular but still radiating warmth.

'You should count your blessings it's not like it was in the war. In those days we couldn't just call up and find out where someone was. There were women who spent years waiting for their husbands, not knowing if they were alive or dead. Smile, Mrs Yolcu. Give us a smile, you're such a kind-hearted woman and so young. Smile – it won't be bad, I can feel it in my waters. You can trust an old lady like me.'

Gül smiles, not because she really understands what Tanja is saying, but more because she's glad she's taking care of them. She smiles because she's not alone. Because Auntie Tanja connects Factory Lane up with the rest of the world.

'Can't you be more careful?' Fuat shouts at his daughter. 'Who gave you permission to go so far away from home? Didn't you keep an eye on her? What did you have to do that was so urgent?'

Ceyda doesn't say a word. Fuat pours himself a large whisky and adds a dash of Coke, then sends Ceyda to bed and moves on to Gül: 'They're still at primary school and you can't deal with them.'

'Oh, but *you* can,' Gül says. 'You can deal with them so well, the perfect father. Like when you sent Ceren to school with toothache. You pretended you'd pulled her tooth like you were outwitting a toddler. And the teacher sent her home – she was whining with pain at her desk. Is that the way you want me to take care of them? You want me to follow your example?'

'She wasn't in pain when she left the house.'

'We should be thanking the Lord that Ceren's alive, that they'll probably let her out of hospital tomorrow, that she's healthy and we have plenty to eat here every day. You should be grateful for your whisky, for this house and the one we're building in Turkey.

You should be grateful, not constantly shouting and complaining – that won't get us anywhere.'

'Were you sitting with a wise man when our daughter got hit by a car, or what? Listen to you – "*we should be grateful*". If there was one thing that got us here, it was my strong will and ambition. If I'd been grateful for having two arms, two legs and a bit of bread and water, I'd still be cutting the greasy hair of louse-ridden village idiots. But we're here and we're working with wool, finest sheep's wool, soft as a cloud. You think you've got all the answers? You should be grateful to me. If it weren't for me, we'd be living in my parents' house, we wouldn't have a car parked outside, and we wouldn't have laid the foundations for a house. The girls wouldn't have so many toys or even a room of their own. You think all these riches come from Adam's rib? You're only ever grateful to the Lord, aren't you? What about the work of my hands and the sweat of my brow? You don't get it, do you? You ungrateful woman.'

A short while later, Gül hears a car starting.

'Ceyda, poppet, wake up, shh, don't wake your sister.'
'What?'
'Shh, quiet, get up and put something on.'
'What's happened?' Ceyda asks once they're outside the room. She's pulled a cardigan over her nightdress. It's dark outside.
'We've got to get your dad inside – I can't do it on my own.'
Gül doesn't see the puzzled look on her daughter's face; she's turned round and is already walking down the stairs.
'What's wrong with Baba?'
'He's fallen asleep in the car.'
'Why?'
'Why? Why? Because he's been necking poison like there's no tomorrow.'

Ceyda only realises what her mother means by 'poison' once she's opened the car door. Her father's sitting in the driver's seat, one hand on the steering wheel, the other next to the handbrake, his head at an unnatural angle, eyes closed, snoring.

'Can't we wake him?' Ceyda asks, her father suddenly looking bigger than usual.

'I've already tried,' Gül says. 'It's a miracle he made it home. God must have protected him.'

She had even considered just leaving him there, but she doesn't want the neighbours to see him first thing in the morning. She shakes Fuat, who's started making noises but still won't wake up.

'Should I get Ceren?'

Gül shakes her head.

'She's not strong enough yet to be of any help.'

Gül's confidence in the strength of her now twelve-year-old daughter makes Ceyda feel proud. At the same time, Ceyda makes a decision that night: *No matter what happens, I'll never marry a man who drinks.*

'Up the stairs?' Ceyda asks. 'We'll never manage that.'

'Just as far as the living room, over to the sofa,' Gül says, while Fuat tries to shake her off and mumbles something that might be words.

Gül curses the extra pounds she's carrying, as she grabs her husband under the armpits and pulls him out of the car. She curses every pasta dish and piece of baklava, while Ceyda holds onto her father's feet.

I would eat less, Gül says to herself, *but to what end? To be more attractive for my husband, to make it easier to heave him out of the car?*

Once they've deposited Fuat on the sofa, Gül sends Ceyda back to bed, removes her husband's shoes and trousers, places a blanket over him, and slides a pillow under his head.

Then she sits in the kitchen, lights herself another cigarette and thinks back to the day when she ate handfuls of chocolates and drank alcohol for the first time. She threw up that day, and she hasn't been able to stand the taste of alcohol or the smell of spirits ever since.

That man's in a bad way, he's gambling with his life. He'll spend tomorrow laid up in bed but then he'll go on drinking – why is that?

It's not the longing he had in Turkey, that curious yearning for drinks he only knew of from films. That longing must have been quenched long ago.

It's not the fire of youth, which needs drink to burn all the brighter. The man's over thirty now – he'll soon be halfway along his path, as they say.

Gül's father is said to have drunk a lot when he was young, boozing and roistering and putting the fear of God into everyone with his Herculean strength. They say he got so plastered he could hardly stay in the saddle, and in this condition, he managed to find opponents, apparently, who he'd throw to the ground, knowing he'd have lost a fight on his feet.

His horse, they said, ate what he'd thrown up and then couldn't find the way back home. Gül reassures herself that was allegedly the only time the blacksmith found himself sleeping on the side of the road.

Timur made a respectable man of himself, and he was a good father. Lord, let it be the same for Fuat – don't let him spend his life wandering the way of the bottle. Lord, let him learn his limits.

Gül's prayers will be answered, but not until they have lost all urgency.

When Ceyda takes off her cardigan without turning on the light, Ceren asks: 'Where were you?'

'Dad was very tired and fell asleep in the car, so Mum and I brought him in.'

'Why didn't you tell me? I would have helped.'

'Next time,' Ceyda says, with no inkling that there will be plenty more next times, and the three of them will often have to drag their father's slack body into the house.

'A very good morning to you,' says Serter, who has popped into the kitchen through the back door.

He's now living in a little flat, and the word is he won't let anyone in. He accuses potential visitors of wanting to spy on him – he believes that one or other of his acquaintances is co-operating with the CIA, or MİT, the Turkish National Intelligence Agency; that they want to kidnap him, drug him and frame him. At work, he has two padlocks on his locker, and he washes his hands twenty times a day. Everyone calls him *that loony* now. That loony uses three bars of soap a week; that loony thinks they've installed CCTV at work to keep an eye on him; that loony doesn't even trust God, even though he hears his voice now and then.

But that loony does his work just like all the others. He gets his wages, and buys food in tins or jars; garlic, which is more widely available now, is the only thing he'll buy unpackaged. 'You can't poison garlic,' he claims, and sometimes people flinch at his breath.

He goes to the cinema, meets up with other Turks who find his antics amusing, drinks from time to time, plays cards, and goes to a prostitute every fortnight. She's very fond of this strange little man, who can never really relax but is clean, generous, polite and never rough with her.

'Is Fuat up?' he asks now, as Gül is chopping aubergines. She doesn't break off from her work; Serter never shakes hands.

'No,' says Gül, 'he's still asleep.'

Fuat woke up about two hours ago and came down to use the toilet. He went back upstairs and got back into bed without so much as nodding at Gül.

'I'll come back later then,' Serter says.

'I hope it's good news. What is it? Can I help?'

'Oh, nothing, sister,' he says. 'Just a silly thing, I'll just come back later. Just a silly thing.'

'Perhaps you'd like to sit and wait for a bit? Are you hungry, would you like something to eat?' Gül asks out of habit, and even as she's speaking she thinks she probably shouldn't have offered. But Serter seems to consider for a moment.

'These pastries, did you make them?' he asks.

'Yes'

'All by yourself?'

'Yes,' Gül lies. Ceyda helped a bit.

'In that case, I'll have one,' Serter says. 'I'm sure it won't kill me.'

Gül would like to believe he's joking. But somehow, she feels honoured when Serter doesn't turn down her offer of a second pastry.

'The Germans,' he says, chewing, 'you've got to keep your eye on the Germans. This business won't end well.'

'What do you mean?' Gül asks, not understanding what he means by 'this business'.

'They don't like you lot, the Germans.'

'Just us? What about you?'

'My wife threw me out. I don't live on this street, and I don't have anyone else. They're not afraid of me. But you lot… You stick together. My landlord died,' he says, 'I live right under his old flat. He was a good-natured old man – God rest his soul. I went to his funeral, a German funeral with women and crosses and all that. And there was an old woman there who looked like my old landlord, and I asked who she was. She was his sister. I've been living there for nearly four years, and I hadn't seen his sister there once. His blood sister. Maybe the Germans only get together for funerals or Christmas. They don't stick together. That's why they're scared of you lot – because you stick together and because you're strong. And it's because they're afraid of you that they don't like you.

'I've got no one, I'm afraid of everything. My own wife wanted to poison me! And all because I heard the voice of God. You've got to be careful with these Germans. You'll remember what I've said one day. They'll say you don't belong in this country, that you're Muslims, that families have too much say over individuals.

They'll try to break you, they'll try to take away your language, your unity, your sense of pride. Just another couple of years or so and I'm going back home; it'll be unbearable here by then. They're hatching their plans as we speak, mark my words.'

He says all of this with his mouth full. Then he reaches out and takes a third pastry. 'These came out well. And a woman like you, you'd never poison me.'

'No one wants to poison you,' Gül would like to say, but it's not just Serter's bedsit that's small; the space inside his mind isn't much bigger, and it has no windows either, so the thoughts can only ever move in one direction.

'Do you hear the voice of God?' Gül asks him instead.

She believes wholeheartedly in God – she knows he sends her signs and would never forsake her.

No, it's not that she has no doubts – though that's easy enough to say. Sometimes she feels lost, alone, unsupported, and not just in her faith. *But such is the way of God's creations*, she thinks at those times, *it's in our nature*. If you could hear God's voice, would you find peace or would you go mad?

Serter chews and nods.

'Do you hear it?' Gül asks again.

'Mmhm.'

'And what does it tell you?'

Gül doesn't know whether she means this question seriously or not, or whether she just wants to see how Serter will react. Everyone says he's mad, but you never know.

Serter looks up, swallows, and stares her in the eye.

'Sister,' he says, serious now, 'you're a servant of the Lord. If he was going to speak to you, would you run around blabbing to everyone? Now I'm no prophet, I'm not here to preach. What God says to me is between me and him, it's not a matter for idle gossip. Honestly!'

He shakes his head and Gül's body is flooded with a wave of warmth; her cheeks flush.

She feels hotter still when the door opens and Fuat walks into the kitchen, even though she hasn't done anything untoward. It would have been a problem when she was unmarried: a man and a woman in a room together, alone. But now that she's married, she has more freedom when it comes to spending time with men. She gets the feeling it's the other way around for German women.

The two men greet each other. Fuat, nursing a hangover, skips the polite banter and gets straight to the point: 'What brings you here?'

Serter looks at him a little irritated at first, then he says: 'You and me, last night we sat down and played cards, right?'

'Right,' Fuat says.

'For quite a while, too.'

'Right,' Fuat repeats, running himself a glass of water from the tap.

'And you lost.'

Fuat drinks the glass of water in one gulp and says: 'You win some, you lose some.'

'You were well away, eh?' Serter says. Then he turns to Gül: 'Could I have an egg to take home? I'm sure your hens' eggs won't be poisoned now, will they?'

'Let me check the coop,' Gül says.

Out in the garden Gül sits on a stone, wondering how much Fuat can have lost this time and how it can be that God speaks to Serter and also lets him win at cards.

She wonders what'll come of Fuat and his drinking, but there's no talking to him about these things.

'I'm not an alcoholic,' he says. 'I only turn the lights on at the weekend – it's hardly that much after a whole week's hard graft. No drinking, no smoking, no eating. Our mouths are more than just flowers in a meadow. We've got to be able to indulge once in a while, we're not plants.'

It's true, he only really has two or three drinks after work on weekdays.

Gül can't kick Fuat out like Mevlüde did Serter. They didn't have any children, and Serter is genuinely mad. How could she throw Fuat out? And what if it had been her who left – where would she have gone then? With two children? How would she pay the rent, who would look after the girls, and what would she say to her father and her sisters? And if she just went back to Turkey, what would she do there? How would she live?

The voices in the kitchen grow louder, until Gül hears that familiar sound: Fuat shouting, his lungs and vocal cords about to give out.

Serter steps out of the back door, looks at Gül, and simply says, 'As God is my witness.'

Then he leaves.

A little later Fuat comes out, a lit cigarette in his hand.

'It's not eggs he needs, it's a screwdriver, 'cos he's got one loose. That maniac turns up claiming I owe him. Who's going to believe him?'

Gül doesn't react. Fuat looks at her backside for a few seconds; the expression on his face could be mistaken for a smile, but Gül knows better.

'You know, I really prefer slim women,' he says, 'I mean, I'm not one of these country bumpkins who thinks a plump wife is a sign of wealth. Those days are long gone. But I suppose if they're saying I'm unlucky at cards, I must be lucky in love.'

Two weeks before New Year's Eve, the children on Factory Lane start asking their parents: 'Are we going to Auntie Gül and Uncle Fuat's house this year? Will we be celebrating with Ceyda and Ceren's parents again?'

It's not just the children; the adults like going to the Yolcus' as well. The women appreciate Gül's calm warmth, her affectionate smile and how eager she is to make her guests feel at home. When Gül laughs and her belly and breasts wobble, many a woman wishes she could laugh like that too, so relaxed, as if her laughter were just another kind of floating. The women also admire the way that, minutes later, Gül might wipe away a tear after hearing a story, suddenly gripped by melancholy or grief. Some of them even think Gül feels things more deeply than them, because it never looks like she's making a show of her emotions.

Though the men who come to the Yolcus' house might not admit it, they're impressed by everything that's on offer there. Fuat is unduly generous every day of the year, but on New Year's Eve he throws his money around even more than usual; the alcohol and snacks never run out, and the amount he spends on fireworks is almost as much as his wife's housekeeping budget. That's one of the reasons why the children love seeing in the new year at number 52. With so many rockets and bangers at midnight, even they get to throw some too.

Fuat's mood lifts days beforehand. Pushing a trolley full of whisky, cognac and fireworks to the till, he beams so brightly you might think the house in Turkey is fully built now, with a sports car parked in the garage. And even while he's handing over three, four or perhaps five hundred-mark notes, he looks like he's finally won the lottery.

'Working our fingers to the bone has to be good for something; we don't want to vegetate like grass in a field. God gave people good sense, and that's a wonderful thing, but sometimes you just have to stop caring for a while or this life will eat you up, hide and hair.'

The faces, the happy faces of their friends, the laughing faces of the children – these are not things you can buy with money, and if you can, there's nothing wrong with that. It's a house full of happy people with good resolutions and bright hopes, a house buoyed up by joy, where all cares and yearnings are forgotten.

Number 52 floats on air on New Year's Eve, and Ceyda and Ceren look forward to the evening and the night once Christmas is finally behind them.

In theory, the Christmas holidays could be like Sundays on Factory Lane; other than Auntie Tanja, there are no Christians living there. The Spanish, Yugoslavian and Greek families have moved away, most of them leaving Germany.

If Christmas was like a Sunday, you could wash your car, turn up the music, visit each other as usual, watch TV, cook, crochet, play cards, nurse your hangover, do the kinds of things you do on the weekend. But at Christmas, all is quiet as the grave on Factory Lane.

Perhaps it's because the television schedule is different, perhaps it's that the silence in the streets descends on the whole town, perhaps it's that the residents have an unconscious or at least unspoken respect for the festivities. Perhaps they're afraid of gossip – surely the Germans would notice if they were noisy. Or perhaps a place that seems almost abandoned is always awe-inducing, perhaps it's because they can't leave the street – why go anywhere else if everything is shut? Most of the people on Factory Lane are bored over Christmas, while Auntie Tanja sits at home alone, wishing her neighbours would come and visit.

It'd be better if they let us work and then gave us time off on Eid or over Ramadan, some of them think.

But perhaps the exuberance, laughter and jollity as they play bingo on New Year's Eve is partly down to those days of Christmas, which feel like obstacles they have to negotiate before they can start the new year with new promises.

Bingo, which Gül had assumed was played all over Turkey on New Year's Eve, was new to some of her friends and neighbours. But before long, numbers are drawn all along Factory Lane at the end of the year.

This year, Yılmaz stares at his bingo cards, his eyes vacant, and in all the chatter no one seems to notice that he's been silent for some time. When Gül skips a round to empty ashtrays and fill glasses, she sees that Yılmaz isn't covering up the drawn numbers on his card. She thinks the game must be too dull for him, assumes an educated man like him must feel above it.

When they all get up to welcome the new year, like everyone else in the town, with plenty of fireworks, Yılmaz simply stays put. Gül seems to be the only one who notices. Saniye has drunk two whisky and Cokes. Seeing her now, tittering like a tipsy teenager, no one would guess what a story she has to tell. No one would believe that her eyes could dip into an unimagined darkness mid-conversation.

Gül goes back into the kitchen, at quarter to twelve on a mid-1970s New Year's Eve. Yılmaz is sitting motionless in his place, staring at his bingo card.

'Would you like to come outside?' Gül asks him, cautious.

Yılmaz raises his head and looks at her, his gaze empty.

'Or would you rather stay inside on your own?'

'I'll come outside,' he says. 'I'm coming outside.' He rises slowly and carefully, propping himself up on the table. Once he's upright, he picks up his cigarettes and puts them in his shirt pocket.

'Shouldn't be a problem getting a light out there,' he says, grinning at Gül.

'Do you know why they all have long hair here?' he asks out of nowhere.

'Who?'

'The students. The left-wing students. Just because you're a lefty, doesn't mean you have to run around looking like a girl. I don't get this country. Growing your hair has nothing to do with the revolution. What will my child learn here?'

Gül feels inferior to people like Yılmaz because she only got her basic schooling. She doesn't know what got Yılmaz onto the subject or how to answer him without sounding stupid.

'Children can learn anything they want here,' Gül says.

They don't get expelled from university, she thinks of saying but doesn't.

'Who gives a shit,' Yılmaz says.

He speaks deliberately, and only when he starts moving does Gül realise the man is drunk.

'My feet were round last night,' Fuat says on mornings after he's spent the night walking like Yılmaz is now.

'Come on,' Gül says, putting an arm around Yılmaz's hip to help him leave the room without bumping into the furniture. Outside, she deposits him by the garden fence where she waited for the postman all those times, and she tells him: 'Wait here a minute.'

In the general half-cut chaos, no one takes any notice of Yılmaz. Gül keeps an eye out for Saniye, who is holding a firework in her hand, giggling, and struggling to get her lighter to work.

'Saniye,' says Gül, 'Saniye, your husband's sloshed – maybe you should go and have a look. He can hardly stand.'

'What, again?' Saniye says, glancing at Gül. Then she refocuses on the lighter in her right hand.

'I can't take care of him right now, just get him to have a lie down, the old drunkard. It's always the same, every day. I want to have a bit of fun, it's the one night of the year when I have a drink. What do I care if he can't stand up?'

Gül looks at Saniye rather incredulously, but her friend smiles because she's just got a flame out of her lighter, and now she's holding it to the fuse.

Every day? That would be more often than Fuat. She can't believe it. Saniye chucks the banger into the darkness and beams at Gül. Glancing back over to the fence, Gül sees that Yılmaz has turned around and is vomiting on the ground. As if unsure what to do, Gül stands still, surrounded by bangs and whistles and pops, the smell of burnt fireworks, scraps of voices and laughter, children screaming. She knows it must be her imagination, but she can smell vomit, even though she's a good fifteen paces from the fence.

The whole world seems to be in motion around her, but Gül doesn't move a muscle. The very thoughts in her head seem to stand still, two thoughts side by side: *Yılmaz is a drinker. Saniye's not taking care of him.*

Gül sees Ceren run into the house with a cheerful squeal, and then two things happen at once: a bang so loud it hurts Gül's ear, and a sudden sensation, like someone has smacked her on the hip. She doesn't move, she just looks down at herself. Smoke billows out of her jacket pocket, which now has a hole in it, and there's a smell of singed fabric.

She didn't notice that someone had put a banger in her pocket. She could make a song and dance about it, hold her hip, and curse such typical pranks out loud, but all she does is turn around and go over to Yılmaz, who is wiping his mouth with his hand.

'Let's go inside, I'll make you a peppermint tea.'

'Can I go over to Gesine's?' Ceren asks, and Gül says, 'Yes, go, but think about what I said.'

'I'm not to go over too often, and I have to be home by five.'

Gül smiles.

'Off you go, and bring Gesine back with you sometime soon.'

Gesine and Ceren met at the hospital, when Ceren was hit by the car. They shared a hospital room. Ceren only had a broken rib and a few bruises and scrapes. Gesine, who is Ceren's age, had climbed up onto the sink to get a better look at herself in the mirror. The sink came away from the wall, and Gesine broke several fingers and one of the bones in her foot.

Gesine is Ceren's first real German friend. She doesn't meet up with her German friends from school in the afternoons, she just chats to them in the playground. She prefers to play with the other children from Factory Lane.

It's different with Gesine. In the evenings at the hospital, when everyone had gone home, Gesine would say to Ceren: 'Come on, come and sit in my bed,' and she'd throw back her blanket. 'It's hard to walk in this cast.'

Ceren was a little startled. Sometimes, if she'd had a bad dream she'd creep into her sister's bed, or occasionally her mother's, but Gesine was a stranger.

'Come on, I won't hurt you.'

Gesine tucked them both in and said: 'Imagine we're in a rainforest, on a raft, just you and me, and we're floating along. There are crocodiles all around us and we're really scared, so we have to breathe really quietly and make ourselves as little as we can. Did you know it's hot in the rainforest? Do you know how hot it is?'

Gesine pulled the blanket up over their heads and whispered: 'We have to be completely quiet. I'll let you know when it's as hot as it gets in the rainforest. The air's so hot there, you can hardly breathe.'

It was as if their smells and their bodies blended in the silence and darkness, as if they became one in a bed that really was a raft, gliding downstream in a lush, humid forest.

'Now,' Gesine finally whispered, and Ceren found that she could hardly breathe. She didn't know when she'd ever been this close to a stranger before, and not just physically.

A couple of minutes later, Gesine cautiously lifted the blanket.

'Okay, no more crocodiles over here.'

Ceren looked about on the other side.

'None here either.'

By the time they came out from under the blankets, the crocodiles had vanished and the whole world seemed a little safer.

Ceren won't tell her mother that they crouched under the blankets together and their friendship began on a raft in the rainforest, surrounded by crocodiles – not until years later, on a winter's evening by the stove in their house in Turkey.

These days, Ceren often has lots of questions to ask when she's been to Gesine's.

'Mum, what do Germans eat for breakfast?'

'Bread or bread rolls, butter, jam, cheese – what do you think they eat?'

'But they eat that in the evening.'

'Did you eat there?'

'Yes.'

Gül isn't sure.

'Maybe they have soup for breakfast,' she says.

'So not jam and sausages.'

'I don't know,' Gül says. 'You'll have to ask Gesine.'

Ceren looks at her mother, disappointed. Gül is always encouraging her daughters to ask questions, but sometimes she's at a loss for an answer.

'And I'll ask Auntie Tanja,' Gül says. 'We'll soon find out what the Germans have for breakfast.'

Gül wants Ceyda and Ceren to learn as much as possible, so she buys them books: children's editions of classics, bound volumes arranged next to the toys in the big supermarkets; Robinson Crusoe, Treasure Island, Moby Dick, Winnetou.

She wants her daughters to be better educated than she was, to have more doors open to them in life, to know more and be better able to choose. Gül finds it odd that her children can speak such good German, but they don't know what the Germans eat for dinner.

And Ceren is astonished to notice, whenever she's at Gesine's, that there are certain German words she still doesn't know. She doesn't have any problems at school; she always gets good marks in composition and dictation, and she basically feels her German is as good as that of the children who speak it at home. She doesn't even have an accent, unlike Ceyda.

But when she's at Gesine's, she learns words like *Suppenkelle, Kehrblech, Feudel, Bücherbord, Nudelholz*.

The day Ceren learns the word *Abendbrot*, she's sitting on the steps outside the front door, watching the sunset and trying to understand why there's only one letter difference between *Abendbrot*, meaning supper, and *Abendrot*, the red glow of sunset, now bathing the street in a light that seems softer because it isn't reflected on flagstones and tarmac.

Ceren thinks about her dede's summer house. She remembers sitting on its front steps when she was little and how she thought her dede's street and Factory Lane couldn't be that far apart because neither of them was tarmacked.

'What's all this?' Fuat asks. 'How am I supposed to get it in the car? It beggars belief, all this stuff you've bought. We're not going to a war zone. It's not enough that you're so fat, now you want me to load up the car with everything the German shops have on offer too. The car will be scraping the ground. What is all this? What's in the suitcases? Surely a few changes of clothes would be enough, wouldn't it?'

Gül doesn't reply. She's in the bedroom surrounded by bags and cases, wondering where her husband has been over the past few weeks. He must have noticed her holiday preparations; she's been shopping for over a month now, filling bag after bag.

'It's the same every year,' he says. 'What's in there? What is it? I asked you a question.'

'Presents,' Gül says.

'Who for?'

'For your parents, my parents, our nieces and nephews, for your brothers, my sisters, for everyone.'

'Wouldn't it be enough if you just brought along something small for everybody? Does it have to be' – he tugs a zip open – 'does it have to be a toaster? Can't they just toast their bread by the fire or use the gas cooker? Does anyone there really need a toaster? Honestly. And what's this? Nutella?'

'The children like it.'

'Five jars of the stuff? No, six. What's wrong with your mother's good old rose-petal jam, is that not good enough now? And this: Maggi. What are we taking Maggi for?'

'They don't have it in Turkey. That's why we came here, isn't it? Because there's work and money and opportunities here. Why shouldn't we make the most of those opportunities?'

'A car's no different to a donkey, you know. One day now it'll collapse under the load.'

'When you bought the Mercedes, you were boasting about what a great car it is. Not an old banger like before; proper quality workmanship, not like what you get in Turkey. You were going on about how many horsepower it's got, how it hugs the road. And now you're trying to tell me the car will collapse because of three jars of Nutella? Are you saying the Mercedes wasn't worth the money?'

'Hold your tongue, stop pretending you're a mechanic. I'd like to see you repair the car with your woman's intuition if the axle breaks.'

'I don't meddle with your car stuff, do I? And this here, this is domestic stuff, this is my business, and I say we're taking these bags and cases with us. Why else did we get a roof rack? You should have taken a look at it a while back instead of waiting until two days before we leave. Now I can't unpack anything without someone feeling hard done by.'

'You wouldn't have been able to take all that stuff on the plane. I bought a car to make things easier, but then nothing's ever easy with women around. Women,' Fuat says, 'women, nothing but dead weight. Even on their own hips.'

Two days later, the two of them still haven't exchanged a friendly word – but the car is loaded up, Ceyda and Ceren are yawning on the back seat, the day is dawning, and Fuat is sitting behind the wheel smoking while they wait for Saniye and Yılmaz.

'Women,' Fuat says again. 'Yılmaz would get here on time on his own, but he has to wait for his wife.'

The rest of the year, it's rare for every family member to be in the same room together for more than an hour, and now they're going to be spending almost three days cooped up in the car. Just like every time they travel to Turkey, they'll get there exhausted, and just like other every time they arrive, their joy will outweigh the exhaustion.

The Granada turns onto Factory Lane, with Yılmaz at the wheel, and Saniye and Sevgi, who is almost two now, on the back seat. They pull in, then they all get out of the car and say good morning; the women ask God that the roads may be open for them, and before they get back in, Auntie Tanja comes out of her garden gate at this early hour, holding a bowl. She smiles.

'Have a good trip,' she says. 'And come back safe and sound. No one else is here to do it, so I'll pour the water for you.'

'May God reward you,' Gül murmurs in Turkish; she doesn't know how to say it in German. Then she adds a *Danke* and hopes her good wishes can be heard in her voice.

Tanja has seen her neighbours pouring water on the road behind travellers many times before, wiling them to find their way as easily as the water. That morning, she splashes a salad bowl of water onto the street after the cars. Gül turns around and looks through the rear window, sees the old lady standing in the road alone with the empty bowl in her hand. As the sun rises slowly behind her, Tanja waves. *That's a good sign*, Gül thinks, but she says a quick silent prayer just in case: *Lord, let us reach our destination without mishap or misery.*

They make their second stop just south of Munich. Ceyda and Ceren break off their game of cards to look for Sevgi and play with her a little, but she's asleep on the back seat. For the next leg of the journey, Saniye gets behind the wheel of the Granada while Yılmaz tips the passenger seat back and closes his eyes.

Gül knows Saniye has her driving licence, but she's never seen her friend driving before. Nor has Fuat, who gives no sign of having an opinion on the matter.

The sisters return to their game. They play quietly, sensing that loud words might get their father even more riled up. The two cars have almost left Austria behind them when Fuat lights a cigarette with a yawn and says, 'Will you look at that, those two share the work: sometimes he drives and sometimes she does. And me, I've been behind this wheel for sixteen hours flat, like a lorry driver; my bum's gone numb. That wouldn't be a problem for you, you've got plenty of padding. That Saniye, she hasn't just got a smaller backside – she can drive as well. These women, it beggars belief.'

At least if he gets worked up, he won't fall asleep, Gül thinks. We've been on the road so long – he's right, poor thing, it can't be easy driving all that time.

'How often have I told you: you need to get your driving licence.'

'I'm scared,' Gül says. 'I can't do it.'

'Scared,' Fuat says. 'Oh yes, scared of taking a wrong turn, scared of driving, scared of learning to swim, scared of dogs, scared of coincidences. The question is: what aren't you scared of? You can't conquer life if you're scared – you have to go up to a fire with the bellows like your father. You can't keep running away when things hot up.'

But how could Gül ever drive a car? She's constantly on edge, even in the passenger seat. She tries to relax her muscles whenever she notices herself tensing up, but she doesn't look away from the road for a second; she doesn't daydream, let alone fall asleep. And it's rarely more than three miles before her whole body stiffens again and she starts to hold her breath, thinking another car is driving too close or Fuat is going too fast, overtaking too riskily.

She may well be scared of lots of things, but that doesn't mean the drive is easy for her either. Still, she's never shied away from work, effort or exhaustion – unlike her husband, who has a reputation at the factory for being not half as hard a worker as his wife.

They don't stop for a few hours' sleep until they reach Yugoslavia. Fuat's eyes are small and red, not just with fatigue, but because over the past few hours he's lit a cigarette every time he's felt sleep coming on. Gül doesn't want him driving with the window down; the girls are asleep, and she doesn't want them catching a cold.

As the smoke awakens Gül's desire, she fantasises about the cigarette she'll smoke with Saniye in a remote corner of the resting area. The families eat together: bread and cheese, olives, tomatoes and onions. Sevgi is awake and crying, and while Saniye tries to calm her down, Yılmaz tells the story of the time he left Saniye behind at a petrol station in Yugoslavia, two years earlier. It's a story he likes to tell often. 'Saniye was asleep on the back seat when I got out of the car. I filled her up, paid the bill, took a leak, got back in and drove off. Twenty miles I'd gone before I realised I was on my own.'

'And me,' Saniye says, 'I woke up and went to the toilet, and when I get back the man's gone and I'm left standing somewhere in the middle of Yugoslavia. No passport, no money, just the clothes on my back.'

'She didn't know when I'd notice she wasn't in the car any more,' Yılmaz cuts in, 'so she asked the next Turkish driver if he'd give her a lift until they caught up with me, one way or another. But then good old Saniye spots me on the other side of the road because I'd turned back, and I'm thinking: *Why's that guy flashing his lights at me, what's he trying to tell me?* – until I realised my wife was in his car. She was asleep when I got out – am I meant to check the back seat before I drive off? And then I said something, I think I wanted to wet my whistle, but she didn't react. That was twenty miles after the petrol station.'

He's repeating himself, Gül thinks, looking him in the eye. Only then does she notice Yılmaz is drunk. Perhaps that's why Saniye is driving. Yılmaz's eyes are red too, and now that she's paying attention, she can smell the alcohol on his breath.

Still holding Sevgi, Saniye gets up, gives Gül an almost imperceptible nod, and the two of them walk out of sight. Gül takes a packet of cigarettes out of her pocket and offers one to Saniye.

'Ohhh,' Saniye exhales satisfaction and smoke. 'That does you good after such a long day.'

Gül enjoys her cigarette as well, but then she looks at the ground, unsure whether she should ask her question.

'Fuat must be wiped out,' Saniye says. 'He's been driving the whole way on his own.'

Nothing about Gül's breathing or body language changes, but Saniye apologises all the same. 'I didn't mean to blame you, Gül. I couldn't imagine you driving a car. Everyone does what they can. Come on, Gül, smile: we'll be crossing the border tomorrow night, God willing. There's no one else like you, Gül, not on Factory Lane, not in all of Germany or Turkey. Sister, we're on our way to Turkey, and here we are having a cigarette together in the middle of Yugoslavia – give us a smile, come on.'

Gül raises her head, looks at Saniye and flashes a hesitant smile.

'Who knows what life will bring?' Saniye says. 'You can lose everything in the blink of an eye, and here we are enjoying a cigarette. Let the men drink and shout and act all important with their money or their politics. I'll never find a friend like you again, and one day even you won't be here any more.'

Gül's eyes shimmer, wet in the darkness.

A little later, when they're all asleep in their cars, Gül wakes with a jolt, hearing the Granada's engine start. She's instantly wide awake, but Fuat is snoring and the girls are still fast asleep. Keeping quiet, Gül gets out of the car and walks up to the Granada in front of them.

Yılmaz is lying on the passenger seat. Saniye spots Gül in the rear-view mirror and winds down the window on the driver's side. 'My blasted daughter wouldn't shut up,' she whispers. 'She must have got used to the noise; she closed her eyes as soon I turned the engine on. You go back to sleep – we've got a long drive ahead of us tomorrow.'

Gül catches sight of the empty bottles in the footwell but pretends not to notice. She goes back to the Mercedes, shivering.

They reach the Turkish border the next night. Fuat's eyes had closed twice with fatigue on their way through Bulgaria, but Gül had noticed immediately and shouted, 'Wake up, open your eyes!'

Fuat shook himself awake and ignored his wife's request to take a break.

'We're almost there,' he said. 'I'm not going to wimp out now.' And then he reached for his cigarettes. If he's smoking, he won't fall asleep.

Gül has slept just as little as Fuat; the constant fear that something might happen is keeping her awake.

The officer takes the papers out of Fuat's hand and pulls a hundred-mark note out of his passport, holding it up between his forefinger and thumb through the open window.

'What's this?' he asks. His tone is defiant. Fuat hesitates for half a second, maybe less.

'Oh, that shouldn't be there. I thought I'd lost it – how did it get in with the passports?'

The officer shakes his head. 'This sort of thing is out of order. Pull in over there. And get out of the car, please, all of you.'

With the man out of earshot, Fuat grumbles: 'If it was raining soup, I'd be the only man with a fork. What rotten luck to get the one customs officer in a hundred who won't take bribes. At half past midnight as well! Thanks a bunch. If it was raining pussy I'd get hit on the head with a prick, I tell you.'

Gül looks over at him; she almost never hears him curse like that.

'Don't look at me like that. Now we'll see where being so loaded down gets us. They'll take the whole car apart, they'll look behind every screw, we'll be held up for hours. Yılmaz and Saniye will be snug as a bug at home, getting hot coffee and baklava served to them, while we're stuck here with these guys checking if I haven't hidden something under my shirt buttons. You've got us up shit creek now!'

'Why did you go and give him a hundred marks?' Yılmaz asks Fuat while the guards are checking the Mercedes. 'He'll know right off that you've got something to hide. Look at me – they just waved us straight through.'

His breath smells of alcohol again, and Gül wonders whether the border guards noticed.

'I slip a note inside my passport every year,' Fuat says. 'It's always worked before. Anyway, you gave the Bulgarians a bottle, didn't you?'

'Yeah, to speed things up though; not because we had anything to hide. And they're our neighbours, they see us in a good light. It's always your own people who ruin things for you. Mark my words: It's your own people you have to be afraid of, they don't care about your tears. Trust the Kurds, the Bulgarians, the Greeks, even the Germans if you like, but not the Turks.'

'Yılmaz,' Saniye cautions.

'It's all true,' he says. 'Looks like it's going to take you a while to get through now.'

'You go ahead without us,' Gül tells them. 'But drive carefully. We've been together this far, but the road beckons the travellers. Off you go.'

Fuat pulls himself together while they say their goodbyes, but no sooner has Saniye put the car in first gear and eased off the clutch than he starts up again: 'That man beggars belief, that know-it-all. Hardly sober for a minute all the way here, then he starts giving me advice – that drunken communist, that goddamn traitor to the fatherland.'

He picks up a stone and hurls it after the Granada, while Gül walks over to the bench where Ceyda and Ceren are sleeping, wrapped up in a blanket and leaning against each other. Fuat lights yet another cigarette; this is his sixth pack since they set off from Germany. His head is almost as red as his eyes, and Gül knows he needs someone to vent his rage on. She doesn't mind being that person. *We've got this far without mishap or misery*, she thinks, *and with God's help we'll manage the last stretch as well.*

The officers search the car for four hours, sifting through the cases and bags, making orderly lists of items. Fuat is so tired he nods off on a bench. The sleep gives him the strength, and the customs duties the anger, to rant and rave behind the wheel almost all the way to Edirne.

'Of course: three toasters, two irons, four watches, two mixers, one juicer, one I-don't-know-what, six kettles, like we want to open our own shop. Did you see how much I forked out for all that? Six big ones down the drain, my hard-earned money. Just so our relatives can heat up a slice of bread and wear a nice smooth shirt. As if it's not enough for you to take the money out of my pocket to buy all that stuff. Let them wear what they want, nylon shirts for all I care. I don't give a shit. I don't work my hands to the bone so they can live the life of Riley. That rubbish has cost us well over a thousand marks now. How many nights could I have played cards on that, eh? How many lottery tickets would that have bought me? All the great things you can do with a thousand marks, instead of splurging it on electric gadgets and then paying customs on top. It hurts my soul. How many hours did I graft for that?

'But when we get there, you're not to say a word about what happened at the border, you hear? Not a word to anyone. Make sure the girls don't tell anyone either. I don't want to hear any more about it for the whole of this holiday. Not a word!' he yells.

After a while he falls silent, but his rage keeps him awake until the end of the journey. They arrive in their home town late that evening. Fuat won't eat, only drinks a glass of water, turns down the rakı and doesn't even finish the last cigarette of the day. All he wants is to go to bed.

Fuat looks a bit like a little boy playing at being a big businessman; every once in a while, he can't stop himself pulling a childish grin as he leads his father-in-law through the shell of the building. He acts all benevolent to the labourers who are laying the electricity cables or busying themselves with little plastering jobs.

'The lads have done a good job,' he says. 'It's really looking good. Not as polished as the Germans, who'd have it finished on time too, but what can you do? This is Turkey after all, but they've not half-arsed it. I'm happy to pay a little extra – really they ought to be paying me, for teaching them all about high-quality workmanship. Now we won't have toiled away in a foreign country for nothing. This is no mud hut; it's a proper, solid house, one my grandchildren will be able to live in, their grandchildren too.'

'Here's the toilet, alaturka, like we're used to, but over here we've got another one, a proper European water closet. So anyone can go just as he pleases. You can sit down on this one and read the paper in peace. You know you've really made it when you can crap in comfort.'

Fuat misinterprets the smile on the blacksmith's lips. What he takes to be approval is in fact anticipation.

'The house is as good as done now,' the blacksmith says. 'Another week or so, maybe two. Three if you like. And then you'll come back and live here?'

'No,' Fuat says. 'No, we're not sorted just because we've got a house now. We're going to have another floor added so we can rent it out, so we've got a bit of money coming in.'

'One floor, okay, but the rest is done; that won't take six months.' But the smile on Timur's lips has already died.

'And the children are still at school – they're used to the system over there. They're getting a good education – it's not all learning by rote over there like it is at home; they're really learning to think. If they were boys… Those boys who grow up there and go through school and then on to university, they're the future of this country, you know. They'll all come back and help to turn this into one of the most sophisticated countries in the world. Another fifteen, twenty years and we'll be as great as America, you'll see.'

'If God grants me the time,' Timur murmurs, but Fuat doesn't hear him. 'You'll live out your lives in a foreign country, then,' he says a little louder now, 'lost among people who speak a different language.'

'Just a few more years, God willing.'

Just a few more years, during which Timur and Gül will only see each other for six weeks each summer.

'And here,' Fuat says, 'this is where the reception room will be.' When he sees his father-in-law's face, he says: 'You know, for receiving guests.'

'Yes, of course,' the blacksmith says. 'Do they have them in Germany?'

'No,' Fuat says. 'No, no. The Germans haven't got a clue about hospitality.'

'So when I come over, will you host me in your reception room?'

'Of course, if you like, but it's not really meant for family.'

The blacksmith has seen these sorts of rooms before, usually in the homes of Istanbulites, or people in Ankara, or the rich people of his own town. 'Not for family, no. They're meant for the sort of people you have to show off to.'

Timur turns around and heads for the door. Fuat follows him, his head bowed. He's trying to understand why the blacksmith is suddenly talking like Yılmaz. There's not a university round here, but even his wife's father hasn't managed to escape these left-wing ideas. The whole country is in uproar, and Fuat has no faith in the way things are going. There are leftists in Germany too, a fair few of them, and the terrorists among them have sought to strike fear and horror into people, but the state is strong; it'll make short work of them. The men in power are not the sort whose aim is to bag themselves villas and yachts; in Germany, politicians are honest men of principle.

Later on, Timur tells his daughter about his visit to the house and how modern he thought it looked, how solid, trusty and safe it seemed.

'Oh, if only it could be a home for you here,' he says.

'Why shouldn't it be?' Gül asks.

'It doesn't seem like your husband is planning to come back. The minute he opens his mouth, all he seems to come out with is reasons to stay over there.'

Gül makes to argue, but he waves her off.

'That's the way of the world now,' he says. 'People move faster and faster, but it makes no difference because the roads are always getting longer. I have eight grandchildren now. I used to see my grandfather every day – now I see the newsreader on TV every day, and soon there'll be a television in every home. Do you remember how it used to be? When we were the only ones on the street with a radio? Those voices brought the world closer without taking us any further away from one another. Now the world seems impossible to understand; it gets bigger and smaller by turns and everyone's trying to carve out a corner for themselves. And Fuat's decided that your corner's in Germany. You won't be back any time soon.'

Gül sees her father's eyes shining and says: 'If he won't come, I'll come on my own, don't worry.'

If only we knew which promises we'll keep and which we won't.

Fuat pushes the trolly, and Gül calls out to the girls to tell them what to get as she picks tins and boxes and jars off the shelves. It's the same every Saturday. Fuat gets up as early as possible – no matter which shift he's just worked or how much he drank the night before, no matter how much it feels like his head's about to crack open – but somehow, they still never manage to set off early enough to avoid a rush at the end.

Saturday is the day of the big weekly shop; they go to the supermarket and to the Turkish butcher and greengrocer, which sells almost everything now: aubergines, garlic, watermelons, bulgur, cumin, pine nuts, citric acid, okra, pepper paste, sheep's cheese, Turkish delight. But Gül can get all these things on her own during the week. The supermarket has Coke and lemonade, pasta, flour, rice, whisky, toilet paper, washing powder, washing up liquid, cream cheese, Nutella, underpants and socks. Ceyda and Ceren are allowed to pick books from the children's aisle, and sometimes toys too. Ceyda likes crime stories about murderous old women, terrifying thuggish men and unprepossessing but clever young detectives, while Ceren reads stories about young girls and their dreams, about worlds full of ponies and daring getaways, which she thinks are something all little German girls can have. Gül lets Ceyda pick first, because Gesine has almost a whole bookcase full at home; Ceren likes to read a book as soon as Gesine's finished it, imagining herself and Gesine between its pages.

They buy biscuits, sweets, snacks, spice mixes, breadcrumbs, cream, sugar – Gül's list is long, and the shopping trolley is overflowing by the time they reach the till. Fuat is more or less irritable depending on the day, but they're all impatient. The queue for the tills is always too long, the checkout girl too slow, time too short.

Fuat has a comment at the ready for any driver who threatens to hold them up on the way home: 'Oi mate, I can see from your shirt collar that you can't tell your driving licence from your ID card; the accelerator's on the right, mate, this isn't a cinema, you're not here to sit and watch. I could cut my toenails in the time it's taking him to change gear.'

Every traffic light seems to linger a little longer on red, and every Saturday they have less than five minutes to go as they turn into their still-untarmacked street. Fuat parks outside the house and heads straight in; the television needs at least a minute to warm up. Gül and the girls carry the shopping into the kitchen, but they don't unpack it. It's Saturday afternoon, *Nachbarn in Europa* is on, and they never miss it.

More precisely, they never miss the Turkish part of the programme, *Türkiye'den mektup, Letters from Turkey*. Every Saturday the four of them sit down to watch *Neighbours in Europe* for twenty minutes, and except for the occasional murmur of *It beggars belief*, none of them says a word.

It's the only time in the week when the four of them sit together on the sofa, Fuat in the left corner, Gül next to him, Ceren cuddled up to her mum, and Ceyda on the right, always looking a little indifferent. What does she care if the news is on?

But she also enjoys these moments when the television seems to be speaking just to them, and it's only partly to do with the language being spoken.

Week after week, the family spends those twenty minutes sitting together. If there's been a fight beforehand, there'll be a truce; no one manages to stay grumpy for the duration of the programme. If one of them is in pain, they'll simply forget; all cares shift to make room for the pictures and voices on the TV.

If someone were to ask her afterwards, Gül wouldn't be able to tell them what she's just watched. Most of the time she doesn't remember all that much; she simply sits there and breathes in the peace, the quiet that settles at the sound of the words. It's as though the rhythm and melody of her ancestors' language bring love into her living room, a love and connection to the rich soil of Anatolia; as though its brown earth is transported into the room along with the sounds, the scent of acacia trees and burnt cow manure, even if they only show pictures of Ankara and Istanbul, pictures of concrete and suits and uniforms worn by men you can hardly tell apart.

To Gül, it's like spending twenty minutes on an island of her childhood, a country that is lost forever to all of us but that will never disappear.

Life seems lighter once the twenty minutes are over, and though the mountain of work towers over them, it's just a hill on an island they can never be banished from.

For these twenty minutes on a Saturday afternoon, the whole family is one; they belong together. It's a time of harmony.

Did I ever see my father and my mother together like this? Gül wonders to herself. *When did we ever sit together, except to eat? Thanks, thanks be to the Lord.*

This man might drink, he might gamble and wish he had a slimmer wife, but we're a family and we have a home – who would destroy a home of their own free will?

You can't destroy a good home. So say the ancestors. In this unpredictable world, it's important to have a roof over your head, one you can retreat into, be it only on the sofa, in front of the TV.

Gül doesn't sing. She doesn't even hum, but you can imagine her singing as she cooks the dinner after the programme, her daughters lending a hand. On Saturdays the sun shines inside this house. On Saturdays the sun shines all over Factory Lane, all year round, even during that time of year they all call 'winter'. The summers are only brief; the time between two car journeys that seem to last forever.

It's Saturday morning. Fuat is still asleep when Ceyda comes in the kitchen, where Gül is making the topping for lahmacun. Saniye, Yılmaz and Sevgi are coming for dinner; Gül has already made the potato salad, and all she has to do after *Nachbarn in Europa* is knead the dough. She's got everything under control, but just the way Ceyda walks in is enough to make Gül lose her composure. Her stiff footsteps and their rhythm, a tell-tale sign that she's done something bad, and the way she simply stops and waits mutely until her mother asks: 'What's up? It can't be that bad, can it?'

'I... I've broken the aerial. We were playing in the living room. I ran into it and it broke.'

Gül goes to the sink to wash her hands; she feels like she'll be able to think better with clean hands. When and how is she going to tell Fuat?

'Don't worry, we'll sort it out. Have you turned the telly on?'
'Yes, but it's all blurry.'

Should she tell him before they go shopping? If she does, he'll rant and rave all the way round the shops. But maybe they can get a new aerial there.

'Let's have a look.'

The two of them leave the kitchen together, but before they get through the doorway, Gül senses something's not right. She senses it the way she dreamed Ceren was drowning. She senses it the way she'll guess in a few years' time that Ceyda is afraid of losing her mind, even though they'll be many miles apart by then. She senses it – it doesn't take skill or talent; feelings and connection are gifts from God.

'Who was it?' she asks in the living room.

'Me,' Ceyda answers.

The aerial has been ripped off the TV and is broken in two.

'How did it happen?'

'Ceren and I were playing around, jumping on the sofa and chairs, and then I thought I was falling, so I just grabbed hold of something.'

'Tell me the truth,' Gül says. 'You know you've always got to tell the truth. We're good people, we don't lie.'

Ceyda looks down at the floor.

When should I tell him? Gül wonders again. *Or might I be able to mend it? No, no it doesn't look like it.*

'The truth, my darling – there's no need to be scared.'

She knows Ceyda is lying, but she doesn't know what really happened.

'It was Ceren. We were playing chase, and she... She was scared of Dad, so I said I'd take the blame.'

How naive Gül is not to have thought of that herself. Feelings and connection might be God's gifts, but other minds work better than hers.

'Go and get her. She doesn't have to be scared.'

Not much later, the three of them are sitting in the living room. The picture on the television is reminiscent of ants marching through snow.

'What are we going to do?' Ceren asks.

'Don't be afraid, we'll work it out.'

'What's Dad going to do to Ceyda when he finds out?'

'Nothing,' Gül says. 'He won't do a thing. If anyone's going to take the blame, it'll be me. I'll say it happened while I was cleaning. You don't know anything about it, alright? I just don't want you two lying to me again, okay? You might not tell me everything; you might even lie so as not to hurt someone's feelings, but I don't want either of you two lying to me, and I don't want you lying just for your own sake. Now go to your room and stop worrying about it. We got by without *Letters from Turkey* before.'

'But you'll be lying to Dad,' Ceyda says.

Gül looks at her daughter; it takes her two blinks of an eye to come up with an answer.

'I'll be lying to protect you,' Gül says. 'I'll be lying because you're children and I'm a grown-up.'

Even before Yılmaz and Saniye get there, Fuat has already poured himself a whisky and Coke.

'It beggars belief. While you were cleaning! Once a week the programme's on, and you go and break the aerial on a Saturday. Couldn't it wait until Monday? Once a week we sit here nice and cosy together and they tell us what's going on back home, once a week. Other women fall out onto the street while they're cleaning the windows, and my wife has to go and destroy the aerial. You must have tugged pretty hard at it, and that's what you call cleaning, is it? You shouldn't be allowed anywhere near electrical devices, you shouldn't even be allowed an iron. Once a week I watch a lovely slim presenter, not like my wife who's so fat she rips the aerial off the telly. Why don't you try dieting?'

It's been like this all afternoon. Gül lets him moan as much as he likes, thinking up answers that go unsaid and smiling to herself because she knows Ceyda and Ceren are playing outside out of harm's way. But after a while she's had enough.

'It's your fault I'm so fat.'

Fuat stares at her, amazed that she's suddenly answering back. He's even more amazed by her accusation, which he's never heard before. Before he can come up with a response, Gül tells him: 'It was you who came along with the pill, "Here you go, I've got something for you, so we don't have to be careful any more." Without me going to see a doctor. It's those pills that have made me swell up, those hormones or whatever they are. Who knows where you got them. And anyway, maybe you don't like fat women, maybe you do want a slim blonde wife. But shall I tell you something for a change? I like men with hair on their heads, not baldies. You can't always pick and choose what you get. You hear me? Men with a full head of hair!'

Fuat jerks his glass upwards, but he doesn't pull back to hit her. Gül stands in front of him and looks him in the eye, and before the defeat she sees there turns into disaster, she leaves the room.

Later that evening, Yılmaz will say to Fuat: 'That's how I like it; you're learning to drink now, my friend, just savouring it in peace, not getting louder with every sip you take.'

And Saniye will say to Gül: 'It's better, honest. The old one drank and beat me, and this one just drinks. God forbid, but if I ever marry again, perhaps the Lord will send me a husband who doesn't do either. But who knows what flaws he'd have then? A man like Serter who's lost his marbles isn't what you'd want either. Your lahmacun is delicious by the way – may your hands always be healthy.'

Fuat will never say anything about Gül's figure again. Nor Gül about his bald head. Women might pose in front of the mirror to inspect their new clothes or put on makeup, but it's men who are made vulnerable by vanity.

'That's not a telephone,' Ceyda says, 'Where are the numbers?'

'This one doesn't have numbers,' Fuat replies.

'What? None at all? So you can only get calls from other people?'

'Who's your dede going to call anyway?' Gül asks. 'Who else here has a telephone?'

Fuat looks at Gül and shakes his head.

'He can make calls too. You know the old black and white films, Ceyda, where women sit in front of a pile of cables and connect calls, they plug this in and pull that out and they say, "Hello, you've reached the Telephone Exchange." You know those old films?'

Ceyda nods.

'This is an old telephone. When Dede turns the crank, someone from the post office will pick up and ask who he wants to speak to. Then they'll connect him to the right cable. It's not fully automated like it is in Germany.'

'So everyone with a telephone has their own cable?'

'No, it's a very complex system, to keep from having so many cables. Very complex. Perhaps I'll explain it to you when you're older. We'll be able to call Dede when we're back in Germany – it'll be much quicker than always having to wait for letters. You know your dede can't write letters anyway; he doesn't know Latin script. He has to dictate them. The telephone will make the world smaller; it takes us three days to get here by car, but the telephone transmits words instantly. It'll be like we're neighbours. This little thing and its crank will change so much in our lives, you'll see…'

Soon Gül will no longer sit with her daughters, reading them the letters her father has dictated or her sisters have written. She won't be able to read each sentence again and again, to savour every last syllable; she won't be able to carry the lines around in her pocket to read them again at lunchtime, to pep her up for work. As always, everything will change.

Gül is glad she can reach her father in this way now. Words soothe that sense of longing, hence all the letters, hence all those lines by the great bards; words connect people, lessen the heart's burden. And what words could be more direct than words that are spoken? What could be more soothing than sound; the sound of a loved one's voice?

Two days later, Ceyda finds herself alone in the room where the telephone is kept. Full of curiosity, she picks up the receiver and holds it to her ear: no sound. She gently turns the crank then puts it back down straight away, shocked at her own boldness.

Only once the receiver is back on its cradle does she hear footsteps approaching. When her mother walks into the room, Ceyda is sitting on the divan, pretending she's been reading a book.

She gives a start when the phone rings. Gül seems a little surprised but reaches for the receiver. The voice at the other end is so loud that Ceyda can hear it.

'Hello, I'm calling from the Post Office,' a woman's voice says. 'Have you just tried to reach us?'

'No,' says Gül, 'we haven't.'

'But it rang on our end.'

'Must be a mistake,' Gül says. 'We don't want to make any calls at the moment, thank you.'

'A good day to you, then.'

Gül hangs up and looks at Ceyda.

'Did you use the phone?'

'No.'

'No,' Gül repeats. She sits down next to her, takes the book from Ceyda's hand and looks at it before setting it aside.

'When Ceren was little but big enough not to poo her pants, we went for a picnic. You might remember. One weekend, with Saniye and Yılmaz – I don't know if Sevgi had been born yet – we drove out into the countryside. And at some point Ceren stopped playing and sat next to me but said nothing. And then I smelled this horrible stench. Worse than in the stable. My father had a cow once, you could tell which one it was from the smell of its dung, he always said. It stank, and I asked Ceren if she might have gone to the toilet in her trousers. I whispered it in her ear so she wouldn't be embarrassed in front of the others, but she just shook her head. And she sat there so awkwardly, on one side of her bottom. She didn't understand that she couldn't hide it.'

Ceyda fixes her mother with a look that resonates with the word *Mummy*, the word which has hurt Gül so deeply. The word her daughter had crammed all her pain into, the word which could never carry as much despair on paper. But it could do on the phone. Ceyda's look seems to say: *What is it you want to tell me, what is it you want to teach me? You left me all on my own. More than once.*

'I'm not saying you're lying,' Gül says, trying to keep her voice soft and gentle, trying to hide the hurt that Ceyda's look has caused her. 'All I'm saying is, we mustn't lie. We can't hide anything from God. We have to be good people. Just look at your nene. You know she's not my mother and we didn't always have it easy with her, and, as God is my witness, even she lies sometimes, but I'll always be grateful that she taught us not to lie.

'It's what we hear that makes this life. We have two ears, but only one mouth, which means we can listen twice as much as we speak. We bought Dede a telephone so we can listen to each other. Everyone says something, but when someone tells a lie, false deeds follow. And the words you speak can never be taken back, they stay there forever. When you say something that's untrue, you'll always carry that unease around with you; you won't be able to sleep, and you'll be unhappy. You mustn't lie, not for my sake but for yours. Because I want you to be happy.'

Gül is a little surprised at how she's just explained this to her daughter.

Ceyda looks at her mother and says: 'I didn't crank it.'

The moment when she tells Gül the truth about the crank will come decades later, when they're at a health resort in Germany.

The problem isn't that you can't get enough of your loved ones' voices when you've been apart so long, the problem isn't all the longing for their scent and their warmth, those calloused hands Gül longs to touch when she hears her father's voice. Phone calls aren't just hard because a voice can quench and feed your longing all at once, they're not just hard because they cost a lot of money and you always feel rushed. No, the real difficulty is being unable to reach each other. She can't just dial the blacksmith's number and let the phone ring in his house until he picks up the receiver and says *Gül* because no one else calls him.

First, she has to request the call at the post office in Germany because there's no option to direct dial. And then she has to wait. If she's lucky, it'll be an hour, or maybe two or three, until the phone rings and she's connected.

If she's less lucky, it might be seven or eight hours, and then the phone will ring in the middle of the night, and the voice at the other end, which sounds as if it's coming from the bottom of a well on the other side of the world, will be accompanied by a drowsy air and, in the blacksmith's case, an edge of fear, because surely it could only be someone calling with bad news at this hour.

For the first few years, phone calls are no better or easier than writing a letter. And yet weeks and months later, Gül still finds herself telling people about the conversations they have, like the night when she fell on the stairs because she'd been dashing to the phone; how she winded herself when she fell on her backside, that stabbing pain in her back; how tired Timur sounded at first; how he told her about Sibel's miscarriage, the third one by then, just three months and she'd lost the baby again; how she forgot about the pain in her back and cried; how she looked at the clock in astonishment as she hung up – it had been twenty minutes and Fuat was going to curse her when the bill came – and how she could hardly make it back up the stairs. Some things she'll keep to herself, though: how long the bruise lingered; how the left side of her bottom went from purple to blue to green to yellow over the next eight weeks.

How she stood in front of the mirror craning her neck and wondering whether that purple was the same shade as the rings beneath her mother's eyes before she died.

How Fuat came into the bedroom when she was standing there, knickers around her ankles, nightdress hoiked up, and said: 'I see you're displaying your wares,' and how gentle he was that night.

But it won't be any easier when the business with the switchboard falls away, because she won't be able to get through. Gül, Ceyda and Ceren will take it in turns to spin the dial until their fingers are sore. Usually, they'll hear the engaged tone before they've finished dialling the number. Gül and Ceyda are patient: they manage twenty minutes of dialling Timur's number, one after the other. But Ceren gets restless after four or five goes, and she gives up.

A few years later, Fuat comes home beaming.

'I've just been to the post office. We're getting a new phone, one with buttons. Long live technology! Every day they invent something to make our lives easier, and here we are right at the source, we can share in all these comforts. The only place that's got it better is America, I reckon. Here we are, right at the heart of Europe with our finger on the pulse – you can feel life beating here. This is where innovation happens, not in Anatolian villages. No more sore fingers for us!'

As if he'd ever had them. As if he'd invented the device himself.

Ceren will use the new telephone to develop a method for getting through to Turkey quicker than the others. She won't press the numbers one after another, or even press redial. First of all she'll just dial the international code, then, frowning, she'll listen to the noises on the line, and once she's heard a barely perceptible *click*, she'll tap in the code for Turkey, then she'll hold her breath and listen again. Unlike the others, it'll rarely take her more than seven tries to hear a ringing at the other end of the line. Except at Ramadan, Eid or New Year, when it's sheer luck to get through at all.

Phone calls will get easier as the years pass, noticeably cheaper too, but they'll never bring that much-anticipated change. Decades later, Gül will say: 'Fuat has always believed in progress. That there was always something better, nicer and more comfortable out there somewhere. And we've had it good, the Lord be praised: we're not starving, we've no need to fear having empty bellies one day. But that longing was always there, it's just as God commands. We can just as much escape longing as we can escape death.'

Gül frowns when her colleague Işık adds up how tight money is for her.

This much to pay off the house in Turkey; this much for two hectares of land, the car repair, a little bit for her mother who has no one else to take care of her; this much for a television with a remote control, a new sofa because the springs are poking out of the old one.

'We never seem to stop spending,' Işık says. 'We toil and work our fingers to the bone, but we barely manage to put a couple of coppers aside. Before you know it, another year's passed and you've spent a heap of money on your holiday. The years go by and we don't really notice; they flow by like water.'

'How much did you say you got this month?'

Işık tells her again.

'I got a hundred marks less,' Gül says, 'but we did the exact same shifts.'

She can't help remembering how it was in the sewing factory, where they said she was so badly paid because she didn't have her papers.

Tomorrow morning, she vows. *First thing tomorrow, I'll go to the office and complain. They can't keep on treating me badly; everyone overlooking me and me always holding my tongue like a good girl. Something has to change one day. First thing tomorrow morning.*

That evening she sits at home crocheting a blanket, going over what Işık said. *The years flow by like water.* She remembers the big water they channelled through the orchards of the summer houses in the heat, the stream where her father lost his watch, the water pump where she threw a stone that hit her sister in the eye.

Back then, the years flowed like water too. Perhaps they flow faster now, that much may be true, but something else has changed too.

Back then, the water was free. It had power and strength; they had to steer it or pump it out at the well, but the water flowed and sought its own path. These days, they're all in houses where the water is trapped in the pipes and has no strength of its own. And just like the water, the people are trapped: trapped in this life between work, money, spending, more work, more spending, the factory, the house, the garden, the car, holidays and the children.

Though Timur would spend all day at the forge, you could go and see him there, sit and talk and scratch his legs, drink tea. Ceyda and Ceren sometimes come to meet Gül from the factory, but they only know the gate; they've never set foot inside. And you couldn't drink tea and talk in there anyway.

How often had Gül sat by her father at the forge and watched the blacksmith working, hearing the hiss when the sweat dripped off his chin onto the glowing-hot iron? Now she spends eight hours a day combing wool, never knowing what will be made out of it. She sees the factory walls for longer than her daughters' faces.

But she's not the only one – everyone sees the walls of the factories and offices and shops for longer than they see their husbands and wives and children; everyone lives in a world in which they're trapped like water in the pipes. If even water can't run free, how can people be free here?

Gül pauses for a moment and looks up from her crocheting. She feels herself turning hot, as if someone could have read her thoughts.

What kind of thoughts did I get caught up in there? If anyone knew, they'd laugh.

What do I care about the water and how trapped we are here? I'll go to the office in the morning and ask why they give me less money than Işık.

'We'll take care of it, Mrs Yolcu,' the lady in the office says the next day. Gül goes back to work, unconvinced.

We'll take care of it. They probably won't do a thing. She just wanted to fob me off, but what was I supposed to say? I'll just go back again tomorrow and ask again. I won't let them get away with it. I've worked for that money; I've earned it by the sweat of my brow.

And the next day, she does indeed go back to the office to ask about the issue with her payslip. The woman tells her the same thing: 'We'll take care of it, Mrs Yolcu. Have a little patience.'

Gül vows to go back tomorrow and the day after that. She'll go back every day if she has to. She'll keep going back until it gets embarrassing for them; she's got it into her head now, and she won't give up.

During their break, Işık comes over and asks: 'Did you go to the office and ask about the payslips?'

'Yes,' Gül says.

'Great,' Işık says, 'that's just great! I add up how tight things are for us, and then this is what I get.'

'What?' asks Gül, who can't understand why Işık is so het up.

'They got their sums wrong. They paid me a hundred marks too much, and they wouldn't have noticed if you hadn't asked. They're taking it out of my next pay packet.'

Gül looks at Işık, not knowing for a few seconds whether to laugh or cry. She sees Işık's features growing even harder.

'It's not funny,' she says.

'No, it's not,' Gül admits. 'But don't be upset. It was my fault you lost your money. I'll give you the hundred marks, I just need a bit of time. You shouldn't have to pay the price for me trying to get my lot. That wouldn't be right.'

'I can't accept.'

Gül smiles even more now, because Işık's eyes are saying something different.

'No one could have seen this coming, could they? I'll get you the money, just give me a bit of time.'

Gesine and Ceren are sitting in the kitchen, reading books in which girls not much older than them own ponies, or at least get to look after them and ride them too. They sit on the horses' backs and feel like life can't get any bigger. This world is strange to the two friends. Unlike Ceren, Gesine doesn't know anyone who's ridden a horse, and when she sat on a pony at the circus, she forgot to breathe. She feels close to the heroines in her books; it's just the horses that seem a world away.

Ceren is familiar with horses from her holidays, even if she's only ever ridden a donkey herself. Her grandfather was a carriage driver, and she doesn't share Gesine's enthusiasm for horses. The warnings from her grandmother still echo in her ear: 'Never stand behind a horse – it could kick out.'

There are still a few carriages in her parents' home town, and though she likes riding along on a horse and cart, she'd be scared to sit on a horse. She's not sure if Gesine realises how big they are.

Ceren knows horses close-up, but it's the lives of the heroines in her books she finds strange. They never have to help out around the house, they don't usually have any siblings, they don't have to learn how to knit and crochet, and their freedom doesn't seem to have anything to do with riding horses. It's much bigger than that.

But the two friends like sitting together on the couch by the stove in the Yolcus' kitchen, each with a book in hand, dreaming themselves away to places they don't know their way around, while Gül makes the dinner.

Now and then Gül glances at the girls, and each time it's as if her heart grows a little wider until it no longer fits inside her, until it fills the whole kitchen, until she thinks the warmth of it could heat a whole house. How peaceful and happy they look, and how the happiness washes over her and grows bigger. What could be lovelier than a happy daughter? If joy can't be reflected, it can't multiply. Though your heart might beat in fine fettle, if it beats just for you, you'll be alone in this life that God has granted you.

When Fuat comes in, Gül turns to look at her husband with a blissful smile on her lips. For a moment, Fuat wonders if his wife has been drinking. Gül nods in the two girls' direction and holds a finger to her lips. She looks at her husband; Ceren gets her thick, arched eyebrows, her broad forehead and her high cheekbones from him.

Fuat is her daughters' father, and however difficult things might be with him sometimes, Gül's feelings transfer to him in this moment, and she feels an urge to simply walk over and embrace him, and then stand side by side with him so they can look at their daughter together. She suppresses the impulse. Fuat would make some kind of inappropriate remark and ask if she had lost her mind.

Still, it feels like the blood running through her veins is warmer now. Thanks be to God for this heart, with enough space inside for everyone.

Fuat walks up behind Gül and says, quietly: 'They'll have it easier than we did.'

Gül breathes in her husband's scent and nods. Yes. Her daughters are growing up with both their mother and father, not with a stepmother like she did. They'll have it easier than she did. If God allows, she won't leave them until they can stand on their own two feet.

After the meal there's a knock at the back door; someone must have come through the garden.

'Come in,' Fuat calls out from the table, where they're all still sitting.

It's Serter, and the two girls steal furtive glances at him. They've often heard that he's crazy, but they rarely catch sight of him. And when they do see him, he never seems to do things that seem crazy to them.

Word's gone round the adults that Serter has been going to a German lady of the night every two weeks. He's not the only one who does it, but he's the one who has set their tongues wagging. Fuat gets up, greets Serter and asks how he is.

Gesine goes very shy whenever the Yolcus have visitors. These days, she's happy to sit at the table, even if she doesn't understand the conversation, but as soon as strangers turn up, she feels out of place.

'Would you like to join us for something to eat?' Gül asks, though she's already heading straight to the cupboard to fetch another plate.

'No, no,' Serter says. 'Thanks, really, I'm fine. I love your food, you know that, but I've eaten.'

'I'm sure you can find room for a little something.'

'Come on,' says Fuat, putting a hand on Serter's shoulder, 'come on, I've got to check on the chickens. There's no need for us to stay to watch the women clean up.'

'I'll get you your jacket, it's cold out,' Gül says, putting the plate back and making for the hallway.

'Leave it,' Fuat says, 'I don't need it right now.' He accompanies Serter out the back door, which leads into a corridor housing the toilet and the washing machine.

When ten minutes have passed and Fuat still hasn't come back, Gül murmurs: 'He'll catch cold.'

'He put my jacket on,' says Ceyda.

'Stop peering through the window like that,' Gül says. 'There's nothing to see.'

A further twenty minutes later, Fuat is back in the kitchen.

Gesine said her goodbyes and left a while ago, and now Gül is drying up and the girls are sitting in the living room watching TV.

'Why did you drag him outside in such a hurry?' Gül asks.

'Good God!' Fuat replies. 'What is it you've got running through your mind? That I've got debts again? Gambling debts are debts of honour – I've got nothing to hide. You're almost as suspicious as he is. Can't even trust your own husband. *Why did you drag him outside in such a hurry?* Because his teapot's so cracked, there's no mending it. He's stark raving bonkers. There were three young women in here. Who knows what unsavoury things he'd start saying, what kinds of gestures he'd pull? – the sort that don't belong in a civilized household. He's a bachelor, after all. I was thinking of our daughters: that's why I dragged him outside. You never know with these mad types, and he is mad, completely. Who knows who he got it from? – he can't have come up with these ideas on his own. That we ought to fear the Germans, that they're no better than any other regime. The German secret service killed those terrorists in prison, he says. *They were all Nazis at one time anyway, the Germans – racism's in their blood. They'll butcher us like those lefties, so we have to support the armed struggle.* Would you want our daughters hearing such things? He asked me for a donation, for the people working underground. He's got connections, apparently. The leftists are our future in this country, he says.'

'He's not just crackers, he's the whole bloody biscuit tin at this point. You could talk nonsense for a hundred days and you'd still never come up with the kind of stuff he does. Other people raise money for mosques; he raises money for terrorists. Things won't end well for that man, mark my words.'

'Poor thing,' Gül says. 'He's living in a world of his own. He must be so lonely.'

Fuat goes to speak but says nothing. He shakes his head, pours himself another whisky and Coke, then makes his way into the living room. Gül follows him not long afterwards.

Fuat puts a packet of Lords on the table and kicks back without taking out a cigarette. He smokes Marlboros himself; Gül smokes Stuyvesant – not secretly, but never in Fuat's presence. Ceyda looks at the packet and feels herself turning hot. She avoids looking at her father. The cigarettes were in the pocket of her jacket, hanging behind the back door. Ceyda waits, barely daring to breathe. Waits for her father to say something, but he just watches telly; the most she can make out is a slight grin on his face. He pulls his Marlboros out of his shirt pocket under his jumper and sticks one in his mouth.

Ceyda doesn't know what to do. She can feel herself turning red; she knows there's no doubt in her father's mind as to who the Lords belong to. Should she say something? Will he say something?

Gül soon grasps what's happening. Though she's never seen her daughter smoking, she had more than an inkling. She can feel the heat radiating off Ceyda. Inwardly she scolds her daughter for being so careless.

Five minutes go by. 'I'm tired, I'm off to bed,' Ceyda finally says, and gets up.

The matter won't be spoken about again, but Ceyda will be more careful in future. And she won't smoke at all for the next three weeks. Fuat won't tell this story until his daughter is married and has children of her own.

'Raising kids isn't all that hard,' he'll say. 'You don't have to say much, you just have to do the right things. I knew she wouldn't stop smoking – who stops doing something at that age just because their parents say so? But the fact I said nothing left a bigger impression on her than a lecture. She didn't smoke for days, weeks afterwards. You've got to know when to hold your tongue.'

'Are you sure?' Gül asks.

'Yes.'

'You can carry on in school. To do A-Levels or whatever they call them.'

'I'd need good grades for that.'

Ceyda has never been all that great at school. But she isn't that bad either.

'Why should I go to sixth form? No one from my class is going. It's just for swots who study all day long. There aren't any Turkish kids there either.'

'What do you want to do instead?'

'An apprenticeship.'

'What kind of apprenticeship?'

'Hairdressing.'

'Hairdressing?'

'Yes, I want to be a hairdresser.'

Gül frowns. Fuat was a hairdresser in Turkey, and he never liked the job.

'People go there and you can talk all day.'

'That's it? *People go there and you can talk all day?* You're not even that chatty. Have you thought it over properly?'

'Yes.'

'Really?'

'Yes. You're not in a factory, there's no shift work, you get Mondays off and you can make a bit extra on the side from home. You can do it anywhere: here, Turkey, Italy – it doesn't matter where you are, you can always earn money.'

'You know your father didn't like the job.'

'Yes, but he was a barber, shaving and trimming men's hair. The work's much more varied here – you can do colours, streaks, perms, blow-dries, layering, bobs…'

Gül looks at her daughter. She seems to have given it a lot of thought. And Fuat won't care as long as she learns a trade and makes some money.

'Alright,' she says. 'If that's what you want, then you go ahead and train as a hairdresser. And if you ever change your mind, you can always go to evening classes. I'll support you as long as God gives me the strength.'

Ceyda will never go to evening classes. She will train as a hairdresser, but she'll spend even less time in the job than her father did back then.

When Ceyda leaves the house two days later with several large envelopes to post her applications, Gül sits down on the couch in the kitchen and her eyes well up with tears. She has to laugh at herself too, though.

It's gone so quickly, all of a sudden.

So that's what having children is like.

And they'll always be children, no matter what path they choose and which way they turn.

She didn't have a mother to teach her that. She was already married by Ceyda's age.

Ceyda smokes, of course, and she's probably fallen in love by now. Just like Gül fell in love with Recep when she was young. Ceyda's heart must be much wilder and stormier than she lets on. She's bound to have her secrets, not just about the cigarettes. But Gül always remembers her as a child too.

The child crying *Mummy*, a sound that will stay in the world forever.

Mummy, she'd cried out back then, but has Gül lived up to that cry? Has she done everything a mother needs to do? How is she to know? That's another thing she never learned. She only saw how her stepmother did it. And her stepmother probably wasn't even a good mother to her own children. She never praised them or cooed over them, she never pressed her children to her bosom and protected them from the world. Perhaps because she'd had no one to hold and protect her either.

Gül only had her mother for a short while, not long at all; what are six years when you can barely remember the first two or three? What are six years when you're pushing forty? What are those two or three years she had with her mother? Days counted down, days that passed far too fast.

She couldn't learn how to be a good mother back then. She left her daughters behind in Turkey, but how many others did the same? Were they all young and stupid too?

Her daughters have grown up here, they can choose a job for themselves and earn their own money now, but Gül still doesn't know whether she's a good mother. She does what she can, but there's always more a mother could do; all she knows is that she's done better than her stepmother did, and that wouldn't be difficult.

I'd give my life, she says to herself, *it's just on loan. But that's so easy to say. Who knows if I really could? Would I have thrown myself in front of the car to prevent it from hitting Ceren? What would I have done in that moment?*

I can't save the children from the world, though. They have their own lives. They always have. They came through me, not from me. And yet, if only I could protect them, even though I had no one to protect me.

When she returns to the kitchen, Ceyda looks at her mother, puzzled.

Gül rarely just sits there these days; there's usually at least some needlework on her lap if she looks idle. Ceyda sees her reddened eyes but also her smile – a smile that embraces her and holds her tight; that tells her the sound of this voice, the scent of this body, the touch of this skin will never end. She sits down next to her mother, who puts her arm around her daughter and pulls her closer.

'May everything turn out the way you wish,' Gül says. 'May all roads be open to you, and may you not feel the cold of the opposing wind.'

Ceyda feels her eyes prick. She inhales her mother's smell, that earthy but light scent that gives an inkling of how pale her skin is, how voluptuous her flesh and how gentle her words.

At the same time, Ceyda is glad school will soon be over. She's happy she won't be spending endless hours at a desk any more, staring at teachers who don't understand her life. Hers and the other children's from Factory Lane. Teachers who say things like: *Just look it up at home in the encyclopaedia.* Or: *You could have looked that up in the dictionary.* Teachers who talk about the Second World War over and over again, and who think the kids who aren't interested must be closet Nazis. Teachers who call her Leyla and try to fill her head with things that bore her.

Soon she'll be standing in a salon, talking to people about the weather, about shopping, their children and their brothers and sisters. Soon she'll be earning a wage, and she won't have to ask her mother for money whenever she wants something. Her mother, who doesn't go to her father for the money, but finds a way to fulfil Ceyda and Ceren's wishes. There'll be a bit more money in the house, and Ceyda will be able to put something towards her own trousseau.

'Go and walk your sister home from work today,' Gül says. 'And tomorrow as well. It's better you walk your sister home from work now it's getting dark so early. Don't let her walk past the woods on her own.'

'What about me?'

'Go the long way when you fetch her, and on the way home you can both take the short cut.'

From that day on, Gül stops taking a break with the others on her late shift. Instead, she puts on her coat just before six thirty, packs away her cigarettes and goes out to the yard. She stands by the fence there and watches the path by the woods. She can only make out her daughters by the way they walk, but every time she spots them, her cigarette tastes even better and she thanks the Lord once more.

For a whole winter, she stands there every evening during the late shift – whether it rains, hails or snows – smoking a cigarette and watching two small figures emerge and then disappear from of the beam of a streetlamp, only to reappear in the next circle of light.

For a whole winter, there's that moment when her cigarette suddenly tastes better and she can get back to her work with a smile on her face. For a whole winter, Gül stands in the yard in the evening, one hand on the fence, waiting to see her daughters. Not once is she disappointed.

How would it have been if we'd stayed in Turkey? she asks herself sometimes, as she stands there waiting for them. *Would I be working then too? Would Ceyda be learning a trade? Would Fuat have drunk less? Or more? Would we live on a road where the word neighbour means the same as it does here? Would I have felt better if I'd seen my father every day? Would there have been less longing, less fear, and instead more worries about our daily bread and the roof over our heads? Would Fuat have grown unhappy in a job he didn't like? And would he have been sad he couldn't support his father, out of work now that cars have replaced carriages?*

'The whole world is a foreign land,' Yavuz had said to her the day she boarded the train in Istanbul to come to Germany. He was a farmer, an old acquaintance of her father's, and he often repeated himself: 'We're alive, thank the Lord, we're alive! We're standing on our own two feet. The whole world is a foreign land that we're captured in, captured in the time that passes between birth and death. And everything before and after is eternity.'

Sometimes, being in that foreign land feels like standing on a roof with a view of everything, as though vastness and calm and comfort were all out there somewhere. For the length of a cigarette, you feel peace; peace on the roof of this prison.

'These Spaniards!' the blonde woman says, her hair set in lacquered waves. 'They always talk so loudly, like they're the only people on Earth.'

Her friend is wearing a headscarf, a small, triangular piece of fabric that doesn't quite cover the back of her head.

'I know,' she concurs. 'They come over here, oblivious to the fact that we like a bit of quiet after lunch and on Sundays, and they make a racket late into the night. That might be alright in their country, but there's no place for it here. You can't even take the tram without them making a nuisance of themselves.'

'They're not cut out for life here, they're so hot-blooded.'

Gül is sitting right behind the women and can hear every word they're saying. She can also hear every word the men nearer the front by the door are saying, but she finds the women's conversation easier to understand.

'He'd only been back two days and they stole his car. The goods must have been welded in there. Just think how much stuff must have been in there for it to be worth all that. We could spend years slaving away here until our backs go crooked, but you don't get rich that way.'

'The car's gone, but still, he was really lucky,' the other man says now. 'Imagine if they'd busted him at the border. You can talk as long as you like there, but no one'll believe you, and by that point you'll really be in the shit. Then you can wail all you want, but you'll be stuck listening to the wind whistle through your jail cell.'

'You've got to do it like they do, have a bit of nouse. Find a back-street repair shop in Istanbul where you can say you got your car fixed. Then pull out your proof of repair. You just need a bit of nouse, and you'll be laughing all the way to the bank. I'm telling you' – the man lowers his voice a little – 'we've got to get into this racket. I know a bloke. That's where the money is, not in shiftwork.'

'It must be a real chore taking the tram in Spain,' the woman with the headscarf says, 'having to spend the whole day like that, with no let-up.'

'We've only been once, to Mallorca. There aren't any trams there but it's still noisy.'

Gül's German is still poor, even after all these years. She understands the bulk of what she hears, but when she has to speak, she loses her nerve and words fail her. Not once has she spoken

German for longer than five minutes at a stretch. Where would she speak it? And how?

I don't have the knack for it, she thinks, consoling herself. *If I were more outgoing and not so cautious, I'm sure things would be different. I'd be able to speak like Saniye, with no inhibitions, without being frightened of making a mistake. But I'm just not like that. I can't even call to mind the things I already know.*

Evidently, the two women in front of her have even less of a knack for languages than she does; anything that isn't German sounds the same to them. Gül can recognise Spaniards, Italians, Greeks and Yugoslavians when she hears them speaking, though most of them returned to their home countries long ago, perhaps because the economic situation improved, perhaps because they couldn't stand the longing, perhaps because they know you've got to make do with what you've got.

Those women should thank their God that they've been able to stay in their own country, where there's enough work, Gül thinks. *They don't have to move and find out how hard it is to learn a foreign language.*

She has to get off at the next stop, and now she's standing behind the two men, who have been talking quietly. If they club together, they could get a nice fat payout in three or four months' time, more opiates and heroin than money can buy.

I should be grateful too, Gül thinks, *grateful for a husband who may have his flaws but would never break the law to get rich, no matter how much he dreams of it. He'd never wade into that swamp and drag his family in with him. He'd never bring trouble and woe on all our heads, so his daughters only get to see him at visiting hours. He may have his faults, but he's decent where it counts.*

Gül goes into the shop that Saniye recommended to her, where the baklava apparently tastes like it's been freshly baked in Gaziantep. All the people on the streets, the trams, the buses, the bustle of Bremen irritate and bother Gül; she wonders whether she'd ever find it possible to walk through a city like this and feel relaxed.

Years later she'll live in Bremen, and only then will she say: 'People are capable of anything, we must never be too sure of ourselves, we must always have a little doubt. I thought I could never be a spy or a thief or a prostitute, but now I know anyone is capable of anything. Life can lead you down alleys you'd never dream of. You can never say, "That wouldn't happen to me."'

Gül never says, 'See?' or 'Serves you right!' or 'I told you so.' She doesn't even think it. That kind of satisfaction is alien to her.

But she's also not surprised when Mevlüde gets laid off. Mevlüde, in whose mouth the words 'Oh, it's nothing, they won't even notice,' churn like chewing gum. Mevlüde, who practically never cleaned the rollers on the carts, who did her work but was never happy, constantly cursing the task at hand, the factory, the Germans, Serter, the wool, the sheep, foreigners, the bosses. Mevlüde, who managed to fill her house on Factory Lane with unhappiness.

But it's not just Gül's department that's seen lay-offs. Yılmaz says: 'That's what capitalists do, first they say to the state, "There's been an upturn, we need more workers – let's bring in people from abroad, then we'll all get rich." Except the people from abroad, of course, but the capitalists don't say that – the state just knows it. Then the capitalists say, "Look over there: people are working for much less money. But let's not bring people over here this time, where we have to guarantee them higher pay – let's take the machines over to them. Sod the state and sod the cheap labour here. Look, we're raking it in now." That's how it works. All of us will lose our jobs eventually.'

But Fuat says: 'Germany is a strong country – the Germans are hard-working, ambitious and dutiful. The factory's not about to be shut down just because some of the production has been outsourced abroad. This factory survived two world wars, it's over a hundred years old. Why would it suddenly shut up shop now, when things are going well for everyone? And even if it did, there's always work for those who want it. It's not like it is in Turkey. And there's always the dole, anyway.'

Gül can't imagine the factory closing either. She's been working there for so many years now, she just can't picture the building standing empty.

After a spell of redundancies, calm seems to return to the factory; Gül is relaxed, the work is easier because all the workers who didn't do a good and thorough job are now at home.

Gül feels validated. You don't have to shirk, you needn't worry; you simply do one task after another, conscientiously; you keep your eye off the clock, no slacking, and then the end of the day seems to arrive of its own accord, bringing with it a sense of peace.

There's no need to be frightened of hard work. Gül has done plenty of it, and she can do plenty more. She has faith in her abilities, and to her, being kept on is a reward for her efforts.

She stays until the end. Gül doesn't listen to the rumours; even as more and more people are let go – she simply keeps working and refuses to think about things she can't bring herself to believe, because they're unimaginable. Even when they announce that the factory is closing, Gül is still holding out hope that some miracle will keep everything the way it is.

The first Monday she doesn't have to work, Gül gets up and makes breakfast. She waves Ceren off to school and Ceyda to college, then she sits in the kitchen with Fuat, who got up a little later. He eats his breakfast in silence while Gül is still trying to understand how a person's life can change so completely from one day to the next.

After a cigarette, Fuat pulls his jacket on and Gül asks him: 'You off out?'

'I'm going to the coffeehouse.'

Gül looks at him, surprised. As much as he likes to gamble, he's not one of those men who are always at the coffeehouse, drinking tea and smoking over a backgammon board or with cards in their hands. He might enjoy an hour or two there, but then he wants to play for cash and have a proper drink. And they don't serve those at the coffeehouse.

'I'm going to ask around,' Fuat says. 'I can't sit at home all day – a few weeks' dole is all well and good, but I need to work, and I can earn a bit under the table too. My backside's not made for sitting around.'

He stays out until dinner time and comes home smelling of beer. Gül has tidied the house, cleaned, done the washing, phoned Saniye, done some knitting in front of the TV, and cooked dinner. And since Ceren is at Gesine's house, she walks to meet Ceyda on her way home from work. There's a smile on Ceyda's face much more than there used to be in her school days; she seems to be enjoying her work. It's only on days like today, when she's had to go to college, that she's in a bad mood before breakfast.

When Fuat gets home in the evening, the table is already laid. Gül thinks his grin is from the drink, but when Ceyda is clearing up after dinner, he says to his daughter: 'Make me a nice sweet coffee. And I'll have a cigarette with it, one that tastes so good my lungs'll think it's a Friday. No one could call me lazy. You've got to be smart in this world, a bit smart. Anyway, congratulations are in order: I've got a new job!'

'Really?' Gül says, and almost in tandem, Ceyda asks her father: 'Have you signed the contract?'

'It's not just anywhere either,' Fuat continues, taking no notice. 'It's with the kings of carmakers, the place where quality and performance count, reliability and durability. A brand that's known all across the world.'

He looks around as if to challenge them, but neither of the women says anything.

'Mercedes!' he says.

'Have you signed the contract?' Ceren asks, repeating her sister's question.

'No,' Fuat says, 'no, but there's nothing standing in my way now, I've as good as got it. I was in Bremen today, at the Mercedes offices.' His chest is so swollen with pride that night that it takes a few whisky and Cokes for his shoulders to slump back into place and the tension to leave his body.

Gül thought she'd barely be able to fill her days once she stopped working, but she's surprised how much she used to manage when she was still going to the factory. She spends longer chatting to the neighbours, and she takes a bit more time for her needlework. Fuat bought her an electric sewing machine; she sews dresses for the girls and knits jumpers for her husband, and by the end of the day she's hardly had half an hour with nothing to do. She might not have a job, but she doesn't sit around twiddling her thumbs. It's even rare for her to turn on the new television Fuat has bought, a remote-control colour one.

Gül takes care of the garden, planting courgettes and pumpkins, cucumbers and tomatoes, beans and peppers. And though the earth beneath her hands feels different to back then, though it smells different and is a different colour, though the light is different and the sun doesn't always warm her back, these hours remind her of her childhood and the big mulberry tree in the garden at the summer house. They bring the blacksmith's smell back to life, that smell he had when he'd been working in the garden or the stable. She thinks back to the time her father took her along to someone else's orchard and left her alone there, not knowing she was afraid. How relieved she was to hug him and smell the sweat on his shirt collar when he finally returned.

Gül feels fine without work, and the spring passes swiftly. As swiftly as time passes when you don't notice you're happy until afterwards.

Fuat is proud of his job and drives the car to Bremen and back every day, perhaps even earns a little more than before, buys an even fancier TV, a one-year-old Mercedes, and a brand-new moped; he thinks the latter is safer when he drives drunk.

These are good times at 52 Factory Lane. Ceyda is glad she decided to train as a hairdresser; Ceren brings Gesine home with her more and more often, since she doesn't have to share her room with her sister during the day. All their cares fade, and the bitter words and shouted curses that do still come no longer sour the atmosphere for days on end; the disharmonies hardly cause an echo.

The cracks only begin to form once they're all in the nearly new car, fully loaded once again, to Fuat's annoyance, and driving off for Anatolia. It's only once they're all cramped in together, and the heat and the endless roads and traffic grow unbearable that their harmony starts to falter; only once they're trapped inside the metal box that the harsh words bounce off the walls, and the sun's rays fail to soften their moods. But even then, Gül can still feel the past few months reverberating inside her, and so she smiles a secret smile, making sure to hide her gentle happiness from Fuat so as not to irritate him.

That year, the summer – the time between their car journeys – passes even faster than spring on Factory Lane; it's gone before they can even think *lovely*, and Gül retains her inner smile for the duration of the drive back. She's put on weight again over the past months; her belly wobbles with her every laugh, which sounds like it could chase away all trace of darkness.

Ceyda and Ceren will reminisce about this summer often in later years, never really understanding why it was better than all the others, why the sun shone brighter, why their dede hugged them more, or why the laughter echoed louder and even the sad songs sounded more cheerful, in a language in which grief and summer are only one letter apart.

Suddenly the melancholy struck a brighter chord, whereas even the sunniest tunes had suggested a note of gloom before.

The sisters joined in with singing, *You milked my heart until my knees gave way*, although they themselves were filled with something that was neither yearning nor desire. They'll never tire of listening to the tapes they bring home with them this summer. Songs that will remind them of those five and a half weeks, for the rest of their lives.

Even Fuat sings along during the long drive home, while Gül simply smiles as her breasts bounce with every hole in the road. She doesn't sing along, doesn't hum, but the music is inside her, like she's swallowed the voices.

It feels like Fuat is poking a knitting needle into Gül at a spot she barely knows herself, a place that sends the pain deep into her, when he says: 'You need to get on with finding a job.'

When and how the feeling of the summer got lost, Gül doesn't know; it's autumn but not yet dark enough for Gül to have to pick Ceyda up in the evening, and although Fuat doesn't say it as often as he used to say he preferred slim women, he dampens the light a little more every time he tells her to find a job.

It's not as though Gül isn't looking. The job centre says there's nothing for her, and the other women on Factory Lane are stuck at home and can't find anything either. Even Saniye, who knows so many people, can't help Gül. She's glad she still has a job herself, packing shoes into cardboard boxes eight hours a day.

'At night I sometimes wake up with a start because my hands aren't moving and I think the belt's running without me working,' she says, then laughs. 'We used to get one pair of shoes every other winter,' she says. 'Who'd have thought we'd be living in such luxury one day? I could pinch two pairs a day and no one would notice. And the job's not forever, is it?'

Gül doesn't know anyone who has worked in as many different factories as Saniye. The longest her friend has held a job down is three years – there was always something else she wanted to do, always a change she was looking for. And she only ended up packing shoes because you have to take what you can get these days.

'You need to get on with finding a job.'

Fuat must have noticed over the years that Gül's not lazy. No matter how much she's enjoyed being at home, she'd still like to work, and every time she hears those words from Fuat's mouth, she feels as though being unemployed is her own personal failing.

Soon Fuat's tone will grow harsher, and the accusations will follow, but for now Gül can still let herself melt into the moments with Ceren that her life as a housewife affords her.

Ceren comes home from school in the early afternoon while Ceyda and Fuat are out working, and mother and daughter have the house, and time, to themselves. Ceren talks about the books she's been reading, and Gül often tells long stories as she thinks back. Stories about how she would read the articles or half-articles from the newspapers her stepmother used to line the cupboards. How she'd be sent to fetch a glass and then lose all sense of time, finding herself immersed, half-inside the cupboard, in a report on a baby with two heads. How her stepmother's cousin's baby was stillborn, and how she'd once believed her brother was going to die from a safety pin that got stuck in his back. How Yasemin from the village came to stay with Uncle Abdurahman…

Gül leaps from one memory to the next, and sometimes Ceren can barely get a word in. Many of the stories don't come to a close, and it'll be years before Ceren can tie up the loose ends.

Ceren doesn't get lost or sidetracked when she tells stories. Through her daughter's words, Gül gets an impression of how things look and work at Gesine's house.

'No, really,' Ceren says, 'it's true. Gesine brushes her teeth in the bathroom while her brother's in the shower.'

'How old is her brother? Aren't they embarrassed? What does her mother say about it?' Gül asks, amazed, but then she adds: 'It's their culture, they learned it that way, they mean well.

No one wants bad things for their children. We have to accept people the way they are. Everyone's different.'

Paying no attention to the programmes, Gül sits in front of the TV in the evenings and tries to understand how these things add up.

'Why can't Ceren eat with us?' Gesine had asked her mother. Ceren could hear every word from the next room. 'I always eat at her house when I'm there.'

'Gesine,' her mother had said, 'I've told you this before. Ceren's parents have two incomes.'

And Gesine answered: 'No, not any more. Ceren's mum's unemployed, and they still let me eat with them.'

'But they get money from the job centre,' her mother had said.

No matter which way Gül looks at it, she can't understand it; instead she has to make do with the scant explanation she gave her daughter. As Ceren's friend, Gesine is like a member of the family. That doesn't mean it has to be the same the other way around.

Still, she would never turn a stranger away from her table. Where two people eat their fill, three people eat their fill too, she was always told. Apparently, things are different in this country.

And that brother – she hopes the mother has him under control and he doesn't show himself naked to Ceren too. She doesn't say a word about her fears to Ceren, trying instead to impress upon her, on other occasions, what's right and proper.

Gül values Ceren's trust and she's glad of their new intimacy. Yet at the same time, she also makes an effort to pay more attention to Ceyda. To make sure she doesn't get jealous, she asks how her work has been every evening, and she tries to extend the question into a long conversation. She gives her disposable lighters, and keeps crocheting and knitting away for her trousseau.

Ceyda has always been more private than Ceren, and Gül has to remember her own words: *We have to accept people the way they are.*

The children come through us, not from us, and they're not a colouring book you can fill in with your favourite shades of crayon.

I don't love one of them more and the other less, as God is my witness, I love as my heart permits.

If it weren't for the girls, Fuat's words would cut deeper.

Just as the blacksmith was once the first person in his neighbourhood to own a radio, Fuat is the first resident of Factory Lane to buy a video recorder. But unlike his father-in-law's radio, this purchase doesn't result in a sudden deluge of visitors for the family. The neighbours do come round to look, marvel and wonder at the device, but in a matter of days, weeks at most, almost all of them have one of their own. The blacksmith was wealthy in his time, whereas here, everyone works in the same factory.

Within months, video tapes are doing the rounds; the Turkish butcher, who also sells fruit and veg, suddenly has videos to rent behind the till.

These days, no one on Factory Lane turns on the TV to watch German programmes.

Years ago, in another life, they would all go to the cinema to watch Humphrey Bogart, Cary Grant, Ava Gardner, Kirk Douglas, Bette Davis, Gina Lollobrigida, Elizabeth Taylor, Robert Mitchum. Of course, there were also films with Erol Taş, Fatma Girik, Filiz Akın, Ayhan Işık back then, but for almost twenty years it was the American films that fed their desire, their dreams of other countries and better times. Films that made Fuat strive for a taste of real whisky rather than settling for watching it in black and white on the big screen, not getting so much as a whiff for himself. Films that beguiled Saniye into believing that Europeans jumped into bed with their shoes on at every opportunity. Films, like stories, made them believe in another world, one where life felt different to the one they knew. A life where their hearts would beat to a different rhythm; harder, happier, healthier – a life bigger than this one, with its worries and sorrows, its grief and drudgery.

What sent them searching was not necessity, but that longing for a different kind of life that seemed within reach, always within reach – how else should the others be able to tell them about it?

It was cinema that nursed their dreams twenty years ago, filling their heads with pictures of how things could be, bringing them envy and making the world seem somehow smaller.

Film reels had no trouble crossing the ocean, the roads seemed to be open to them.

Now families sit together in front of the television in the evenings; on the weekends they watch five or six films in a row. It's not a patch on the cinema double bills from back in the day, but the actors in these films don't have foreign names any more. They have names like Kemal Sunal, Orhan Gencebay, Tarık Akan, Hülya Koçyiğit, Yılmaz Güney, Müjde Ar, Türkan Şoray, Cüneyt Arkın, Ferdi Tayfur, İbrahim Tatlıses.

Films where a famous singer plays a musician who's in prison and who sends a songstress pieces he's composed for her; songs that reflect a longing which can only be felt from behind walls like these; songs lamenting that our hearts grow heavier with each passing day – until Fuat can't help but top up his glass.

What is left for us in this world? Night has fallen, and when you're far away from the country you call home, what else is there to do but drink? How could it be a sin? Drinkers die, but does everyone else live forever? Pour yourself another one, and draw the smoke in deep so it settles on the melancholy inside.

Films that tell of the glorious conquest of Byzantium, in which only Christians are capable of grisly misdeeds. Films where wives die in childbirth, and their husbands endure lives of countless sorrows, all to bestow a little happiness on their daughters. Films where the farmer's son falls in love with the landowner's daughter; films about bloody vengeance, where people go grey overnight in prison.

Films with stories that seem familiar; films in which men and women declare their undying love for each other, though their families have been trapped in a blood feud for generations. Unlike most American films, love is not the answer here. It doesn't bridge chasms; it doesn't leave you feeling warm inside when the film ends. It leads to more deaths, more suffering, less hope. Here, love is not a romantic ideal – it's a folly that grabs people and drags them mercilessly to their graves. Films where the heroes die at the end, their blood mixed with the dust on the road, and those they leave behind know that the pain will never truly fade.

Gül watches a film where a young woman is sentenced to death for a crime she didn't commit and who says nothing the whole time she's in court. No one has ever listened to her, no one has ever believed her or in her. Love is a song her grandfather sang to her when she was still little, a distant memory; the sound of a voice cracking, singing out of tune. Everything else is just words with no feeling behind them, like all the muttering in court. She sees no way out and holds her tongue.

And who would you believe: a maid who has been raped countless times and has never defended herself, or rich men?

Gül sits in front of the television and understands; she understands, just as she understood the Anatolian Blues when she was a little girl. Of course you can tell the truth, of course you can be decent and pure of heart, but what does it count for, what does it change? What does it matter when you're standing before men in robes who believe themselves able to pass judgement? The reward for a good deed is the deed itself. You ought not to strive for anything in this world; it gives you nothing for free.

But there are also comedies where, for instance, a man plagued by rheumatism can predict the future and becomes a holy man in his village, feared and revered by all.

These films teach Ceyda and Ceren as much about their parents' country as the American films taught Gül and Fuat about the United States back in the day. These films don't just seem like other worlds; they look like places you could really step into. Places where your heart might find peace, despite all hardships.

Just as the sisters will happily listen to the cassette tape of that summer over and over again, they'll also watch the films countless times over – love stories where the characters sing and fall in love as if they've been struck by a stone.

Gesine also watches some of the films with Ceren; you don't have to understand the words to grasp what's going on, but she struggles to watch two or three in a row.

For two weeks, Ceren tries to teach Gesine Turkish, so she can share the films with her friend, but she soon finds she can't explain how the language works, and Gesine is shocked that she can't memorise the words, despite having no problem with English vocab at school.

Thank you, please, the names of a few dishes, *good,* and *I'm full*: after two weeks of daily lessons, there's little more Gesine can remember of Turkish, and Ceren has to watch the films with her sister or the other children in the neighbourhood. It sometimes takes weeks before the butcher gets the films back, because the tapes are passed between houses on Factory Lane. Everyone lets him know if they've got this or that film, then the butcher notes it down on a greasy index card and collects the lending fees.

'That's technology for you, it's always advancing,' Fuat says. 'Think back to the years when we'd see the MGM lion roar and wouldn't understand a single word after that. Think of those hectic Saturday mornings when *Letters from Turkey* was on TV, and the episodes didn't last much longer than an actual letter themselves. Gone are the days when we watched *Marriages on Trial* because there was nothing else on, wasting our time with husbands and wives rowing over money and kids, with the Germans and their accusations, betrayals and infidelity. Now we can decide for ourselves what to watch on the screen. Technology is advancing: soon you'll be able to live everywhere in the world at once. You'll be able to get everything straight to your living room at the touch of a button; all the films in the world, all the newspapers. Soon you'll be able to get anything; they'll ship it or send it by lorry. Soon you won't have to think, "Oh, I wish I could get this or that," like we did back in the day, "Oh, if only they had aubergines, if only they had the Turkish papers, if only they had mutton." "We haven't got any" will soon be a thing of the past.'

'Plenty, that's what technology brings people: plenty and comfort. We don't have to sweat all the way to Turkey any more, because the car has air conditioning now. Every day they invent something new; they might guard it with their lives, but these Germans, the Americans and the Japanese, they're going to change the world as we know it.'

At the weekend, the residents of Factory Lane gather in one of their living rooms; one, two, three families, adults, teenagers and children. There are pastries and tea, Coke and Fanta, sunflower and pumpkin seeds, roast chickpeas, and conversation. They chat while the films play. If the conversation topic's particularly interesting, the children will be the only ones following the film's plot, sitting on the floor in a semi-circle in front of the TV. The others will lose themselves chatting about southeast Anatolia, trousseaus, Turkish history, or just gossiping about the actors or absent neighbours. When it gets to an exciting scene or a good joke, they'll all be spellbound again, but they soon slip back into chatting, and the hostess ensures the tea glasses and the little crystal bowls of nibbles are never empty. The films make their way up the street and back again, so eventually no one will have missed a single scene.

The films bring changes to the way the children speak – soon they're all cursing like Kemal Sunal. Not the sort of swears for insulting wives and families, not the ones you only utter when you're shrinking back from a clip round the ear, but the sort that are mainly made up of names for animals, the kind of animals you usually find in a stable. Animals apparently deserving of contempt because they've allowed themselves to be domesticated. The children call each other *You big ox!* and *Son of an ass!*

and fall about giggling because they've dared to speak forbidden words; the films' laughter lingers on in them.

Years ago, the blacksmith's radio changed their lives. On summer evenings they would all sit outside their houses, listening to the sound of the radio rising from the blacksmith's roof. It was a while before Gül understood that there were no tiny people putting on a kind of play inside the box her father brought home.

Children's lives are completely different these days. They can work the video recorder even before they've started school, and they know there's no one living inside the telly. How quickly everything has changed, so quickly that Gül sometimes thinks it's been too fast for her to really take notice.

You have to stop and look back, otherwise life flows by like water in a stream. You can't hold onto anything. Even though the water is controlled and pumped through pipes, it flows all the faster here and disappears before you can say 'wet'.

'You've got nothing but films on the brain these days. How nice, eh? – spending all day on the sofa watching videos, while I'm hard at work at the factory. Get yourself a job!'

'God is my witness,' Gül says, 'I've never watched a film on my own. I can't even work the machine.'

'You do nothing but lounge around at home all day. Your year of unemployment benefit is up, and we're not putting a penny aside any more. Thank goodness Ceyda puts something in the kitty, otherwise we'd be in big trouble. It's out of order. This is Germany – I don't care how you do it, just go out and get yourself a job. We're not here to lead a life of Riley, lazing around at home. I've almost given up gambling because we can't afford it.'

As far as Gül can tell, that's the truth.

It's a long time since Fuat stopped singing the praises of his job, the company and technology. Now barely three days pass without

Gül hearing accusations, more and more accusations, different ones every time.

'You're turning my daughters against me,' Fuat has started accusing her. 'It beggars belief, I'm their father but no matter where I am, they're not there. I sit down in the kitchen, and Ceyda gets up and walks out; I come in the living room, Ceren leaves. Not even in the garden – the minute I get there, even if they're working outside, they down tools as if they're making a run for it. You're sitting at home all day long, washing my daughters' brains with soap – soap and antimen shampoo. You're setting up a women's front against me. A man can't even feel comfortable in his own home, it beggars belief!'

Gül sees his pain. She knows the girls do indeed flee from their father, but she's never encouraged them to do so.

'Fuat,' she says, 'Fuat, may God strike me down on the spot if I've done anything to turn the girls against you. I've never said a bad word about you.'

'Oh yeah? So why can't I sit down anywhere without them jumping up? It's been this way since you've been at home.'

That's not true, Gül would like to say, but she bites her tongue while her husband talks himself into a rage, like he has done for as long as she's known him.

That's not true, she could say. *You've only started noticing it now because you've been so unhappy recently. It was like that before too, but you used to go chasing after pleasure; you had more energy for selfish distractions, and there were lots of things you didn't notice. Then or now, did you ever ask yourself why they do it? Do you really think it's because I'm stirring them up against you? How many years have we been living together – do you really not know me? Have you ever asked yourself whether it leaves a mark on the children when they carry their stinking father from the car to the sofa? Whether it hurts to see how generous he is to strangers, and how stingy he gets when it comes to his own daughters?*

She would say it; it's not that she doesn't dare. That might have been the case in the old days, but now she has the courage.

Yet she also has the certainty that he wouldn't understand. She doesn't know, with the best will in the world, whether that's because he can't understand it or because he doesn't want to.

He has limited horizons, she will say of her husband in later years. *I've never really understood him, but I do know he sees the world through a very small window. And he only uses one eye.*

What she sees is that Fuat has had enough of someone always being in when he comes home. She sees that he wants some peace and quiet to himself. The only thing she can't tell is why that is.

Ceyda has watched a lot of love stories on video over the past few years, some of them over and over again. Gül can't say whether her daughter has romantic ideas; whether she inhabits an inner world that she barely lets show. Whether she thinks the right man would change everything.

It's the last year of her apprenticeship, and the first young men have started coming over with their parents to ask for her hand. Some of them Gül knows Ceyda has never spoken to before, others she's not so sure. Is there someone Ceyda is in love with, as Gül once was with Recep? If so, can she help her daughter to see that someone in private? Or even to marry him?

These days, Gül can read a lot of people; she can predict what they'll do next, guess their thoughts and motivations, including those they'd never dare say out loud. She's no longer the young woman who came from Anatolia to Factory Lane, amazed at how different people are, how they lie and tie themselves up in knots, how two-faced and deceitful they can be, how they put on an act as if life were a stage with nothing behind it.

Yet when Gül steals a glance at Ceyda and wonders what the secret thoughts in her head might be, she knows so little of them that she almost instantly feels like a bad mother.

And so she says straight out, walking her daughter home from work, 'Ceyda, is there someone you know or would like to get to know?'

She looks away, so that Ceyda won't feel she's being put on the spot. Her eyes wander to the closed-down factory, to the place by the fence where she always used to stand.

'No,' Ceyda says, 'there isn't anyone.'

'I won't tell anyone. It's normal for you to be interested in certain things – you're at that age. I was no different, but my mother never talked to me about it. Times were different then.' *And she wasn't my mother.* This she doesn't say. She doesn't think her own mother would have talked to her about it either.

Ceyda says nothing, and the only thing Gül can sense is that her daughter would like a cigarette. But even if Gül offered her one, she wouldn't smoke in front of her.

'You didn't want those few men who've come so far. But if there is someone, I'd like to help you. You're still young: you can turn down dozens of men and not marry for two, three, four years yet. You can go back to school if you like.'

Gül says this even though she doesn't know how she'd explain it to Fuat. Still, she'll find a way, there's always a way.

'You can go to university. If you like.'

Ceyda nods but says nothing. Perhaps she'd like to tell her mother about her vow never to marry a man who drinks; perhaps the only thing holding her back is fear her mother might see it as a reproach.

Three weeks after this conversation, another young man comes over with his family. Adem is twenty-two, a mechanic, and works in a factory that makes cigarette vending machines. He's tall and thin, and his family comes from the same province as the Yolcus; they know some of the same people. Adem doesn't seem shy but he's not talkative either; instead, he looks at Ceyda with a certain level of interest. His father says he has no bad habits.

'He doesn't even smoke,' he says while Adem has gone to the toilet. 'Really. These young people do everything in secret. His younger brothers smoke and think I don't know what, but Adem doesn't seem to like these things.'

There's something about Adem that doesn't quite sit with Gül. Almost like she dreamed of him once and didn't like him.

It feels like lead suddenly forms in her stomach the next day, when Ceyda says that she'd like to marry Adem.

Why? Gül asks herself. *Because he doesn't drink? Because she wants to leave home, where her father complains every day? Because she's seen too many of those films? Because he doesn't gamble? Because he seems quiet?*

'Are you sure?' she asks her daughter. She remembers what her father said to her back then: *I'll have to make you a husband at the forge. You've found something wrong with every one of them!*

If only she could forge a husband for Ceyda, who now says: 'Yes, I'm sure.'

'There are other men without bad habits. Maybe you should wait a bit.'

'No,' Ceyda says. 'I want to marry Adem.'

'You don't need to move out. No matter how much your father talks about money.'

'It's not that.'

Gül would like to know what it is, but her father never tried to influence her choice, so she simply holds her tongue. Unlike his wife, Fuat is thrilled by his daughter's decision.

'Come on, let's drink to him!' he says, pouring Ceyda a whisky and Coke. 'We'll have a wedding that wants for nothing, where everyone can eat until they're out of breath. Bottles on every table, as many as people want; a marriage hall; a proper function hall; live music. We'll get it all videoed so we can watch it again years later. They say you become a man when you join the army, or you become a man when you get married, but you're not a proper man until you marry off your children. That's how it is. Here, have another sip!'

'You've got to be a bit smart. I'll start looking for a hall tomorrow. Now this is good news! Ceren, dial your grandmother's number so we can tell her all about it.'

Perhaps it's the whisky that makes Ceyda feel excited and relaxed. Or perhaps it's something else.

'You'll have our room to yourself,' she tells Ceren while the sisters are getting ready for bed.

'Yes.'

Ceren doesn't want to say any more; she knows there will be tears in her voice, even though she's not crying.

'You should be happy.'

'Yes.'

'Look, they live no more than a hundred kilometres away. I'll get my driving licence. We'll see each other all the time. We won't be apart.'

'Yes.'

Ceren's voice sounds better already. Perhaps because she's pulling herself together.

We won't be apart.

If only we knew which promises we'll keep and which we won't.

Gül is sitting in the kitchen, thinking of her days in the kitchen of their two-room flat. Back then her daughters were far away, and she wanted nothing more than to have them with her. Now they're here, and the older one is about to go again. But they can get in the car at the weekend and be at Ceyda and Adem's door within an hour; they live in a two-bedroom flat on a new estate, a few streets away from Ceyda's mother-in-law. She's got a job at a salon, she's earning money, she's bound to be fine. She's not under anyone's thumb, being bossed around like a maid – all she has to do is look after herself and her husband.

Everything seems to be fine; there's no reason for Gül to sit in the kitchen prodding at the pain to work out precisely how it feels and where it might be coming from. Whether it's the separation, the uncertainty, the emptiness, a lack of trust, or the niggling feeling she has about Adem.

How easy it must be to be like Fuat, she thinks. He could hardly speak straight by the end of the wedding, but he certainly put on a good show. While all the guests were still there, he went from table to table, his chest puffed up with pride, genuinely concerned about everyone's wellbeing. Later, as the hall began to empty, he helped the belly dancer up onto a table, and fumbled several twenties and fifties into her neckline and the top of her trousers. She was a slim woman, just Fuat's type, and no one wondered why it was still called belly dancing when there was no belly to be seen, only muscle. Be it technology or women, the world was moving in a direction that kept Fuat happy.

The day after the wedding, Fuat stayed in bed and had Gül bring him chicken broth, painkillers, water and cigarettes. He barely noticed his daughter was gone. He went to work on the Monday, as usual.

How easy it must be to be like Fuat, when the only ache you feel is in your head, and you even know where that pain comes from.

Fuat is at work, Ceren was feeling restless at home and has gone to Gesine's, and Gül is sitting on the sofa; she knows that things are better than they were years ago, back in the tiny kitchen. She knows it, but it just doesn't feel that way.

Hours go by and she doesn't move a muscle; she looks outside and doesn't even notice the light in the garden changing. When Saniye's face appears behind the window pane, she registers the movement but doesn't realise who it is. The image is like another thought that pops into her head, one she doesn't have to do anything about. Only when Saniye waves at her does Gül suddenly find herself back in the kitchen, back on the sofa, back in her body; only then does she recognise her friend and see the young man beside her. Getting up from the sofa, she glances at the clock: still half an hour before Fuat gets home. Then she opens the door to the two of them.

Saniye's eyes are red and swollen, but her whole face is laughing; Gül has never seen the young man before, but he looks vaguely familiar. Before either of them can speak, Saniye bursts into tears and hugs Gül, while the young man smiles shyly.

'I've got wonderful news,' Saniye says, freeing herself from the hug and suppressing a sob. She sniffles and wipes away her tears. 'Do you know who this is?'

'Your son,' Gül says without thinking, without really comprehending what she's saying. *Your son*: that's all that comes out her mouth. Only once they become sound does Gül begin to understand what the words really mean.

'My son,' Saniye says.

'Your son,' Gül says, looking at the man who could be Ceyda's age, but who looks much more grown-up than her daughter. She hugs him and kisses his cheeks.

'Ufuk,' she says, 'Ufuk, you've lifted your mother's heart, may God reward you – come in, come in. I'll make us some tea.'

'It was like in the movies' Saniye says when they've sat down. 'The doorbell rang and I opened it, we laid eyes on each other, and it was as if all of a sudden the music stopped. "Ufuk?" I said, and he said, "Mum?" And then my knees went weak – I had to grab onto the doorframe, I thought I was going to faint. He looks just like my first husband did when we got married. I felt dizzy and I thought, "The floor's gone from under me, there's no ground." Then Ufuk hugged me, and I just let go. You know when you're falling asleep sometimes, you get that feeling like you're falling? It was a lot like that, except I wasn't scared. Thanks be to God, a thousand times over, for letting me see this day.'

Gül has tears in her eyes. 'God bless you,' she says to Ufuk. 'Who knows what you've gone through to get here. May your hands and feet always be safe from harm.'

Later on, in a voice that is bright and young yet somehow sounds very adult, Ufuk tells them about growing up in his grandparents' house, how he first learned what had happened to his family when he was twelve. How he ran away because he wanted to visit his mother's father in prison, and how he actually managed to find the old man and got to speak to him a few days before he died. How much he longed for his mother in all that time, how desperately he wanted to see her, how little he cared about his grandparents' claims that she was the daughter of a murderer and probably a whore. 'Whore or not, she's still my mother,' he said. 'And nothing and no one can stop me, I'm going to go to Germany and find her.'

His tea goes cold while he's telling them how he hitched a ride from a lorry driver transporting freight to Germany, how he spent the long journey thinking about the fact that he would soon be standing at his mother's door, laying eyes on the woman who gave birth to him. How scared he was when he stood outside the house, a fear so great he almost wished he could turn right round and leave; how, even as he rang the doorbell, he thought he could pretend he was someone else. How he wouldn't wish their separation on his worst enemy.

As Ufuk speaks, Gül has to keep wiping the tears from her eyes.

All her worries are gone; she lets herself be moved by a story all about another kind of grief, a grief so close to her heart it's as if it's always lived there.

'What did Yılmaz say?' she asks.

'Yılmaz!' Saniye says, startled. 'I completely forgot about him! When Ufuk turned up, I was so giddy that I didn't know what to do, so we came to you. Yılmaz must be home by now, he'll be wondering where I am. I'll call him and tell him to come here.'

'Alright, Fuat and Ceren will be home any minute – we can all eat together. Or are you tired, son, perhaps you'd like a little lie-down?'

'No, no,' Ufuk replies. 'How could I sleep now?'

'It beggars belief,' Fuat says when he hears the story. 'It really beggars belief. You'll go far in this life, my boy. Anyone as ambitious, wily and brave as you is bound to grow up to be a proper man. Your mother needn't worry about you. What do you fancy drinking? A whisky, or perhaps you'd prefer a rakı?'

Gül notices that Saniye, sitting next to her, holds her breath when she hears this question. She seeks Fuat's gaze to signal to him that he'd be better off not offering anything to Ufuk, but her husband is already opening the fridge, where he keeps his whisky.

'No, thank you,' Ufuk says. 'Thanks, but I don't drink.'

Gül hears Saniye exhale and sees her face relax, but Fuat can hardly conceal his disappointment.

'You're big and man enough to come all the way from deepest Malatya off your own bat, but you won't have a drop? You're not one of those religious types, are you?'

'No, no, God forbid! I just don't like the taste,' Ufuk says.

'How about a beer?'

Now Fuat wants to know for sure.

'No thanks, not for me.'

Yılmaz's eyes are red, but not as if he's been crying. His eyelids are drooping a little, like he's tired; he seems a bit strange to Gül. Saniye hasn't told him anything yet; all she said was that he should come over. When Yılmaz sees Ufuk, his mouth opens and shuts without producing a sound. For a few moments, he looks bewildered, shutting his mouth, opening it again: it's the only movement in the room. Everyone else just looks at Yılmaz, trying to understand what's going on. Just as the silence is starting to get uncomfortable, Yılmaz says: 'I knew your father. You're the spit of him. Come here, son, let me give you a hug.'

Now the others are standing there, mouths agape.

'Mustafa, Mustafa, there are hundreds of Mustafas! How was I supposed to know that Saniye had been married to one I knew? He was still a bachelor when I knew him – we went out drinking together a few times in a pub in Malatya. Mustafa would get aggressive when he'd had too much to drink, but he was a good bloke, may God have mercy on his soul. I don't know what he was doing back then. We were young and one of my uncles was living in the city and trading in flour, so I went to work for him because I wanted to earn some money for my studies. He had me lugging sacks of it around and, in the evenings, I'd treat myself to a few glasses with Mustafa. He was doing all sorts of deals – dodgy deals, if you ask me. And all of a sudden, he was gone.'

'It beggars belief,' Fuat says, turning to Saniye. 'And this is the man you found in Germany: one of your first husband's old drinking buddies. What a world, what a life! What do you fancy drinking, my friend?' he asks Yılmaz now.

'Just a beer.'

'We've got reason to celebrate.'

'Yes, but I'll stick to the beer today.'

'What a world,' Fuat says. 'It's incredible. One doesn't like booze, the other only wants a beer. Come on, Yılmaz, beer? It's basically water. Even a little sip of poison wouldn't kill you. We've got cause to celebrate, surely you don't want me to drink alone? Just a little drop of the hard stuff.'

'OK, but really, just a tiny one,' Yılmaz says.

Now his eyes are red, but there's a glimmer in them too, one Gül can't quite place.

Gül is coming to fear the time when Fuat comes home from work, because they argue almost every day. There's always a pretext – the food's not spicy enough, the Coke's not cold enough, or his wife is obsessed with cleaning. There's always a beginning, and whatever that beginning may be, it almost always leads to Fuat saying: 'Get yourself a job. You can't sit around here all day long, that's not what we came here for. One wage packet and three mouths to feed. We can't get far on that, let alone secure our future in Turkey.'

Gül sits in the kitchen, wondering what to do. Perhaps Fuat is annoyed that he has to go to work every day while she stays at home. Perhaps he doesn't like his job. Perhaps it's really all about the money.

But no matter how hard Gül tries, she can't find work.

A few families from Factory Lane have taken the government's repatriation grant and moved back to Turkey. Maybe they ought to do the same.

Fuat rarely gambles these days and the sum he spends on his weekly lottery tickets is modest, but he still dreams of the kind of wealth that will put an end to all their cares and worries.

The Germans pay a lot of money if you promise not to come back to Germany, and one evening, before the usual fight can break out, Gül says: 'I've been thinking, you know.'

'What've you been thinking? That you'll get a job by sitting around at home?'

'No. We've been here so long now. We've got a finished house in Turkey, we've got fields and a plot of land. Why should we go on working our fingers to the bone here, when we've got everything we need there? Maybe we should apply for that return money as well. It's a lot of money, we could…'

Fuat interrupts: '…we could sit around all day because there's no work over there. How many years would the money last us: three, four, five? And even if I did have a job, you hardly earn anything there. I'm not stupid, I'm not quitting a job at Mercedes just because my wife can't find work in Germany and wants to go back home with her tail between her legs! You can forget that. You women, the ideas you have. Me, leave a good job to go and twiddle my thumbs back home in Turkey? Does that make sense to you, does it? You're welcome to go if you like.'

Gül looks at him. 'Would you come later?'

'Yes,' Fuat says, 'I'd come later.'

He doesn't look at her while he says this; Gül prefers to hear the words and not his tone of voice as he speaks them.

More and more, Ceren and her mother sit together on the couch in the kitchen, their legs touching. Ceren leans up against Gül, feels her arms around her, rests her hand on her mother's thigh. She tells her about school, about Gesine, how she feels with her sister gone, about her dreams, a joke she heard the other day, the strong wind last night, little things that fill a whole life because they're always there. Gül, though, talks about things past, about her grandmother's eyesight that got worse and worse until she went blind, though she could still tell everyone by their footsteps and even knew when Gül had put on weight. The grandmother who had many complaints about her first daughter-in-law, Gül's real mother Fatma, until the blacksmith came up with the idea of pretending to beat his wife behind closed doors to allay his mother's jealousy. Gül talks about her father, who always said his first wife was as beautiful as a piece of the moon, and who, after visiting the cemetery, had wished his new wife and his dead wife could change places.

In the hours on the sofa, a world comes alive for Ceren, one she's never experienced. Set against familiar backdrops – the summer house, the house in town, the graveyard – colours and sounds and events shift, all from her mother's mouth. The result is landscapes that exist outside of time; places they can always visit.

Sometimes they just sit side by side wordlessly, the warmth of their bodies mixing, scents intermingling, peace and comfort becoming one, and instead of words, it's the silence that connects them.

And into that silence, Gül says one day: 'Would you like to go to Turkey with me?'

The land of the stories, Turkey. The time that lasts six weeks, Turkey – a single season and so many colours in Ceren's mind, even more than in her big Pelikan paint-box.

'Yes,' she says, not hesitating. 'Yes, Mum.'

'You won't get to see Gesine or your other friends if you do, you'll have to start at a new school and make new friends, you won't see your sister as often, it won't be easy to settle in. Have a good think about it.'

It won't be any different in Turkey to here, where almost everyone on our road is Turkish, Ceren might think, *except that people speak Turkish in the shops and at school as well.* Gül imagines it won't be difficult to get used to it herself; she grew up there, after all. She imagines a shared life will be easier than one spent alone; she'll see her father every day like she used to, smell his sweat and feel his stubble.

Sometimes we try to see into the future, and it looks like a mountain we can't ever climb, and sometimes it looks like a path laid out for us. But it's never as it seems.

Over the next few days, Ceren keeps saying she wants to go to Turkey, while Gül doesn't tire of repeating her doubts. Four weeks after they talked about it for the first time, the two of them decide to leave Germany. Not now, in the middle of the school year, but in the summer holidays, which means Ceren will have almost three months off. Her life in Turkey will begin with her having school holidays for as long as the children there.

'Back to the country we call home,' Serter says. 'Back to our homeland. May God's blessing be with you. That path's closed to me now.'

Gül has bumped into him at the grocer's. He has a tin of white beans in his hands and is turning the can around and peering at it, as if looking for some sign that the contents are poisoned.

'Don't say that,' Gül says. 'Who knows what will happen? Maybe it's on the cards for you too.'

'It's got nothing to do with the cards,' Serter says. 'It's just that place holds no happiness for me now. Look,' he says, putting the tin back on the shelf. 'Just look around, we don't belong here. They've been hatching plans to get rid of us for years. And now they've got this repatriation grant – it's great for people who leave willingly, but one day they'll resort to harsher means. I told you before, they're scared of us.'

'But you said you'd go back to Turkey too.'

'Yes,' he says, 'I deluded myself into thinking that. But if you look at it rationally, the truth is: you're going back to be with people who are like you, but people think I'm mad – I don't belong anywhere now. That's normal for me as a foreigner in this country, but if I go back there, where I ought to have a place but don't, I'll get depressed, you hear me? Depressed. Anyone with an understanding of human psychology could work that out. It's part of my life in Germany to not be wanted, but in Turkey it would push me into an abyss that not even the voice of God could brighten. That path isn't open to a man everyone thinks is mad.'

'And what will you do if they do resort to harsher measures?' Gül asks, not because she believes it but because she doesn't know what else to say.

'I'm well prepared,' Serter says. 'How? I can't reveal that to you. But that scheming woman Mevlüde never managed to poison me. All these adversaries of God who are out for my blood, they've failed. I won't let the Germans grind me down. Don't you worry about me.'

On the way home, Gül wonders whether Serter is the loneliest person she knows. And whether he feels lonely himself, or whether the proximity of God is enough for him. She wonders what the poor man could do about it and why the Lord has punished him like this. Nowhere to call home, no family to speak of: she can't imagine anything worse.

A week before Gül, Fuat and Ceren board the plane for Turkey, Auntie Tanja dies. One morning, she simply doesn't wake up. All the residents of Factory Lane who aren't on holiday yet go to the funeral. For almost all of them, it's the first Christian funeral they've been to. They've seen a few on telly, of course, but here the sun blazes down, their smart clothes don't quite fit, and there seem to be a lot of shades between black and dark blue. Their tears are real though, the grief on their faces not for show.

It's the first funeral Ceren's ever been to, and she's amazed to think there are dead people lying in the well-tended cemetery, full of flowers and candles and ramrod straight paths. In her mind, the dead belong in cemeteries like the one where her grandmother is buried. A jumble of chaos, where simple pieces of rock serve as gravestones; a graveyard where the size of the graves tell you where the children lie; a graveyard where you have to keep your wits about you to make sure you don't accidentally step on a grave and dishonour the dead. A graveyard where you feel afraid.

Everything here is meticulously ordered, as if they want to put death in its place.

Ceren thinks back to the day when she was hit by a car, and her mother came with Auntie Tanja to the hospital. She remembers Auntie Tanja pouring water out on the street as they left for Turkey. How she'd give the children chocolate bars, and how she'd stand out in her garden leaning on her cane at New Year, smiling and repeating the Turkish words *nice yıllara*. She cries at the grave, she cries but she thinks: *I probably never would have seen Auntie Tanja again, whether she had died or not.*

She'll see Gesine again one day, she's sure of it.

Two days after the funeral, they all fly to Turkey together, and it looks like they're flying off on holiday: Fuat, Gül, Ceren, Adem, and Ceyda, who's now pregnant.

III

'What a nation of liars; what rotten, greedy people! What kind of morals do these people have?' Fuat complains once he's put the phone down. 'Where are the men like that border guard who refused to take my hundred lira that time, men like the ones who spent hours taking our car apart? Where are the upstanding men who serve their fatherland? Has there been an earthquake? – did a crack open up in the ground and swallow them up, all ten or twelve of them, or however many there are? I think I'm losing my mind, I've got to restrain myself. Restrain myself, d'you hear?' his voice rises to a shout.

Gül is sitting on a chair in the kitchen. There's a cooker but no fridge, no cupboards, no table, no plates and no cutlery, just one other chair, and that's borrowed from the neighbours, as is the one she's sitting on. The living room is just as bare as the reception room. The master bedroom has two mattresses on the floor, and there's one for Ceren in the second bedroom. There's not a stick of furniture in the house, their words echo off the walls, and they can't help feeling lost as they fall asleep at night. They've been living like this for three weeks now.

Fuat terminated the tenant's contract in good time. And the tenant moved out and took everything with him. All his furniture, right down to the coal stoves, which belonged to him about as much as the taps did. But not just that – he'd also removed the doors from their hinges and taken them with him or sold them before running off to Istanbul with his wife and children.

'If he'd stayed in town, I'd have given him time to buy bandages before I gave him a whupping,' Fuat said, 'but he decided to run away like a woman instead. Taking the doors with him – the cheek of it! May he choke on the bread he eats, that thieving bastard.'

They'd had to order new doors from the carpenter, and shortly after that, they heard the lorry was being held up at customs, even though all the formalities had been seen to. The fridge, the shelves and cupboards, the two televisions, the video recorder, the three-piece suite, the mixer, the crockery, the beds, the clothes: in short, everything they need for their house is in that truck. It's all checked and stamped, and the papers are in order, but Fuat refuses to take the hint.

'It might go faster with a bit of lubrication.'

'I'm sure you know a solution to the problem.'

'You know how the living conditions are in this country, especially for government employees.'

'My son's going to university next year and scholarships are few and far between in these parts.'

'When I tried to bribe them that time, they wouldn't take my money,' Fuat says. 'They left us to stew on the border, tired as we were, and they even took off the hubcaps to check we didn't have a TV hidden under there, a radio or our life savings. And now I've had enough. It's our right, for God's sake. They're not getting a penny from me, they have to let the truck through. We'll see who's more stubborn.'

Ceyda and Adem are staying with Adem's grandparents in their village; Ceren spends her days in the summer house gardens and usually sleeps at her grandparents' house. Though all the children on their road used to play together, they split up into girls and boys now and only mix in the evenings, if that, to play volleyball or dodgeball on the street while the adults sit on the steps outside their houses, nibbling sunflower seeds. They're content just to watch – apart from Melike, who always joins in the volleyball games. The teenagers respect her, not just because she's much older but because she's one of the best, most driven players, who chases down every ball.

Ceren is now the same age her mother was when she got married. As they read photo stories together this summer, Ceren sees her friends from the summer houses with different eyes, knowing she'll be around them all year long.

She's lived through winters in the town, but she was so little she can't remember what it was like. She and her friends sit in the shade of the trees in remote corners of the gardens, smoking cigarettes and scrumping apples, apricots and pears, but she always feels like crying and she doesn't know why.

She would never have seen Auntie Tanja again anyway, her and lots of the others. Most families moved out of Factory Lane after the woollen mill closed; her father has given up the house now as well, to move to Bremen. She doesn't know who or what she's crying for, apart from Gesine. Didn't she do exactly the same things in Germany as she does here? Except the gardens were smaller and the weather colder, except she had to go to school and didn't see her dede, her dede who now hugs her almost every day, puts his nose to her neck and says: 'You're dark like your nene, but you smell a bit like your mother when she was young.'

Other than Melike, all the blacksmith's children are pale-skinned like him. Ceren is his only grandchild whose skin is almost the same cinnamon colour as her Auntie Melike's and the grandmother she never met.

The weeks go by with cigarettes in the gardens, phone calls to customs, sun and sweat, making cherry jam, evening ball games on the street, conversations, endearments and playful teasing, jokes and cut fingers from chopping vegetables, naps in the midday heat and one or more glasses in the cool after sunset, homemade popcorn in front of the TV, and Sezen Aksu on the radio.

Fuat rages almost every day, and towards the end of his leave he has to admit there's nothing for it: he'll have to grease the wheels with a few notes if he doesn't want his wife to be sitting in an empty house for much longer.

Gül is much calmer here. It's not like her first days in Germany, when she sat in the tiny kitchen while Fuat slept in the next room. Now she's in her own four walls, and when her father comes to visit, she puts one of the plastic plates she's bought on a stool and serves his food from the two saucepans her neighbour has lent her.

'Thanks be to God' she says. 'Did we have a fridge in the old days, and was life any worse for us?'

'May the hands that cooked this never suffer,' the blacksmith says. 'It's delicious, where did you learn to cook like this? Not from Arzu, that's for sure. You cook like your dear departed mother. But a fridge,' he adds, 'a fridge makes life a lot easier.'

They've had electricity in the town for many years, but the lines to the summer houses were only laid a few years ago, and since then there's been a television in all the living rooms, a fridge in every kitchen, and the blacksmith has a bare light bulb hanging from the ceiling of his stable so his wife can milk the cow at dawn without the pneumatic lamp.

Gül is calm. The truck departs a few hours after the customs men get their money. She'll make this house a home, she'll see her father every day, she'll send Ceren to school every morning, Fuat will become a voice on the telephone, it'll be up to her to fill this house with joy. A task she looks forward to with confidence.

There are all these people; Gül could ask any one of them, and any of them would be able to help her. But instead she keeps trudging on, feels herself getting hot from the inside out, and it has nothing to do with the sun, and of course it reminds her of the fence around the building site, the one that was there on the Friday and gone by the Monday. She remembers getting lost in Germany, how strange everything had seemed at first, how she didn't know enough German to ask the way. But now, here, where she could ask for help? She feels embarrassed to have lost her way in a small town where there are no buses or trains, just a few taxis and not one traffic light, in the town where she grew up. *The streets looked different back then*, she thinks, and the shopping bags in her hands feel heavier with every step. Why did she decide to try a shortcut, what reason did she have to turn off into this maze of side streets?

Gül has almost no sense of direction. In Germany she could blame getting lost on the unfamiliar surroundings, and then later it was only a short walk to the factory. She never walked long distances on her own, at least not the first time. Even here, in all the previous summers in her home town, she hardly ever did the shopping all by herself. If Fuat wasn't around, one of her daughters or sisters would go with her.

Gül turns right at the next corner, and she's relieved and exhilarated to see her house further along the street. She tells herself it was good that she didn't ask for directions: she was so close anyway, what would the neighbours have said?

She comes here all the way from big old Germany and ends up getting lost in a side street not eighty yards from her house. She's probably so out of touch that everywhere looks the same to her.

'Can you believe it?' Gül says to Ceren when she gets home from school, laughing as she tells her about how she got lost in the side streets with the shopping in her hands. Ceren doesn't even smile.

'What's wrong?'

'The others are always laughing at me. I look completely stupid because there's so much I don't know,' Ceren says. 'They know all the sultans and when they lived off by heart, and all we learned about in history was the Second World War and the Weimar Republic. Today I didn't know the word for "ruler", I'd never heard it in Turkish.'

'Yes,' Gül says, taking her daughter in her arms. 'And I got lost, like I did in Germany in the beginning. Do you know the story about the fence? It's normal, we've moved to another country, we have to be a little bit patient. And now you know what a ruler's called, and tomorrow you'll learn something new.'

Ceren presses herself to her mother and she might be close to tears. Their bodies say: we have each other. Nothing can happen to us.

When they let go, the world is a little lighter.

There's now a garage where Timur's forge used to be. The blacksmith hasn't worked his trade for a few years, because these days you can get everything he made cheaper on the shop shelves, and you don't have to wait.

Just like the coachman Faruk, his son-in-law's father, Timur relies on other opportunities to ensure he and his wife have at least some modest income. He has cows and an orchard, he sprays the other orchard owners' trees with a canister attached to his back to keep pests away, and he does a spot of trading with the farmers in the surrounding villages. Nothing is left of his riches, and like the coachman, he relies on his children for help.

Sibel, who works as a teacher, lives with her husband, a cement factory worker, a little way from her family on the edge of town. She presses a tidy sum into her father's hands every month. After three miscarriages, her marriage is a childless one, and the couple live modestly; they're probably the only people in town not to have a television despite being able to afford one.

Melike lives with her husband and two children in Izmir and sends her father small sums at irregular intervals.

Nalan married a barkeeper in Istanbul and has a daughter by him, and the whole town gossips viciously about how she's apparently been sucked into a swamp of night life and wears outrageously low-cut dresses. When she visits in the summer, always without her husband, she's perhaps a bit more made-up than the other women. She acts like she's a classy lady who grew up in the city, but if she really is leading a dissolute lifestyle in Istanbul, wearing clothes that go against all sense of decency, Gül doesn't really notice.

She also sends money now and then, much less often than Melike, but generally she sends a lot more.

Emin works as a teacher in a province in the east and doesn't send his father any money. He's the youngest, so he sees it as his elder sisters' job to give the blacksmith a helping hand. Gul's options are limited because she has to make do with the 400 marks that Fuat sends her each month, but even she never fails to put a little something her father's way occasionally.

As a child, Gül spent a lot of time in the forge with her father. Later, when she was newlywed, Timur would come to see her at her in-laws' house almost every morning. Now he usually comes by in the afternoons and sits with his daughter in the kitchen which, like the rest of the house, has finally been furnished. He puts his cap on the table, and while Gül prepares lunch, they talk about old times, about how scattered the siblings are now, the weather, the apple harvest, the cows, the enormous German fridge, about Ceren and school, about Ceyda and how the baby will be coming soon, about how Fuat's now living like a bachelor in a little apartment again, about life on Factory Lane, about drying apricots, the caterpillars in the walnut tree, about grandchildren and nephews and nieces, about Suzan, who lives in Italy and doesn't even visit in the summer any more.

All their words resonate with a joy that can't be found on the telephone. How can you quench your longing when your eyes can't have their fill?

Gül hears the sound of her father's moped outside the house, she hears him killing the engine and pushing down the kickstand, and every time it feels like everything in her softens and relaxes, like she's walked half-frozen into a hamam, where warm plumes of steam take away the weight of the day. It's nothing like the telephone ringing in the middle of the night when the connection's finally been made, starting up out of sleep and walking down the stairs in a daze, trying to keep it brief.

Those scheduled calls stopped long ago. Fuat dials the number in Germany, and the telephone in Gül's living room rings shortly after. The couple talk on the phone at least once a week, although usually not for long because phone calls are still expensive. They don't write letters now like they did when Fuat was in the army. People don't write letters any more. Neither Gül nor any of her siblings sits down to put pen to paper; they are connected by words which are spoken.

When Gül feels that longing, she doesn't have to take a letter out of her pocket, one she's known by heart for weeks. She can just speak to her father or her sisters, but not to Emin, because there's no telephone in the village where he works.

The sound now has space, and father and daughter feel free and relaxed. But in this space, feelings emerge that weren't there on the phone and in those summers.

One day, when the blacksmith stays for lunch, his eyes moisten before he takes a bite. They're having green beans with a little mince, and bulgur. Perhaps it's the dish, perhaps it's that the leaves have fallen from the trees, perhaps Timur has spent the whole morning indulging in reminiscences, perhaps this is what happens when you get old. He looks down at his plate, but doesn't sniffle, and nor does the rhythm of his breathing betray him. Gül can't say how and why she notices the glassy tears threatening to run down his cheeks.

'What is it, Baba?' she asks.

The blacksmith looks up and smiles; there are two little tear tracks on his cheeks now.

'I was just thinking about your mother,' he says. 'You know, you were all still so little when she left us. And I hardly blinked twice, and you were all grown up and married. No-one begrudged you it, that's just life: children grow up, get married and leave home. But you didn't just leave home, you went to Germany. Your mother disappeared altogether, but you came in the summer and it was like a dream – then it was as if I woke up at last and you were gone. Then I heard your voice on that bloody telephone, but what difference does it make if a voice comes from Germany or from the Beyond? The others left too, that's the way of things, but I know where they are, I know the names of the cities and sometimes the smell of the streets. How should I know if Germany even really exists? It's harder to believe in than heaven or hell. It's not the distance, my darling Gül – three hours on a plane and then another six hours on the bus, you say. You can't even drive to see Emin in that time, he's further away than you were, but he was still here. Here, in a village without electricity; I even know the accent they speak there. You know what they say, Gül, you know what they say: May the Lord save you from suffering for your children. You're all living, the Lord be praised, but may the Lord never send a parent's child to a foreign land.'

A tear falls into his food now, and Timur sniffs.

Why didn't I ever bring him over to Factory Lane, Gül wonders. *No matter what Fuat said, no matter how much it cost, I should have had him come to visit so he could picture that foreign land, recall its sounds and smells, so he didn't feel he was on the phone to a voice from the Beyond.*

Her eyes are moist, but there's joy there too.

'We'll spend this winter together,' she says. 'And the next one. And the one after that. I live here now, I've come home. For good.'

How hastily we speak such words. How little we look to the future.

Soon both of them will often think of this meal, of the green beans with a little mince because the money doesn't stretch to a decent portion of meat, to the bulgur with tomatoes, on a day in late autumn in this little town in Anatolia. 'Do you remember?' they'll say. 'Who'd have thought it would come to this?'

They'll smile, like they smile on this day, but without the wistfulness, without the pull of past pain. Until a new pain marks the beginning of another chapter.

Ceren doesn't know quite what to say when İlkay asks if she's ever played basketball. Too often over the past few weeks she's been a source of hilarity – when she didn't know what the word for 'ruler' was, when she briefly forgot that a 'one' wasn't a good grade like in Germany, when she fluffed the words to the national anthem, forgot to stand up when a teacher entered the classroom, couldn't rotate her pen between her fingers, didn't understand innuendos, and a thousand reasons more.

It's not that the other kids in her class target her for their ridicule because they don't like her, Ceren knows that. In fact, most of them are extremely nice to her, frequently offering her their help, especially the boys. But whenever she does something inappropriate, the upshot is bound to be peals of laughter.

Ceren has never played basketball, and she doesn't know whether it's a trick question, so she asks her why she's asking.

She doesn't say: *Oh yes, that's that game with the baskets.*

'We could use you on the school team,' İlkay says.

Ceren doesn't reply, waiting. For a laugh, a joke, a catch she hasn't picked up on, as usual.

'Ceren, sweetie, I'm not taking the mickey, I'm being serious,' İlkay says. 'I play point guard, but even if you've never played, we could still use you because you're so tall.'

Ceren is just over five foot six, making her at least a head taller than most of the girls in her class. She towers over her mother and sister, and if she grows another inch or two, she'll soon be taller than her father. She takes size 40 shoes, which will cause difficulties in this small town over the next few years.

Ceren likes İlkay, a short, exuberant girl with hips slightly too wide, and apple cheeks. İlkay has a deep black ponytail and big teeth, often on show because she laughs a lot. She had to repeat a year once, so she's the same age as Ceren, who started college in the bottom year to be on the safe side, even though she'd be a year ahead of that in Germany.

İlkay is quick to make friends wherever she goes; unlike Ceren, she has no inhibitions with strangers and she's a good point guard, as Ceren will come to realise. Over the next few years, basketball will deepen the two girls' friendship. For Ceren, being close to İlkay is reason enough to start playing. But she needs more reasons so as not to stop right after her first match.

She begins by going along to training sessions with İlkay, learning to dribble, lay up and jump shoot, and to fish the balls the other girls lose out of mid-air above their heads and hands. Her height is an advantage and she's a fast learner. After only six weeks, she's in the centre circle at a match against another school as the whistle starts the game, her opponent just a hand's breadth shorter and Ceren terribly nervous. Her mother, who has never seen a basketball match before, is in the stands inside the poorly heated hall, getting even more worked up than her daughter.

Gül sees the referee toss the ball high in the air, sees the two girls leaping and stretching their arms, Ceren rising slightly higher than her opponent, batting the ball to her teammate outside the centre circle, landing, getting the ball passed back to her and dribbling towards the basket, alone.

Ceren is surprised that no one runs after her, though she knows she's faster than most of them. *I can't be that fast*, she thinks, and shortly before the free-throw line she concentrates again. One last dribble on her left, then a step with her right foot, another with the left, jump, throw, and: the ball is in.

Neither Gül nor Ceren understand why the whole hall resounds with laughter. İlkay comes running up to Ceren and hugs her, but she can't suppress a smile. Based on the fact that her daughter is now blushing down to her fingertips, and from the scraps of conversation she hears on either side of her, Gül works out that the score is now 2:0 for the other team, after four seconds' play.

That's the start Ceren gets off to in basketball, and she'll be grateful to İlkay for putting so much time and effort into persuading her not to give it up immediately. That's how it starts, but soon enough the other teams have nothing to laugh at, and they learn to fear her, a player who can win entire games all by herself, if need be.

After living with Fuat for so long, Gül always has Coke in the house, but it sits undrunk in the fridge for weeks until a friend visits with children, who down whole glasses of it greedily and then wipe their mouths on the back of their hands, just like they've seen on TV. A drink for kids and grown-up alcoholics. Years later, Yılmaz Erdoğan will joke on stage about drinking Coke in Ankara as a young boy and how, during summer holidays in eastern Turkey, he struggled to explain what kind of drink it was.

Children and adults probably drink it for similar reasons: because it's sweet. Perhaps Fuat doesn't like the taste of whisky, even though he thought it looked irresistible back in the day when he saw Humphrey Bogart drinking it on screen. So he pours sugar into it, discreetly. For Bogart, it seemed as if masculinity and civilisation began at the moment of distillation, but Coke offers the taste of freedom and adventure. Why shouldn't the two go together?

Gül takes the empty bottles to the shopkeeper on the corner to return them.

'Thanks,' says Hayri, whose shop has almost everything, except for fruit and veg and meat. Bread, washing detergent, pasta, drinks, sweets, chewing gum, rice, flour, bulgur, washing-up sponges, bleach, rat poison, sheep's cheese, yoghurt, sugar, salt, pepper, children's toys.

Hayri makes no sign of paying Gül back, and Gül stands there at first, dithering a little.

'Is there something I can help you with?' the shopkeeper says.

'The deposit,' Gül says, hesitating.

'What deposit? Why should I expect a deposit from you, Gül? – you shop here every day. You're pulling my leg, aren't you?'

He laughs.

'But I paid a deposit for the bottles,' Gül says.

'Then take them back to the place that took your deposit.'

'You took my deposit.'

'Gül, I've told you, you shop here every day! Why would I charge you a deposit? I don't do that with any of my customers. Where would I be if I did? We live in the same district– I'd get nowhere keeping deposits.'

'We didn't know each other when I bought the bottles. It was in the summer, and you charged me a deposit'.

It's only six little glass bottles, the money's hardly worth mentioning and Gül doesn't tend to stick up for her rights. It must be something about the way Hayri sits on his stool; the way his stained jumper stretches over his large gut; his unshaven look and his sneaky, unsavoury grin, that keeps her from just leaving the bottles and going.

'In the summer? How am I supposed to remember that? Come on, now.'

'You don't need to remember, I do. You charged me a deposit for these bottles, I swear, as God is my witness.'

It seems a bit excessive, even to her, taking the Lord's name just for six little bottles. And Hayri clearly feels the same.

'Leave God out of this,' he says. 'What does He know about Coke? Or deposits, for that matter? I can't remember. Why didn't you bring the bottles back two days later? Why did you hang onto them for months? If you'd brought them back sooner, I'd have still remembered, but anyway… Just leave them here. Is there anything else I can help you with? Do you need anything?'

'My deposit.'

'Oh Gül, enough about this deposit. Did you come all the way from that fancy Germany just to argue with me about a deposit? I never charge deposits, Gül. Never.'

Gül knows that she paid a deposit, here, to Hayri. That's the only thing she's sure of right now. She doesn't know whether to laugh or cry, leave the bottles there, or take them with her. Whether to scold Hayri or smile at him.

She simply turns on her heel and leaves the shop.

Outside, the first flakes are falling. How long has it been since she's seen winter in this town? Is it twelve years, thirteen, fifteen? Who can know for sure, and what difference does it make? She's just starting to enjoy the snow, but her anger at Hayri shoves its way back to the front of her mind instantly. *It's ridiculous*, she thinks. The lack of order here, the way whims win out, the habit of rewriting the rules every five minutes. Hayri deceived her; it doesn't matter how small the sum was. The man she buys bread from every day cheated her and grinned as he did it, and there's nothing she can do about it. She could start going to another shop from tomorrow, but people go to Hayri's shop every day, and those same people like to gossip.

She knows what Hayri would say: 'Here comes that fancy-pants Gül, all the way from Germany. She builds herself a big house complete with a Bosch fridge and a Grundig TV, a Sony video recorder, and crystal glasses in her living room cabinets, and God knows what else – and she's so stingy and mean that she demands a deposit from a poor shopkeeper who she never paid in the first place. It's always these wannabe rich types who chase every penny; they're shameless.'

Hayri has never been to her house, of course, but people like to talk, a lot, and Gül is conscious of the looks some of the neighbours give her. She senses the envy and yet she can't convince them that hasn't just returned from paradise; the kind of paradise she can recreate here too, because she has the means to do so.

But isn't it her fault they think these things? Didn't she used to turn up each summer with the car loaded up with everything the shops had to offer? Didn't she spend every summer smiling with happiness and contentment? How were people to know the reason for her good mood was right here and not there, where neither milk nor honey flows?

She told them about the little kitchen she sat in, the street she lived on, the shifts and the rules that never changed, but that kind of thing never got round as quickly as the details of how she'd furnished her house.

Hardly anyone knows how little money Fuat sends her each month; she has to buy coal like everyone else, and a new winter coat for Ceren, and it's a scandal what the shoe shops here charge for a pair of women's boots in a size 40.

When she gets home, Ceren's already back from school, sitting by the stove wrapped in a blanket, her lips blue, shivering.

'What's wrong my girl?' Gül asks. 'Has the school run out of firewood?'

Ceren looks at her, astonished.

'How did you know?'

'I went to school here too, you know. A few things have changed since then, but some things are still the same.'

She hands her daughter another blanket, adds some coal to the stove, sits next to Ceren, kisses her on the ear and says: 'You'll warm up soon enough, don't you worry.'

She tells her about the days when the blacksmith would send wood to the village school, so the children didn't freeze. The school had one classroom and just one teacher for all its pupils. Ceren attends a school that her mother would get lost in, and at the end of the month, Gül doesn't have enough money left to spare more than a dozen logs.

'I almost cried during my typing test,' Ceren says. 'I couldn't feel my fingers any more, I could hardly hit the keys, but I forced myself to. I forgot all about the i and the ı, but when the teacher dictated the first word with a ç, I realised I'm used to a QWERTZ keyboard, the German one, not the Turkish one with an F. There was a sheet over the keys; we had to do it blind, and I got it all wrong. All of it. Every letter.'

In two years' time, Ceren will be able to impress people by touch-typing on both keyboards without making a single mistake, hitting 100 characters a minute on a mechanical typewriter; she'll be even faster on an electric one, but with the advent of computers, the F keyboard will be done away with altogether, becoming little more than a memory, a memory of this test, which she doesn't pass.

Her grades are generally worse than they were in Germany, where they were neither good nor bad. Here she finds herself wondering if she'll pass the school year, and Gül blames herself for having brought her daughter with her.

She's doing fine herself. Or is she? She sees her father every day, she sees her sister Sibel regularly, she's no longer constantly afraid of not understanding something, and she can get everywhere on foot and doesn't get lost any more. When she leaves the house, it feels like she's stepping into a world where she truly exists and isn't just present; where she's more than just a name on a filing card in a factory, another case at the job centre, another recipient of troubled glances because she looks different.

When she goes out in the streets, she feels like she's more real than she was in Germany.

But she still goes to Hayri's every day; she sees the looks she gets in the neighbourhood; sees her visitors surreptitiously feeling the sofa upholstery, inspecting the knick-knacks in her cabinet, the porcelain figurines you can't get here, crystal vases that look more expensive than they are. She notices people eyeing the video recorder, which she never uses when she's by herself. She prefers to listen to the radio while crocheting, or to read short stories by Aziz Nesin or Muzaffer İzgü, which tell of the country's adversities, but still manage to cheer her up.

That winter, Gül sometimes wakes up at night, breathes in and sighs, delighted not to smell alcohol.

All the same, she asks herself over and over whether she made the right decision. For instance, the time Ceren comes home with a huge cold sore on her lip. The size of a five-mark coin. There was no sign of it when she left for school in the morning.

Gül takes a horrified breath. 'What happened?'

Ceren laughs and shows her the palm of her right hand. 'I was scared of this.'

Gül recognises the mark left by a ruler, and her instinct is to run to the school, grab the teacher by the collar and ask him who he thinks he is.

She has never hit her daughters, neither one of them, and her husband has never laid a hand on them either. Who does this teacher think he is, going further than the parents? These aren't little children he's tapping on the wrist; they're young adults, slapped mercilessly on the palm of the hand with a ruler. Gül got hit with a ruler herself, but never so hard that it left a mark. She feels like grabbing that teacher and shouting that she'll wipe the smile off his face if he ever dares to hit her daughter again.

Ceren's laugh, meanwhile, turns into tears. Perhaps because she sees the look on her mother's face. 'You're not angry with me, are you?'

Gül remembers that feeling.

Every moment contains a truth. Yet moments and truths are fleeting; they don't last. Some moments, though, are so strongly linked with a feeling, that the truth they hold never changes. Gül remembers she found the slapping sound of the ruler worse, back then, than the pain. She remembers crying because she thought her mother would be angry with her.

That feeling comes back to visit her, and Gül wraps Ceren in her arms. That feeling speaks the words through Gül, without her having to do anything: 'No matter what's happened, no matter what happens in the future, I'm your mother, I'll back you up. Always. Even if you end up selling yourself on the street, I'll still be your mother and I'll do what a mother does, even though it'll hurt.'

For Ceren, that moment will be forever tied to the feeling of her mother's embrace. Those soft arms and the scent of her hair; that moment when she is relieved of all burdens, all fears, all disgust, all doubt. Gül's old feeling becomes a new one for Ceren – one truth grows into another, fear becomes love, and every moment is forever, even when it passes.

Of course, when they let go, Ceren's cold sore is just as big as it was before.

Ceren tells her mother how the class unanimously decided not to do their maths homework, which no one had understood. They didn't even attempt to solve the equation on paper. What could the teacher do if they all turned up with no homework done? And they had all stuck to their word, even the teacher's pets.

The teacher called them up one after another, handed them a piece of chalk and gave them a chance to solve the equation on the board. Anyone who didn't manage it got slapped with the ruler. Few of them even went up to the board, simply putting the chalk down and holding out their hand instead. Some of them tried in vain to solve the equation and faced the teacher's ridicule.

Ceren sat at her desk at the back of the room, knowing she was going to be hit, for the first time in her life. She hadn't told her mother that she hadn't done her homework. She wasn't sure she wouldn't burst into tears in front of the whole class, to top off all the embarrassing and shameful situations she'd been in since the start of the school year. She knew crying would be far worse than scoring an own goal.

Every time the teacher called a pupil up, he asked who was responsible for their disobedience, whose idea it had been. No one owned up to it, and as the teacher's anger grew, so did the number of blows each person received.

Ceren cramped up more and more, leaving no room for the bad feelings inside her. Twenty minutes she sat there, like someone waiting to wet their pants in front of everyone, and it got worse with every whack someone else was given. Then she saw

İlkay's horrified face staring at her lower lip. Ceren touched her lip, felt the cold sore, and noticed the itching almost simultaneously. A wave of disgust and desperation washed over her, as the sore seemed to grow and grow, and her body got stiffer and stiffer.

'If only it'd been my turn sooner,' she will say later, 'I wouldn't have had to sit there for so long. The waiting was the worst part.'

Not everyone had had a turn, though. After Ceren, İlkay stepped up to the board with the chalk, and although she knew she wouldn't be able to solve the equation, she stalled for almost a quarter of an hour, uninterrupted by the teacher. Either her approach wasn't entirely wrong, or he was clueless too. Cenk did the same after her, but the teacher cut in after a few minutes: 'Put the chalk down, that's utter nonsense. Show me your palm instead. No, no, the left hand, the one you held the chalk in.'

The school bell saved eight students that day.

'It'll be their turn next class,' the teacher announced; he didn't want anyone to say he wasn't fair. Or that he didn't use every opportunity to teach his students maths.

Gül looks at the biggest cold sore she's seen and ever will see in her life, and she wonders whether she made the right decision. And she asks Ceren too.

'But we're together,' her daughter says.

Sometimes Gül thinks the town seems like Factory Lane, only bigger. Like it's gained side streets, none of them tarmacked, and the side streets have branched out further, like the shoots and young branches of a tree. Everyone knows everyone here too – if not always directly, then perhaps by way of one or two others. Kadir the cook's cousin, who lives behind the hospital; Nesrin the teacher, whose uncle Kemal works for the town administration; one of the pipe smoker Fatih's sons. If you go back a couple of generations, there's always a moniker you can use to work out where a person fits.

Gül knows that once upon a time, she could just say she was the blacksmith's daughter and everyone would know what she meant, but she was still little then, and the town seemed enormous to her. Back then she couldn't really imagine that everyone there knew everyone else. She was shy and quick to feel scared.

In a few days, she'll be a grandmother; now people sit politely and don't smoke around her. She was a young woman when she went away – everyone called her kızım: my girl, or bacı: sister. Now she's back, and it's not just her sisters who call her abla: big sister, but lots of people; they greet her with respect. What is it they say? There are things you can't earn without waiting your turn.

I shouldn't be scared any more, Gül tells herself. *I shouldn't feel small just because I only had a bit of schooling and didn't get a proper education.*

The notion that you learn more about life and can make better judgements when you've had a good education will stay with her all her life. This belief falters for a moment at most but never leaves her, not even when she reads that a professor has sexually coerced a student, or when Melike teaches her children to lie because honesty doesn't get you far in life and you have to be a little flexible with the truth. This insecurity will see her grow wise, truly wise, because she doesn't run the risk of being too proud of her wisdom.

'You two are related,' Hayri the shopkeeper says, 'even though you don't know each other. Aysel's grandmother was one of Timur's father's cousins. Aysel went to Germany a few years after you did. She's back for good now too; she *was* married to Medet, the grocer's son.'

Gül doesn't like the way he stresses the word *was* while eyeing Aysel, but she pretends not to notice.

A few words exchanged in the shop on this occasion develop into a chat in the street when they next meet, and before long Aysel and Gül are sitting on the sofa together, drinking tea.

Gül suspects that, beneath her headscarf, Aysel's hair is as jet black as her eyebrows. She has a round face, but her body is rather bony, and even her soft cheeks can't distract from the deep lines on her brow and at the corners of her mouth.

'When we arrived in Germany, we worked in the vineyards,' she says. 'In the evenings, our eyelids would be drooping before we'd got in the door. Back then I thought, *if we work like this for a year or two, we'll be spent, done in.*'

'Vineyards?' Gül tries to reconcile her image of Germany with the idea of vineyards. Where would they have vineyards over there?

'Vineyards,' Aysel confirms, without elaborating. She's not about to let these sorts of questions distract her from her need to tell Gül her story.

'Medet was already hitting me back then – I'd be black and blue all over, to the point where I could no longer tell which bits hurt and which didn't. I had five miscarriages over the years, he beat me that much. He must have had a pact with the devil, to have so much strength left over after work. We moved after a year; Medet started working at a paint factory, and I did cleaning jobs. He wanted children so badly, but how's that supposed to happen when you keep kicking your wife in the belly? He blamed me, said I was barren, insulted me. If our neighbours had been German, I'm sure they would've called the police. I don't know what was wrong with the man or where all that rage came from, he could never quite swallow it. But after he broke my nose and, later on, my arm, I decided to leave him. What made me stay with that animal, the devil's sidekick?'

Gül remembers the pain of breaking her nose, back when she was little. How the doctor had set the bone back into place with a jolt, a jolt that went through her whole body as if the pain wanted to claim her all for itself.

'There was no reason to stay. "Never leave hearth nor home," they say, but I was lucky we had no children. It wasn't a home either; it was more like a boxing ring, except I never hit back.'

Aysel looks at Gül. The expression on Aysel's face could be a smile, but there's something else in her eyes: hope, perhaps, or relief, or maybe amazement that she stayed for so long. Perhaps it's all those things at once.

'We don't really know each other,' Aysel says, 'but for some reason I trust you. I got a divorce, but did things get any better afterwards? Medet met a couple of people and was hoping to get rich quick. He was caught with drugs on him, and now he's in prison. I had no livelihood, and I was sitting there in God's own hell, in Germany, all alone, without any proper work. What was I supposed to do? Spend all my time signing on at the Sozialamt?'

She says it in German, *Sozialamt*; she can't translate it.

'What was I doing in that country anyway? I never wanted to go, it was Medet's idea. I thought it was best if I came back here, to where I grew up.

'My parents are old, they've hardly enough money to live on themselves. Oh, Gül, it's so hard sometimes, even trying to scrape together enough for your daily bread; in Germany I would've got benefits. I thought the people here would at least be warmer, more willing to help, friendlier. But you know how the men here treat divorcees? Like fair game. Have you noticed how that disgusting Hayri gawps at me? He even pats me on the behind; after all, I've no husband to give him what for. I don't even have a brother here, and my father's too old. I thought it would be enough if I left Medet, and then I thought it would be enough if I came back here, but neither was true. I need a new world, a brand-new world. You have to leave everything behind, start again. Ideally in a different language, one you can't be insulted in. But who really wants to start all over again? Who wants to forget the faces of their parents, their siblings, their nephews and nieces? Who wants to stay in Germany forever? It's hard for a single woman here. But in Germany, they would never have seen me as one of their own. Just like it is here, with the Greeks. Just look at them: they've got Turkish names, they don't speak a word of Greek any more, and they've lived here for generations, yet we still call them Greeks and won't let our daughters marry them. But they prefer to marry each other too. You have to leave everything behind, but you never really arrive, Gül,' she says, her eyes so full the tears might flow at any moment.

'I don't know why God has laid this burden on me. If I'd never gone to Germany, Medet wouldn't have made such a mess of me, would he? His brothers, his parents, the neighbours, someone would've helped me, I could've sought refuge somewhere. Remember how I said he broke my arm because I held it up to his face? "Think you can raise your hand to me, do you?" he said.'

Now she cries with abandon.

'Oh, Gül, I'm sorry, I've got no one else.'

Gül hardly dares to breathe. There's so much she doesn't know about, not just the vineyards in Germany.

When Gül thinks of Fuat, when she talks to him on the phone, even when she feels the abscence of another person before she falls asleep at night, there's no longing for him, no matter how much she listens out for it inside herself.

She misses having someone by her side when men stare at her in the street; she misses being able to ask for money again when it gets towards the end of the month; she misses having life in the house, footsteps, cupboard doors opening and closing, the sound of water running into a glass, a sigh from the next room, the unexpected scrape of a cigarette lighter; but longing, the kind of longing she once felt for her children, that hunger that hollows out the soul, makes it fragmented and empty, that ache in the chest, the pain that stays in place even in sleep – she doesn't have that.

She's all the more amazed by her reaction when she sees Fuat again in the summer. He has lost a little weight, which suits him. It must have been sunny in Germany; his face is tanned, and his brown eyes have a cheerful shine to them.

Sudden joy as she sees Fuat getting out of the car, a man who shows no sign of his long journey. Gül is so astounded by the feeling that she can't move, at first. The joy fills her utterly and completely; for one or two seconds, any movement is impossible; her heart seems to be bursting.

Once she can finally put one foot in front of the other, she forces herself not to run the couple of yards to her husband, forces herself to keep face so as not to reflect that joy. She walks towards Fuat, smiling – that she does – and hugs him. She's too busy holding back to tell whether the joy is mutual. Only after two breaths in their embrace does she notice that Fuat is using different aftershave, and her joy is dampened; she feels cheated.

'How was the trip? Are you hungry? Come in – Ceren's gone to the shop, she'll be back any minute. You've got new aftershave,' she adds, and sees Fuat smile.

That's him, stopped at a petrol station outside of town after a 36-hour drive, used cold water in the toilets to arrive smooth-shaven. Not like Hayri, who sits on his stool with fourteen days' worth of stubble, and trousers so covered in stains they'll never get clean.

Ceyda and Adem arrive two days after Fuat, and Gül sees her granddaughter Duygu for the first time. She's surprised this time, too: though she's long been looking forward to this moment, she didn't think it would make her skin fizz as though her happiness wanted to find a way out, in the end settling for tears. The first time she holds Duygu in her arms, she senses she will miss this child; her happiness is tinged with an inkling of the pain to come. Ceyda and Adem drive to Adem's parents' village just five days later, but Gül will have one last chance to see her granddaughter before they go back to Germany.

Gül feels good, even though she notices Fuat has changed, even though she senses he enjoys life alone in Germany. She keeps intending to, but over the whole of the holidays she won't ask him how many years he thinks he'll stay over there. The last few days before he goes back, Fuat grows impatient and short-tempered. Gül is offended because it's obvious he can't wait to get out of his home town, to leave his wife and daughter behind again.

Up to that point, though, Gül sees her husband spending many happy hours in the summer house gardens here and there, praising the weather and the taste of the fruit, the freedom in this country, the freedom not to have to turn up for a shift at six on the dot, the freedom to buy a rakı from the shop at ten o'clock at night, the freedom to enjoy life.

Gül sees him drinking tea, throwing the backgammon dice with the thievish joy born of a certainty he'll win, singing hymns of praise to Germany, spouting tirades against the weather there; speeches in which he impresses his listeners with his verbosity and his comparisons, like unheard records fresh off the press.

She sees his chest growing broad and his heart opening up, and she savours this image of her husband; she savours hearing him beside her in bed, even if the room smells of aniseed liquor, worse in the morning than at night.

But Gül also sees that Ceyda isn't happy, even though she's never sure what's going on in her older daughter's mind. She watches Adem, that young man who doesn't drink, doesn't complain about his work, talks a lot about football, and sometimes seems rather absent. She wonders what kind of problems Ceyda might have with him. In the few days when they see each other, she has no opportunity to ask, but there's a shadow over Ceyda's mood, a shadow that disappears for moments when she holds Duygu.

Gül has no chance to talk to Ceyda in peace, but she does take Ceren aside and say: 'Try not to get jealous because you see that I'm happy. Your father and sister don't make me happier than you do. If you hadn't agreed, we'd never have come here; I don't know how I'd have managed it without you. And if you do feel jealous, then think of all the hours we spent by the stove and…'

She looks for words but can't think of any that could describe those hours by the stove, yet she can tell by Ceren's eyes that her daughter understands her anyway.

The joy of the past weeks doesn't linger on when Fuat has left; instead, things come to her attention that she was aware of before, but that hadn't seemed so important when there was life around her; family life. Melike and Mert also spent a few weeks in the summer house, Nalan was there with her daughter, Sibel and Aziz came by often, and Emin stayed almost two months with his wife Meryem – the blacksmith beamed from morning to night, life rushed past and sought its own path like wild water.

Now that they're all gone, Gül sits alone at home, when Ceren is at school, and wonders why she feels like crying all day long. Not even the sound of her father's moped coming to a stop outside can cheer her up.

When the first leaves fall, she wonders where she belongs, why she still feels so lost in the world at over forty years of age, whether her mother's death cut so deep into her heart back then that it won't ever stop bleeding. Whether she will ever forget the sound of the spoon her father hurled against the wall when he was told of her death. Whether people raised by their mothers feel this way too, never truly whole. Whether their longing weighs so heavily too. Whether it's better to know something and then lose it, or never to have known it. Whether Sibel, who can't remember their mother at all, might not have it worse because she doesn't even know how to quench that longing.

Gül sits at home, held hostage by questions that have no answers, questions that push a person further and further out into an ocean of yearning. Melancholy: a pursuit to block out the emptiness.

It doesn't last long. A few weeks after school starts, there's something different in the air at home: a mood, a vibration that Gül can't quite place at first. She doesn't know if it's to do with the light, whether perhaps she's secretly looking forward to another winter, or whether it's because her father has been embracing her more often because he senses her gloomy thoughts.

She wonders about this change for a couple of days, until one evening she looks across at Ceren sitting in front of the telly, and notices that her daughter isn't following the film; that the images in her mind have lent her face a blissful expression, a gentle smile, as if life were without limits.

She observes her daughter quietly out of the corner of her eye, and her questions and her pain soften at her daughter's smile; Gül is content to mirror the happiness of others.

Only later, once Ceren has returned from the world inside her head and the two of them are getting ready for bed, does Gül ask: 'What's going on?'

'Nothing,' Ceren replies promptly, a little too promptly. 'What makes you think something's going on?'

'How should I know? There's something different about you.'

Red blends into the cinnamon colour of Ceren's complexion, heat washes over her, and she feels the first droplets of sweat appear at her hairline, but she doesn't know what to say.

'Maybe... maybe... maybe I'm tired... or looking forward to next summer... or...'

They're standing in the hallway in their nightdresses.

'Come,' Gül tells her, then walks back into the living room and sits on the couch. 'Come here.'

Ceren's footsteps are uneasy, as if she's forgotten how to walk. She sits down next to her mother, who takes her in her arms.

'Whatever it is, I won't shout at you, and I won't make a fuss. What is it?'

'İlkay's brother, Mecnun, you don't know him...'

Ceren takes a long pause, and Gül wonders how she didn't work it out for herself.

'I'vefalleninlovewithhim.'

Gül chuckles.

'So his name's Mecnun, like from *Leyla and Mecnun*. So you've found the one, then? Have you ever been out with him, to the cafe or the park?'

'No.'

'Have you ever been alone with him?'

'Yes, at İlkay's, but only briefly.'

'And is he in love with you?'

'I think so... yes.'

'What sort of a young man is he?'

'He's calm and kind. Not a show-off and not a ladies' man either. He smokes and he drinks, but not too much, as far as I can tell. He doesn't gamble. He wants to be a teacher. He reads *Cumhuriyet* like Uncle Yılmaz. Some people say he's a leftist. And he has these deep, dark eyes, a bit like a child's eyes, so soft and curious.'

'How old is he, this man?'

'Twenty-one.'

'And what does he do?'

'He's studying German.'

Silence reigns for a few seconds. Cautiously, Ceren turns to look at her mother.

'Where is he studying?'

'In Adana.'

Gül nods.

'And he comes home at the weekends sometimes?'

'Yes.'

'Has anyone seen you together anywhere? You must tell me the truth.'

'No. Definitely not.'

'Good. We must have a few rules. I've got nothing against you seeing this Mecnun, but not in public. And not at İlkay's house too often. This is a small town – we're not to become the talk of it, we don't want to make life difficult for ourselves. Your father can never ever find out about it. Under any circumstances. We'll find a way for him to come here without all the neighbours spotting him straight away. Perhaps we could have him run errands, carry coal for us or something. I'll do whatever I can to create opportunities for you to meet, but I don't want you to abuse that, alright? And if you write each other letters, they must never fall into other people's hands. You can't give anyone an excuse to attack you.'

There are tears in Ceren's eyes when she hugs her mother; she doesn't know whether to laugh or cry, whether it's happiness she's feeling, or relief, joy, love, or an incredible feeling of boundlessness like she might fly.

How wonderful, Gül thinks. *How wonderful that we're here and I can give her this choice. On Factory Lane, we lived right on top of one another; we were trapped.* The town was small too; they wouldn't have been able to meet anywhere in public there either, not without being seen sooner or later by a neighbour. Bremen, they'd have had to meet up in Bremen, and that would have made Gül nervous: two young people in a big city, so far from where she could keep an eye on them. It seems easier here. How wonderful that Fuat is so far away. Tears prick Gül's eyes too, memories come, and that night, mother and daughter sit up until almost two, wrapped in blankets in the living room. Gül tells her about meeting Recep at the village primary school, how he popped up unexpectedly one day in town when she was working for Esra, the dressmaker, and how all her thoughts took on the colour of his eyes. For the first time in her life, she shares the story of the letter Recep wrote to her and which she never read; the letter she threw in the river before she could make sense of the words, because she'd heard footsteps ring out suddenly behind her. She tells her about the lottery ticket he gave her, how it won, and how she had no explanation for how she'd come by it and so told no one. She tells her about the days when she was younger than her daughter is now, and even though Ceren can't imagine her mother at that age, she's fascinated by the pictures that Gül's voice paints in her head. *How wonderful that we're here*, she thinks, too. *Otherwise, I would never have met Mecnun.*

On this night, Gül senses that the path is wide open to her. Her feeling will prove right, but no one can guess how a common path might fork again. No one can see the pain of the future; if they could, they'd be afraid to live, and they wouldn't sit up talking until long past midnight.

'At least yours was here for a few weeks and you got to scratch your itch, but how on earth does that Aysel manage? Once you've tasted baklava it's not easy to go without it for the rest of your life. Once the floodgates are opened, you always need something to plug the gaps. That Aysel, I don't know,' Hayri says, and Gül stands there like someone has poured lead into her legs and rubbed her brain down with ice. Did the shopkeeper really just say that? How dare he? How can he speak to her like that? How can he talk about Aysel that way, and what can she answer? What on earth?

This is the way she'll tell the story later on. None of these questions have entered her head yet – she's so appalled and amazed that, right now, there are no words, just shock. Her stomach hardens and her thoughts freeze, but she senses she has to say something. She has to stand up for herself, otherwise she'll lose face, otherwise Hayri will harass her even more next time. She can't just pretend she didn't hear.

'I don't think that's any of your business,' she says.

'Oh, come on, Gül, you know what I'm talking about. You women talk about it too. Women, all you do all day long is gossip. Why can't I join in, what have I done wrong?'

'You should be ashamed,' Gül says, 'you should be ashamed of yourself.'

She turns on her heel and is just on her way out of the shop, when Hayri says: 'Wait, wait a minute!'

Gül pauses, Hayri leaps up from his stool, and Gül is just about to turn back to him, when she hears him say: 'Aren't I telling the truth, then? Or has she got some man I don't know about?'

Gül heads for the door, hoping he can't see her hands and lips trembling, hoping her back doesn't betray her rage, powerlessness, and the tears about to fall.

Afterwards, she can't remember how she walked the two minutes home, whether people saw her, whether anyone said hello, whether she really held back the tears until she was through her front door.

What should she do? Go to her father? To Aysel? To Fuat? She knows where she won't be going any more. To that shameless Hayri. Never again. Let him gossip around the neighbourhood as much as he likes.

She understands Aysel better now, but she doesn't want to go to her. It wouldn't change anything. There is no Hayri any more. She simply crosses him out of the book of her life. Draws a line.

'We won't be shopping at Hayri's any more,' she tells Ceren that evening.

'Why not?' Ceren asks.

Although she might have expected it, Gül hasn't reckoned on that question. For the second time that day, she's speechless. But this time she's neither appalled nor enraged, nor does the ground swallow her up. Searching for the right words, she looks Ceren in the eye.

'We won't be shopping there any more, alright,' says Ceren. 'You don't need a reason for everything. I won't go in there any more.'

The first time Mecnun visits the Yolcus, his sister comes with him. As he shakes Gül's hand, he blushes and lowers his eyes. He's a lanky man with long limbs and bushy eyebrows that meet in the middle; he looks more mature than a 21-year-old.

'Thank you,' he mumbles awkwardly, but then he looks up and searches Gül's face. His own gaze is open, vulnerable, but confident too.

He speaks quietly and slowly while the four of them sit together in the living room, choosing his words with care and expressing himself well. 'He's nice to listen to,' Gül will say later, but what seems more important is the way he pays attention to little things, like when he hides his tea glass with his hand when he finishes before the others, so that Ceren won't have to make an extra trip to the kitchen to refill it. The way he lowers his eyes but listens carefully, the way his little questions show he's trying to draw a precise picture of the situation in his mind. The way he makes sure not to command too much speaking time, though he's obviously more educated than the three women. In fact, he's more educated than almost anyone Gül knows; perhaps aside from Yılmaz, who doesn't have Mecnun's sense of tact.

'İlkay, come and have a look at my new lace doilies,' Gül says, and the two of them go to the bedroom, leaving the lovebirds alone for nearly an hour. Gül impresses on İlkay too that no one must ever find out, not under any circumstances.

'Who would have thought it; Ceren and your brother?'

'My brother is a very special person, I admire him,' İlkay says, 'and I'm very happy for them both.'

'We went to Germany, so we'd have better chances in life,' Gül says. 'Better chances for us and our children. You can never know what the Lord has in store for you, you can never guess where the paths that seem to lie ahead will actually lead you. I couldn't have given Ceren this opportunity in Germany.'

'Germany, Germany! Oh, Auntie Gül, enough about Germany!' İlkay says. 'That was then; you live here now. Maybe you were Deutschländers to begin with, but now you're just Turkish – stop comparing everything. When Uncle Fuat comes back and settles in properly, you'll forget all about Germany, like we've forgotten the village we first came from. When I think back, all I can remember is a few colours, nothing else.'

She's still very young; life looks easy to her, Gül thinks. She wonders whether this girl, whose great-grandfather fought the Russians on the border, has travelled even further than her, from the mountains of Erzurum to Anatolia, where people speak the same language and yet her family still don't belong. But Gül is glad that İlkay sees her as one of her own, even though she still doesn't feel that way and perhaps never will.

Later, after they've waved İlkay and Mecnun off at the door, Ceren looks at her mother with a silent question. Gül nods.

'He looks trustworthy. And his eyes, the way he looks at you sometimes – it's not fire, it's embers that will burn on and on, let's hope. May the roads be open to you both.'

After this first official visit, Mecnun returns often, usually alone. He comes after darkness falls, quietly, making sure no one sees him, or during the day with some excuse, helps to lug coal or repairs something in the house, and Gül always watches out that none of the neighbours has any reason to say he comes and goes as he pleases or that he's had any opportunity to be alone with Ceren. She knows they're taking a risk, she knows it, but what else is she to do: stand in the way of lovers?

The snow swallows sound. Even if Timur had come on his moped, Gül still wouldn't have heard him arrive. He knocks at the door and calls her name. Gül rushes into the little reception room where they've spent much of the winter; the living room is too big to heat all day.

'Into the bedroom,' Gül says, 'and not a peep. My father's at the door. Take blankets with you,' she whispers to Ceren and Mecnun; there's another knock at the door, and the blacksmith calls his daughter's name louder now.

Gül opens the door, a little out of breath, her heart beating so hard she can feel it in her throat. Her hands are trembling, and she doesn't know where to put them.

'What's wrong? Didn't you hear me? Did you want me to freeze to death?'

'I must have nodded off by the stove,' Gül says. 'Come on in and get warm. What're you doing here at this time of day, anyway?'

He rarely comes by in the afternoons, especially not on weekends. Gül wonders when she last lied to her father. It must have been when she was still a child.

The blacksmith sighs. Gül realises he's in a bad mood, and she feels a little relieved: he's too concerned with his own problems to notice how nervy she is.

Timur takes off his cap, brushes the snow from his trousers and jacket, and walks into the room that Ceren and Mecnun were sitting in just before he arrived. It still smells a little of cigarette smoke, and Gül places a piece of orange peel on the stove as she passes. Her father seems more than just a little moody; he shoves a cushion behind his back as if wanting to punish it for something, and exhales hard. Gül has an inkling of who his anger's meant for.

'Tore it, I did,' he says, 'tore that bloody cardigan to bits with my bare hands. Who does that woman think she is? Fatma and I didn't argue five times in five years; with Arzu, it's nearly five days a week. I ran all the way here, but my temper didn't cool off in all this snow. I'm all hot and bothered, and that woman tries to foist another cardigan on me anyway. What's it to her if I catch cold or not? They want to control you – that's what they want, all these women: "Put this on, do that, don't ride your moped, you're too old. You need a shave, have a wash, buy bulgur, eat less fat, don't stand so close to the stove, don't do this, don't do that, sort that out!" The kids are barely out of the house, and already she's looking for somebody else to boss around.'

Gül has seen her father furious often enough, including the times he's argued with Arzu. But something changed when they lost her grandmother, Timur's mother, four years ago. The blacksmith had been stubborn and proud before, of course, but he was used to listening to women. When his father died young, his mother had run a tight ship at home. She was the reason he married Fatma, and as long as Timur listened to his first wife, things had gone well: their home had been blessed, and they were never short of money or happiness.

He had listened to Fatma and then later to Arzu, but he always used to say that when he lost Fatma, his luck ran out. Ever since his mother died, he's been arguing with Arzu more and more; he's grown headstrong and seems to do the opposite of what she wants, just to spite her.

If she asked him not to ride his moped in the first snow, you could be sure he'd be taking it for a spin soon enough. If she said it was too late to fix the stable roof, that he wouldn't be able to see what he was doing in the dark, he'd take up his tools and get to work. At night he would get up and eat straight from the fridge, making a mess on the floor. He'd wear the plastic shoes he wore to work in the garden, on visits to other people's houses, and explain away the tears in his trousers by saying there must be moths in the cupboard; he certainly hadn't crashed his moped, whether Arzu believed him or not.

And now he's sitting at Gül's while there's a torn cardigan lying in the bedroom at home, a cardigan he didn't want to wear, because he was perfectly capable of deciding when he'd catch cold and when he wouldn't.

'Longing,' the blacksmith says, 'that's how life passes. First your mother left us, and I took that other woman for my wife so I wouldn't have to give you away. Then you left: one by one, my three big girls, Fatma's daughters, left home. And do you know what the teacher said the third time Emin had to repeat a year? "Blacksmith," he said, "blacksmith, your other children weren't like this. What's wrong with this one?" "This one grew from a different field," I said. You went away, all of you. You furthest of all, then Melike moved to İzmir, and Sibel – yes, she lives here, but how often does anyone actually see her? She sits at home painting pictures, a paintbrush in her hand all the livelong day. You all left, all the women in my life have gone, and that woman's the only one left, God love her. You know what I think sometimes? What would the world be like if it felt good to miss people?'

Gül looks at her father, dumbfounded at the question: what would the world be like if it felt good to miss people?

The blacksmith sighs. 'The ones you want are far away, and the one you never wanted makes your life a living hell. Come, put the kettle on – we'll warm ourselves up with tea as dark as rabbit's blood. Just let me sit here a while; I'm not up to going to the coffeehouse. And I'm not about to go home either.'

Gül gets the kettle and puts it on the stove.

After two glasses of tea, Timur starts yawning and says, 'I'll just have a little lie down; it helps to sleep off the anger, sometimes the longing, too.'

He gets up and Gül hastens to say: 'Why not stay in here? It's cold in the bedroom, icy cold. Have a lie-down here on the divan, I'll get you a blanket.'

Even as she's speaking, she realises that she's doing exactly what makes her father angry: *It's too cold. Put a cardigan on.* She doesn't know how he'll react now, but nor does she know how he'd react if he discovered Ceren and Mecnun. She tries to breathe, but she can't. Her heart's racing, yet her ribcage refuses to rise and fall.

The blacksmith doesn't sit back down; he stands there, hesitating.

'It's not all that cold outside,' he says, but Gül's heartbeat slows; she's got a feeling he'll lie down here after all. He still listens to women, if not his own wife.

'I've got…' Gül can't finish what she's saying; she tries to take a breath again. 'I've got things to be doing in the kitchen anyway, you won't be disturbed in here.'

Gül heads for the bedroom as soon as she hears her father snoring. Mecnun is white with cold, *the poor boy, he's as skinny as a beanpole, of course he's cold*, she thinks, though she's almost forgotten what it was like to be slim.

She puts a finger to her lips and notices Mecnun's jaw muscles tensing under his skin; he's probably clamped his teeth together to keep them from chattering. Gül isn't happy having him leave the house in this state, but what else is she supposed to do?

Once Mecnun has gone, without any neighbours spotting him, Gül feels lighter, much lighter, almost thin. She sits in the kitchen with Ceren, and they listen to the blacksmith snoring. *That's my father snoring*, Gül thinks, *that's why it sounds like music to me, not like when Fuat snores*. She gets up and stands at the foot of the divan, observing her father, the few remaining grey hairs on his head. Some patches might still be blond, but you can't tell any more, whereas his stubble was always a little darker than his hair, and the wrinkles on his face make it hard to shave now.

When Gül left for Germany, everyone was still calling Timur 'blacksmith' or 'abi', or sometimes 'uncle'. Hardly any of the younger ones know what trade he once had now; people still treat him with respect, but they call him dede: grandfather, even though he's still a good head taller than most of them.

To Gül, it seems as if she turned her back on her father for a moment, and now he's grown old. What would the world be like if it felt good to miss people?

Mecnun is in town all summer on his university break, but he has fewer opportunities to meet up with Ceren now. They don't want to be seen together in public; they can't be. Remote corners of the summer house orchards aren't safe either, and Fuat could turn up at any moment at home. The lovers end up seeing less of each other than they did in winter. Gül passes on the letters they write, and every time she hides an envelope, she remembers how the cold paper felt on her bare skin with Recep's letter hidden under her sweater.

To find out how her husband will react to Mecnun, Gül says to İlkay: 'Why don't you come and visit us at Eid, bring your brother along, say you're just popping in on the way to your aunt's? That way, Fuat will have seen Mecnun once already and he won't be taken aback when… when the time comes.'

And so Gül, Ceren, Fuat, İlkay and Mecnun sit in the Yolcus' reception room on the second day of Eid, drinking tea and eating baklava while Fuat gets himself in a lather about Turkish work ethics.

'A week ago, a whole week ago I went to the pastry-maker and ordered a tray of baklava. "Of course," he said, "of course, no problem, it'll all be ready at ten o'clock on the big day." And he got me to pay half in advance on the spot. And what happens yesterday? Not at ten, not at eleven, not at twelve, it wasn't until the afternoon that I got my tray – he'd sold it all by the time I got there just after ten! And I had to pick the tray up myself in the afternoon. Has the man never heard of customer service? How can he have the cheek to demand money up front and then sell my baklava to someone else? It's a holiday, he knows he's going to sell more and do good business, but here they just take the money and put their feet up. That's the kind of country we are. As soon as we hear the W in *work*, we start looking around for a wall to hide behind. Cheating bastards, from the pastry-maker to the president, a nation of thimbleriggers, that's us! And he doesn't know how to apologise either. "Fuat," he says, "Fuat, you know it's a holiday, I do what I can. You can't ask more than that." Yes, you idiot, that's why I ordered in advance and made a down-payment – because it's a holiday! If honour was custard, he wouldn't even have milk, that pastry-messer-upper. Honestly, I don't know.'

'Everything works properly over there, doesn't it?' Mecnun asks. 'That kind of thing doesn't happen there. That's why they're an economic powerhouse and we're not.'

'Right,' Fuat says, 'exactly, you've got that right. You summed it right up, even though you've never been there – it's as simple as that, but that pastry man doesn't get it!'

Gül doesn't think Mecnun is trying to get in Fuat's good books, but she's also a little surprised by his reaction, and she's even more surprised by the turn the conversation takes next.

'Some things are clear to see,' Mecnun says. 'They're an economic powerhouse, a state that offers social protections, a state where a lot has been done for workers' rights, especially under Brandt and Schmidt.'

'Hm,' Fuat says, equally bewildered by this whippersnapper, who can't have been two years old when Willi Brandt became chancellor. Is he one of those young lefties? What's he doing here in this small town?

'But nothing's done for the rights of the working class here,' Mecnun continues. 'There's no state safety net here. The only help here is from the family, and other than that it's dog eat dog.'

'Right,' Fuat says, 'no unity. Everyone's out for himself, for tuppence more profit – no one can see further than that.'

'Some things, as I said, are clear to see, but there are other things I don't understand. May I ask you, Uncle Fuat, is it the case that they don't accept us over there, that they look down on us? That we're like second-class citizens?'

What kind of a student politico has descended on Fuat's house on a holiday?

'Racism,' Fuat says. 'You get racism everywhere. Over here, over there, it's not bright sunshine everywhere; the only place there's no shadow is in the desert and that's why you die of thirst there. No, it's not always easy for us there, but with their help we've built all this,' – a broad sweep of the arm. 'If a person's willing to work it's a good country, Germany.'

'Uncle Fuat, forgive me for asking, I've only read a few books and I've never been abroad, but as far as I understand, what the Germans want is for us to be like the heroes in their books. People critical of the world around them, who develop out of their surroundings, strike out along new paths, against the will of society if necessary. In their books, they have people who emerge from struggle as different characters. But people aren't like that, are they? You can't have a whole society like that. That's just what they want to see. We, on the other hand, describe town or village life in our literature, and we rail against the state, seeking the guilty party there. We're not individualists, we don't stand up against society or the family, we stand up against oppressors. But we're a bit behind in that area, isn't that right, Uncle Fuat?'

There's a brief pause, and Mecnun murmurs 'Sorry'. He doesn't usually talk so much; he must have got carried away and taken up too much of everyone's time.

'Yes, you're right,' Fuat says, 'we're not individualists, we're not as selfish as the Germans. We know when to be ashamed. I used to have this workmate, Helmut, and every day I brought him a coffee, every day. My friends started taking the mickey out of me. "Forget it," they said, "he'll never learn – he just goes home after work and tells his wife what an idiot you are. He'll never ever get you a coffee, and he'll never get embarrassed; he'll just keep saying thank you until the end of his days." And I told them I'd go on getting him a coffee every day until he started to feel uncomfortable. Selfish or not, they're human beings just like us. Eight weeks it took, not a word of a lie, eight weeks before Helmut bought me a coffee. By that point I thought it'd never happen. He let me treat him to coffee for two months. Every Monday, I'd think: *surely this week he'll want to return the favour.* All my friends cheered and clapped, but believe it or not, Helmut just grinned, he wasn't embarrassed at all. We'll never be like them. But if we're stubborn enough, they'll end up like us. We have more riches, you see. We're a rich nation, just not economically.'

Mecnun seeks Gül's eyes for a moment, and his look says *Sorry*. He will have many more conversations with Fuat, but he won't get carried away like that again. He'll stick to football, even though his view on that is very different to Fuat's as well, but football isn't played on thin ice; no one runs the risk of breaking through and making a fool of themselves.

It's not until the next day of Eid that Ceyda, Adem and Duygu arrive. They're spending most of the summer in Adem's parents' village, and Gül blames Ceyda's obvious discomfort on that. They've left Germany for a village where they're less particular about hygiene; where everyone sleeps in one room and there's no running water; where Ceyda is constantly worried about Duygu and wants to keep her daughter from catching a bug or getting diarrhoea or typhoid; where, at night, the unmistakeable sounds of someone relieving themselves can be heard. Life in the village isn't easy – maybe that's why Ceyda looks so battered. She looks pale and tired, and when she smiles, the corners of her mouth are all that move.

Eventually, after a couple of days, Gül finds an opportunity to spend some time alone with Ceyda. They're sitting in the kitchen, stuffing vine leaves. Ceren is playing basketball; she's pursued her hobby far beyond the school team, and now she spends hours practising jump shots, layups and crossovers. She likes it when her sweat drips onto the concrete court and the ball slips noiselessly into the bare ring.

Fuat is sitting down by the river with a few friends, doing all the things they used to do there back in the day: drinking rakı, eating sheep's cheese and melon, smoking and chatting. Adem's joined them; he's the only one not drinking. 'The smell makes me feel sick,' he says, pulling a face when someone sticks a glass under his nose.

Duygu is asleep in the bedroom, and the bottom of the pot is covered with stuffed vine leaves by the time Gül says: 'Something's up, isn't it?'

'Yes,' Ceyda says, without looking up. 'I'm pregnant again.'

Gül puts the vine leaf she's holding down, gets up and hugs her daughter, taking care to keep her hands away so as not to stain Ceyda's clothing.

'But that's wonderful,' she says, trying to convince herself that Ceyda's mood is down to hormones.

'Yes,' Ceyda says, smiling for a few moments. Moments in which her eyes fill, despite her attempts to keep her face in check. Then, for a brief moment, half a breath perhaps, it sounds like she's about to laugh. Instead she bursts into tears, and Gül wraps her carefully in her arms again.

'Don't cry, sweetheart, don't cry, there's always an answer to everything. Don't cry, my love, tell me what's the matter. Hush now, that's it,' she says, but she's also aware they haven't been this close for a long time. Cool-headed Ceyda, the one who's got such a good handle on things. Gül remembers her crying *Mummy*.

Memories of sounds bring pain to the surface.

Time heals no wounds. It doesn't let us forget past hurts; it simply buries them under yet more living. But just as the sound, once uttered, exists in the world forever, so too will the pain. It reverberates, and even when you think you've forgotten all about it, music will dredge it back up and hold it to your heart, as if it were a glowing coal riddled with nails.

Hearts don't break, though that's what they always say, and sounds and hurts never leave us. Hearts are soft, they can't break. They simply grow heavier and heavier, and sometimes Gül thinks she can hardly carry hers any longer.

'Don't cry, sweetheart. I'm here.'

It takes several tissues before Ceyda calms down. Her eyes are red and swollen, she sniffles, and once she's washed her face in the sink, Gül gives her some cologne to help her freshen up.

'So what's wrong?'

'We're having another baby,' Ceyda says, peering into the pot of vine leaves. Gül remembers her would-be third pregnancy and the tears she cried over it then. She appears patient when her daughter looks at her, but her head is filled with storylines playing out one after the other, horrible, frightening, harrowing, racing along at such speed that Gül can hardly catch hold of them. Rape, beatings, alcohol, humiliation, broken crockery, split eyebrows, bruises, cheating, the milkman's child, revenge, honour, infidelity – there's almost nothing that hasn't occurred to her in the time it takes her daughter to find the words.

'He doesn't drink,' is the first thing Ceyda says. 'He doesn't drink, ever. When we pulled Baba out of the car all those years ago, I swore to myself that I'd never marry a drinker. And I didn't. He doesn't drink, he doesn't hit me, but sometimes I almost wish he would. He's indifferent to me, completely indifferent. And even though I'm always telling myself it's not that bad, it could be much worse – it still hurts. It hurts so much. I'm not asking that he appreciates the fact that I do all the housework and look after Duygu; that's my job. And I'm not asking that he takes me out or even notices when I'm wearing a new dress. But when I've got a migraine and I've spent half the day throwing up, he comes home from work and asks me why the curtains are shut. I tell him why and all he says is, "I see." Then he opens the curtains and plonks himself in front of the TV. Mum, it's driving me mad! "I was at the doctor – Duygu's had diarrhoea for days," I'll say, and he goes, "I see." Always just "I see." I've never known anyone to be so disinterested. And now we're having another baby, and he's completely indifferent to that too. If he drank or went wandering the streets with his mates, if he worked overtime or he gambled, if there were something that meant I could say: Alright, that matters more to him than I do. But there's nothing. He watches the football and reads the paper, but he's not fussed if he can't do either. It's almost impossible to imagine someone like that, Mum! – it's like he's living under glass, nothing moves him.'

Ceyda shakes her head, pats a little more cologne on her neck, and then she says: 'He doesn't like pasta. Can you imagine! He eats everything else, but he doesn't like pasta. What sort of man have I married? You haven't had it easy either, I know, but at least Dad looked after you when you were sick, he knew when something was wrong at home, he was obsessed with technology, he asked questions now and then, he was present somehow; he'd crawl under the car with a screwdriver in his hand, he fixed things around the house. But me? I live with a ghost. I can only tell Adem's home from the fact that the remote has moved. Mum, sometimes I think I'm losing my mind; he doesn't respond to me or Duygu at all.'

Not a sound; tears run silently down Gül's face. What is she supposed to say? What can she do? What would happen if they got divorced? How would Ceyda manage, all alone out there with two little children? In a small town where all her in-laws live, a small town where she has no one? Was she supposed to go back to her father's house, where she'd be greeted as a burden? Should she return to Turkey? How should she advise her daughter now, how can she help her? She can't say what she'd most like to say, because it would be a lie.

Do what you think is right, consider it well, and act with care; whatever you do, I'll stand by you and I'll support you.

She's standing by her daughter now, of course she is. But her hands are empty.

Gül remembers those times when Fuat was on military service and his parents treated her like a housemaid. Back then she had Suzan to advise her, but who does she have now? Now she has to offer the solid support that Suzan once offered her, but she feels helpless, weak.

The helplessness and pain are wrenched from her in a sob, a sob that Ceyda will struggle to forget, just like Gül has struggled to forget the sound of the word *Mummy* that summer, sixteen years ago.

At Aysel's, Gül is tempted to talk about Ceyda and her problems. Ceyda is back in Germany and Aysel is someone she can trust;

she wouldn't gossip. But at the same time, she has her father's words in her head: *If you don't want people to find out about it, you mustn't tell anyone about it. Not even your best friend. Not even if he's on his deathbed.*

As though Timur had always been cautious, as if he'd always followed his own advice.

Gül is tempted to talk about Mecnun and Ceren, and about Fuat, who continues to evade her questions about when he's moving back. Soon, soon, just another few thousand marks, not much longer – really, do you want an exact date from me? Fuat, not softened by this summer like he was the last one, has instead done nothing but complain since Eid about everything that is wrong in this country. He says everyone is workshy, as if they'd heard too much hard work might make them sweat – but never experienced it first-hand. 'What chaos reigns here,' he says. 'It's a miracle they even have professions, because nobody knows how to do them properly. The painter can't paint, the baker can't bake, and the electrician has nothing better to do than tell his apprentice to get used to electric shocks, they're just part of the job.'

Gül would like to talk about Mecnun and how he apologised to her for being so talkative at Eid; she'd like to talk to feel freer, lighter.

How long has she been friends with Aysel now? And all the things the woman has confided in her. Hasn't she wept in her arms because the past is music you can always hear? Why shouldn't she tell her everything? Why shouldn't she share as well, then breathe easier for a few hours?

Aysel stands to top up their tea glasses, and Gül takes a deep breath and thinks she can at least tell her about Ceyda – only that, she vows, only that and nothing else.

But when Aysel sits down again, Gül notices her friend gazing at her tea, gathering her thoughts. She wants to say something, and Gül decides to wait. *Listen to her first. God gave you two ears but only one mouth, so you can listen twice as much as you speak.*

Aysel looks up and brushes a strand of hair underneath her headscarf.

'Gül,' she says, 'Gül, I think I'm going to leave. There's nothing for me here. No money, no friends apart from you, I'm dead to my husband's relatives, what do they care that he's in prison? My parents are so old, my brothers and sisters have all moved away, what's keeping me here? Yes, I was born and bred here, but look, everything's changed, nothing's the same as back then; now everyone's prepared to betray their neighbour for a handful of lira. There's no point in staying, I'm going to leave. Five people came to visit me at Eid, five altogether. That dirty grocer Hayri sent me meat. Five kilos, even cutlets. That's the way it is now, I'm one of the poor now, and the man goes and says: "Make us the cutlets, I bet you're better than my wife. I bet there's plenty of things you can do better than my wife. When shall I come over?" I've put up with a lot from him, but at that moment I wished Medet was there to give his face a polishing until it shone like a jeweller's display. I wished he was there to beat Hayri up so badly no one would recognise him, disfigure him for life. That revolting, lewd fat bastard! He behaves like his wife doesn't know how to open her legs.

'There's no point any more, Gül, I'm crawling through life here. I'll never be able to hold my head high in this town and stand on my own two feet.'

'Back to Germany?' Gül asks, and she doesn't know what upsets her more — that Aysel wants to leave and won't be there for her any more, or the idea that the way back might still be open, that it might actually be better there than here.

'Oh no,' Aysel says, 'not Germany. I closed that book long ago. There's no blessing for me there. No, I'm moving to Istanbul.'

'To Istanbul?'

That option seems even more remote than Germany to Gül. Moving to a huge city where you can get lost? Where the streets are so complex that Gül could lose her way day after day? Where there's all that nightlife, all those drugs, easy women, lowlifes and thieves? A lone woman? Moving to a concrete monster of a city?

'Really, Istanbul? Have you lost your mind? That city grinds people up before you can stop to think. Do you know anyone there?'

'No,' Aysel says, and looks at Gül with a glance that says she's not ground down that easily. She's put up with more than Gül, much more, but she has more courage, too. Perhaps simply because she sees no other way out.

'No, I don't have anyone there, but it's a big city, I'll find a job. I'm not lazy, I can do cleaning, look after children, I don't mind washing nappies all day long; none of that bothers me. Istanbul is big. Rich people live there, and where there are plenty of rich people, there are crumbs enough for us.'

'Istanbul's a place for city people,' Gül says. 'It's not for us.'

'Oh, Gül,' Aysel replies, 'how many Istanbulites are there in Istanbul? You're thinking of the sixties. Half of Anatolia lives there now. Some have got rich, others have to bow and scrape like us, but there's no need to be scared of the city, it's practically ours now. It's not like in Germany, where there were only a few of us. Istanbul is full of Anatolians, Kurds, Laz, Circassians, whatever you like – the only people you hardly find there these days are real Istanbulites.'

'Who says so?' Gül asks, amazed to hear Aysel speaking so knowledgeably.

'Mecnun says so – İlkay's brother, you know him, don't you?'

Gül wonders whether Aysel is hinting at something, if perhaps she has an inkling or even knows something.

'Yes, I know him. He's a student, isn't he?'

'Yes. He's a clever young man. Everything he says makes sense. Don't you think so too, Gül? Don't you think Istanbul is full of Anatolians?'

'Yes,' she says, 'yes, how else could it be? That Mecnun boy's probably right. Istanbul is getting bigger and bigger, where else would all those people come from? Did Mecnun advise you to go there?'

'No, I just happened to hear him talking about it. I've always wanted to go there. There are no answers for me here.'

Gül nods. 'I'll miss you,' she says.

Were someone to see these two women, almost crying and smiling at the same time, filling the space between them with something for which no name exists, not even a sound; were someone to see them like that, the sight of them would lift all weight from their shoulders, the marrow in their bones would run warm through their body, and friendship would sound different forever after.

Gül stares at the painting, and her mouth hangs open. No sound comes from her throat, her eyes don't grow moist, her heart doesn't beat faster; you might well think nothing is happening at all. Sibel stands behind her, off to the side, and if Gül were to turn around, if she could turn around, she'd see how unpleasant this situation is for her sister. But she can't move, she can't even breathe. The picture has drawn her into another time and now it won't let her go.

Sibel has loved to paint and draw ever since she was little; when she didn't have enough paper, she'd use the edges of newspapers instead. And now, as a married woman with no children, she's been devoting more and more time to painting; she's bought herself an easel, ordered oil paints from Ankara and painted picture after picture, which are marvelled at and praised by the few people who get to see them.

Gül knew all of this. She'd seen a few of the pictures, and she will never forget how Sibel once said to her: 'You can learn how to do it. It takes plenty of time and patience, but with a bit of practice there are some things you can get better at, all by yourself. That horse looks alive, doesn't it, almost like it could gallop off at any moment?'

Gül nodded, thinking it looked a little like a horse her father once had.

'Look,' Sibel said, 'All the life is in the horse's eye.'

She covered the eye, and Gül had to admit she was right; now it was just a picture of a horse, one she'd seen often enough before, and not a sight that instantly conjured the sound of hooves.

Gül knew that Sibel was a masterful artist, but she didn't know how many paintings her sister had done. Or what kinds of motifs she painted. She had only meant to pay a visit to Sibel at her house on the edge of town. No one had responded to her knocking, but the door wasn't locked, so Gül just walked in. There was no one inside, and the door to the little backyard was open; Gül went through and found Sibel in the building that had once served as the stable, its gate to the street bricked up long ago.

Gül always assumed that Sibel and Aziz didn't use this space, but she finds it full of pictures. Gül can't even hazard a guess as to how many there are, all leaning against each other and piled on top of one another with little care. Two hundred? Three hundred? More than that?

In the picture that captures Gül's eye, on the large canvas just to her left when she enters the room, there is a breakfast scene. A cloth is laid out on the floor and there are people sitting in a circle around the spread of bowls of jam, butter, olives; a little girl is standing next to a man, who is lunging to throw the spoon in his hand at the wall.

The longer Gül stands, motionless, before the picture, the hotter Sibel starts to feel; she switches slowly from one foot to the other, wishing her sister would finally say something, not wanting to break the silence herself.

Gül turns to face Sibel, who is sheepish and proud, both at once. And all the more sheepish for her pride.

'How… how did you do this, my lamb? Why?'

'You told us about it, didn't you? You told us how Baba threw the spoon at the wall when you told him Mum was dead. I just painted what you told us.'

'It looks as if you were there. Why... how did you manage it?'

Sibel simply shrugs and looks at the floor.

'You're a true artist,' Gül says. 'I knew that already, but this... this one... Have you got more like this?'

Sibel nods.

Two hours later, Gül says: 'If I could paint, I'd paint that too. It's incredible to be able to paint like that. How many pictures have you got here?'

Sibel just shrugs again.

'Sweetheart, don't you want to display them somewhere? What are they doing in the stable? Why are you hiding them? Why haven't you shown them to anyone, not even to me?' Gül asks when they're back in the house, sitting on the kitchen divan.

'Where am I meant to display them? Here, in the town hall lobby, or in the foyer at the administration office?'

'Let's ask Nalan, she knows all those singers and painters and artists in Istanbul.'

'What's the point of the paintings going to Istanbul? And what business have I got with artists and night life? I'm just a teacher at a small-town primary school.'

'I don't know anything about it,' Gül says, 'but your pictures are incredible. The landscapes and animals are fantastic as it is, but the paintings of real life... no one could paint with more feeling than that. And it's not just me, it's not just because I recognise so much of it. Other people would think so too, I'm sure. Other people have to see them, they're so good. That's what's always missing in photographs.'

'Why should I ask for a favour from Nalan, that snooty Istanbul lady? Why do I have to go running after anyone, anyway?'

'Sweetheart, I'd be proud of you. We'd all be proud of you. You don't need to hide away. Why did you paint the pictures in the first place? To sit in the stable and rot?'

Sibel has drawn her feet up at her side and is looking at a spot somewhere in front of her knees, as if there were something written there, on the cover of the divan. It's some time before she speaks. She speaks slowly, softly, but firmly.

'I painted them because I wanted to paint. And because I can paint. Not because I wanted anyone to admire me or feel proud of me. I like painting, you know, I like the feeling of holding the brush in my hand, spreading the colours. Many days it's like I look back at the canvas and I can't believe that I've painted the picture in front of me. It's not like God is guiding my hand; I've had to learn a lot, but something happens that I can't understand or explain. It's like I don't exist anymore, just the picture and peace, and I don't stand between them. That's why I paint, not because I want to show anything to anyone else. Or prove anything. Or earn money.'

'Sometimes Aziz comes home from work and picks up the guitar and plays. It doesn't matter to him whether I listen, if anyone listens, if no one listens. He plays and sings. And sometimes he picks up the saz too, but it's usually the guitar. He plays for himself, because it relaxes him and makes him happy, because he can lose himself in the music. And that's how I paint.'

'But–,' Gül starts, then realises everything she could say in this moment seems immature, childish, as if her sister is wise and she's a sulky little brat.

Is this the same sickly, weak little Sibel she always looked after when they were little, the child who started school a year early because she cried every morning when her older friends suddenly went off to school and left her on her own? Is this the quiet, shy Sibel who always had to suffer Melike's bullying?

Sibel looks at Gül, who simply nods now because she can't think of any other objections.

'It hasn't always been like this, you know,' Sibel says. 'I wanted things to be different for myself once, as did Aziz. Do you think he really wanted to work at a cement factory? But he has his music, and it's helped him. Do you think I've never dreamed of putting on exhibits in Istanbul? Or in New York? Do you think the two of us didn't want children? All people have dreams and wishes they hold onto, but I don't want to exhibit my paintings any more. I don't want anyone saying anything about them. I just like painting them.'

Maybe I never should have moved away, Gül thinks.

Like the negatives of the photos they used to take in the holidays – that's how the summers look now. The summers used to seem long to Gül, though time passed so swiftly. They seemed long to her because they were so full of life; they went so fast because happiness is fleeting, because a laugh sounds brighter and is forgotten more quickly than a dark pain that eats its way into your guts.

But Gül often thought of those summers; of their conversations, the cool evening air, the smell of her sisters and father, the lowing of the cows; of the apples, mulberries and cherries from the garden, the visits to the hamam, the children's voices, the dust dancing in the sunlight, the colour of their hands when they'd freed walnuts from their green shells; of one of her mother's exclamations or just a fart that escaped Nalan in the kitchen and made everyone laugh.

Those summers were a garden planted in her mind, where she could go walking whenever she liked.

But now the summers are short. Even though it's hot for much longer, even though Ceren has three months of school holidays, even though she can savour the whole of them and doesn't have to leave at the end. Fuat comes for a few weeks; Ceyda, Nalan, Melike, Mert, Emin, the children, they're all there for a while. But it seems to be just a couple of days, a diversion, a breath of relief, a break. Now it seems to Gül as though it's not a garden being planted, but a hole being dug. As soon as the others are gone, she falls into a vacuum that makes the summers feel shorter.

So that's what it was always like for Sibel and my father, Gül thinks. *That's how they must have felt all those years.* They stayed behind with a kind of blues, not with a garden full of memories that might help them face the pain of separation.

I thought life here froze to a standstill when I wasn't here, but it was just them getting cold in winter. I enjoyed the summer like I was a raisin, and now I know what it's like to have all the cake around me. Our life wasn't necessarily easy on Factory Lane, but staying behind's not easy either. Not easy at all.

Her pride dictates that she go on telling everyone Fuat won't stay in Germany much longer, but he himself hedges the subject, plays it down and postpones his return to an undetermined date in the future. Her pride dictates that she keep up appearances, even towards Ceren and her father, and even Gül herself believes he will come back; what else is she to think?

That he's glad to be shot of her, that he's living the life he always wanted, that she's worth nothing more than the few marks he sends every month? That she'll grow old alone, and he will too? That they'll only hug their grandchildren together in the summer? That she can be pushed aside that easily? That Ceyda's problems will resolve themselves? Fuat won't take care of them, that's for sure. Fuat, the man who left his daughter behind at the airport in Istanbul.

Gül believes she and Fuat will live under one roof again. She believes it not just because her pride dictates it, not just because families ought not to be torn apart, not just because she sees no other way. No, she believes it because she feels it.

And that feeling will be proved right. Even though Gül can't know that it will be very different to what she imagines.

People like Melike believe they determine their own lives, that they hold the strings, because they can push their will on the people around them. But no one can know where the journey leads, no one gets their ship on the course they wish for – the winds blow whichever way they like, sometimes even backwards, and all you can do is adjust your course. Make adjustments so you don't capsize, don't lose face, self-respect, joy, lustre.

Melike broke with all expectations: she went to university, chose her own husband and moved to Izmir. She's not dependent on her parents and the small-town gossip or the expectations of her former neighbours, but she hasn't reached a safe harbour either. She hasn't got rich like she wanted; she compares herself to her colleagues at the school, to the neighbours she thinks look down on her because she's from Anatolia. She joins in the neighbourhood rat race to show off baubles dangling from wrists, ears and necks, suits made in Europe and cars parked outside the house. No one there cares whether Melike smokes on the street or is seen in male company.

Weddings might be turning points, Gül will think later. At her own wedding, perhaps it was already foreseeable that her husband would follow the call of money to Germany. At Ceyda's wedding, perhaps it was foreseeable that Gül would move to Turkey, that their time on Factory Lane was now over and Ceyda would go her own way.

At Ceren's it was certainly foreseeable, though, she will think later. Anyone could see what changes it would bring. But the paths only seem clear when you stop and look around. When you look ahead, all there is is fog.

Ceren's last year of school is also Mecnun's final year of university; afterwards, he'll train as a German teacher, and he knows that without any advocates or contacts at the ministry, he'll probably first be sent to work in the east.

'Ceren will be finished with school soon. Do you think there's a chance we'll be able to get married this summer?' he asks Gül. 'I know it would have been smarter to discuss it when Uncle Fuat was here. But… I didn't have the courage to bring it up.'

'I thought about that in the summer too, but maybe it's better this way. He might have thought he was being played. You've got to let men think they're the ones making the decisions.'

She only realises who she's speaking to once the words are out her mouth. She looks at Mecnun and smiles. Perhaps he's different. Yes. Ceren is lucky.

'I'll ring him and ask him to come, say we've had a genuine suitor. You'll both have to play your parts well, we can't have him working out that you've known each other this long. Think it over well beforehand, don't make any mistakes, don't blame me, and remember: Don't place stones in your own path.'

Fuat comes home on the plane and only stays for three days. When he sees Mecnun, he can only vaguely remember the young man from his visit at Eid; the conversation with the strange student leftist has all but disappeared from his memory, like many things he finds unpleasant.

Mecnun's parents act humble, flattering Fuat a little, complimenting the house and not making a secret of the fact that they're worse off financially than the Yolcus. But their son will soon be a civil servant, even if a civil servant's salary won't get you far in this country. The children both feel drawn to each other, though, and that seems important to them — they hope Fuat will approve the match and they're sure that gold bracelets, fat as baby's legs, will be slid onto Ceren's wrists on her wedding day. Fuat thinks it over briefly and gives the pair his blessing.

Once Mecnun and his parents have gone, Fuat pours himself a whisky and Coke and kicks back, looking like he's just done a good business deal. He has his dark blue suit on and his face is tanned, but it can't still be from the summer sun. He looks happy. Gül wonders what's made him start going to the solarium, and if he's glad that his daughter is going to marry such a remarkable young man.

'It's nice here,' Fuat says. 'It's been so long since I was here in the winter.' This praise presents an opportunity.

'You could have that feeling all the time, you know,' Gül says, emboldened by his words and his sense of calm. 'It might well be time to leave Germany behind,' she ventures to add. For the blink of an eye, Fuat looks as if he's done exactly what Mecnun and Ceren did so well to avoid, as if he's gone and said too much. It's only the blink of an eye, but perhaps Gül is fooling herself too.

'Yes,' Fuat says, 'yes, leave Germany behind, I will do. I will.'

He takes another sip from his glass, and he smiles.

'Not much longer, with God's help, it won't be much longer,' he says, and looks at the liquid in his glass. Half an hour later, he's with Gül in their bedroom, and Gül realises that something's different. Perhaps it's the long period of abstinence, perhaps it's the solarium, perhaps it's because he seemed so happy this evening – she doesn't know, and can't she put her finger on what's changed. He's not wilder or rougher, not more tender or sensitive; he's just different.

'I wouldn't have expected it of you,' Ceren's English teacher tells her at break time. 'The rest of them, maybe, but not you. Aren't you ashamed?'

'What… what?' Ceren stutters.

It's her final year of school. After all the difficulties she faced when she started, after being the butt of all those jokes, all the times she didn't know how things worked or what those punchlines and innuendos meant, she had grown used to feeling the blood rushing to her cheeks. But now she can go about her business at school freely, confidently. Or at least she thought she could, until her English teacher collared her in the corridor.

'What do you mean, what? Don't act all innocent. You might not have noticed me, but I saw what you were doing. In the middle of the main street. With a young man, and hand in hand to boot.'

Ceren's features relax. She's glad her teacher said 'I wouldn't have expected it of you. The rest, maybe, but not you'. Ceren's glad. Her reputation is unblemished.

'The young man, Mecnun, he's my fiancé,' she says, and shows the teacher the ring on her finger.

'Oh right. Oh, I see…'

The teacher fumbles for words for a moment, then she smiles and says: 'Sorry. You've done well, not even out of school yet and already you've got a handsome man on your arm. Congratulations. What does he do then, this Mecnun?'

'He's going to be a German teacher.'

The teacher falters again now. 'I hope you'll be happy together,' she says at last. 'Everything else is immaterial, everything else is just empty words. I hope you'll be happy, because that's all you need.'

Mecnun and Ceren can be seen out and about together every weekend now; Mecnun comes and goes from the Yolcus without having to keep his eyes peeled for curtain twitchers; the two of them can stroll along the main street arm in arm, and the warmth they bring to each other's lives lets them almost forget the winter. At the cinema, Ceren lays her head on Mecnun's shoulder or rests her hand on the nape of his neck.

'Our engagement is like a great promise now,' Mecnun says. 'The sun seems to shine every day and we're in love, we laugh at how others get it so wrong, and we're ready to take everything as it comes. We can't imagine ever hurting one another, but it will happen. It happened before us and it will continue after we've gone, but I want you to know one thing: I will stay by your side, I'll try my hardest to make us happy. I'll stay by your side as long as I live, you can be sure of that.'

He will keep his promise. But very differently to how he imagined.

Words spoken, plans, premonitions, promises and bad dreams only take on their meaning when you can see the whole story.

Ceren has an almost fiery gleam in her eyes this winter, a gleam that grows in springtime with the anticipation of the summer and the wedding. She doesn't get ill, her face is unblemished by cold sores, and even her grades improve. Gül is happy to see Ceren this way. Every night when she goes to bed, she gives the Lord her thanks. She can't remember the last time she was so pleasantly tired in the evenings, getting into bed without any troubling thoughts.

The days when she speaks to Ceyda on the telephone are an exception.

'How are you?' '
Fine.'
'And you?'
'We're fine too. The usual, you know. I look after the baby. Adem goes to work. Duygu's quite happy to entertain herself.'
'Your sister's doing better and better at school. Shall I hand you over?'

Ceyda's second child is a boy. He's only three months old; they named him Timur, after his grandfather.

Mother and daughter exchange news, but behind the words a darkness resounds, as though each colour were mixed with a drop of grief. You can't see it, but you can sense the heavy weight of worry, the sorrow. Still, the two women don't talk about it, as if to speak it would only make it worse, truer. And it's more than that; Ceyda often assures her she's doing well. Better than in the summer, she sometimes says, on the days when she feels strong enough to bend the truth. They won't say any more on the subject. What use would words be?

Fuat orders everything the wedding planners have to offer, just like he did for his first daughter's marriage. Enough Coke and Fanta to make the children sick, enough whisky and rakı to tip the adults out of their seats, food to feed an army, garlands, streamers, brightly coloured kitsch on all the tables, live musicians who pride themselves in not playing the same old tunes and can take requests from the guests, a team with a total of four video cameras to record the happy day, and two professional photographers.

Say what you like about Fuat, but he's not one to scrimp on special occasions. Why else work so hard, if you can't show it off?

With his tan and the black suit Gül is seeing now for the first time, teamed with a snow-white shirt and a tie with a subtle herringbone pattern, Fuat looks a little like a Mafia boss in a movie. He swaggers around all evening, shaking hands and kissing cheeks, quite the gallant gentleman, dancing with the ladies and posing for photos. It's only when Gül sees his poses that she realises what's confusing her about her husband. It's not his politeness, his slightly insincere charm, not the sophisticated act – it's the fact that he's not there at all.

He walks around and takes care of the guests, he talks, jokes and drinks, but the minute he spots a camera you can tell it's all just a role he's playing. He's not fully present; he's somewhere else, in the place where the films and photos will be shown.

His body is here, Gül thinks, *only his body*.

Like at every wedding apart from his own, Fuat looks dishevelled by the early hours of the morning, once most people have left. He has difficulty focusing, the words slither along his tongue as if it were ice, his tie is loose and his shirt creased. By this point, he has no other option but to hold onto the last vestiges of mental command he can grab, and not send his mind on a journey to who knows where.

'What a shame,' he says to a guest in a similar state as him, 'what a shame I've only got two daughters. If I'd known how much I like these weddings, I'd have had lots more children. Lots and lots. I'd have sired a whole football team, with reserves. It's not like I didn't have the strength for it. But we worked our fingers to the bone, abroad. What a life the rich have: eating, fucking, sleeping, never a care in the world. They don't have to work shifts – they can lie in bed with their wife all day long and get rat-arsed every night. You'd be automatically happy, wouldn't you? Especially if you've got a nice slim one, most of those rich chicks aren't much fatter than a kebab skewer – oh, what a life.

Come on, let's raise a glass to this marvellous party. What, you're not wimping out on me?'

'When are you moving back?' Gül asks her husband later, while he's struggling out of his suit. She hasn't seen him this tanked for a long time.

'Oh, how do I know?' he slurs his words. 'You come back to Germany!'

Gül looks at him. He might just as well have said: *I won't be coming back.*

'To Germany? I took the repatriation money, I haven't got a passport any more. Anyway, what would I do in Germany?'

'Exactly, what would you do in Germany? Stop getting on my nerves with your questions then. We've married off our daughter, you've shed tears because she's out of the house, we've celebrated, now's not the moment to pin me down to a fixed date.'

'Look,' Gül says, gathering up her courage. He's had a lot to drink; perhaps now's the time for truths. 'Look, we got married young, we were both almost children back then. Lots of things can happen in this life. We've brought up two children, we've shared a house and a bed and money and worries, we've spent all these years together. Is there something I should know?'

'No,' Fuat says. 'No, what would that be? What are you talking about? Don't be so impatient, don't keep rushing me, I'll come back, you'll see. God dammit.'

Ceren and Mecnun go on a week's honeymoon on the south coast, courtesy of Fuat. Ceyda and Adem stay a few more days, and both mother and daughter look out for an opportunity to talk undisturbed in all the post-wedding bustle.

On the third day after the ceremony, they sit together on the house's flat roof, halving apricots and laying them out on a cloth to dry, keeping an eye on the door up to the roof. They work in silence for a quarter of an hour. Gül waits for Ceyda to start talking. She anticipates all sorts of things, but not what Ceyda is about to say.

'What will you do? Mecnun and Ceren are moving to Erzurum; you'll be left here on your own.'

'Yes,' Gül says, 'for a year or maybe two, and then your father will come back. He's entitled to his pension here, he'll get a severance package there, and then we'll live here in this house.'

Gül pauses and starts forming the question in her head: *And what about you? What are you doing? What will you do next?*

But before she can say the words, Ceyda surprises her again, saying something Gül heard on the night of the wedding: 'Come back to Germany.'

Gül repeats the words, murmuring.

'How am I to do that? I took the return money, I haven't got a passport any more, no residence permit. And I don't know if…'

'There's bound to be a way if you want to find one.'

'Germany?' Gül says, doubtful. 'Germany, I don't know.'

In a little over fifteen years, Ceren will be back in Germany, in a region with vineyards. As if the country were a magnet with still enough pull, even when the call of money has long since fallen silent and the Germans' murmurings of discontent can barely be ignored any more. As though the country were a drug you can never kick. A curse you can't shake. A promise you don't want to forget. Or a comfort you wouldn't want to go without. Perhaps a home, too, where you value the orderly calm, even though you long for exuberance and warm chaos.

'Think about it,' Ceyda says, and it doesn't sound like a throwaway comment. 'Take your time to think about it, and I'll ask the immigration office what we can do. I'm there, Dad's there – there'll be some way to sort it out. Just do what you think is right.'

Ceyda looks down at her apricots, and Gül lays her hand on the little heap of kernels, some of which have already dried in the sun.

'And what about you?' she asks.

Ceyda looks up.

'Don't you worry about me. Really. We're cut from the same cloth. We don't strike our colours.' It doesn't sound like she's talking up her own courage or anyone else's; it sounds like melancholy music coming from deep inside her.

Music that Gül hears inside herself too, after having laid back content on her pillow for so long. Gül's horizon stretched as far as the wedding, and now she feels like she's already waking up every morning alone in this house, where loneliness echoes off the walls and mingles with worries.

We don't strike our colours. This boat will find a way, the water is wide and the world's a big place.

By the end of the summer, Gül gets used to leaving the TV on all day so the voices can keep her company. She rarely looks at the screen; there are all sorts of new channels, but she takes no notice of what's on. Other people leave their TVs on too, even when they have visitors. Video hire has gone completely out of fashion since the private channels started up, and now all the video shops are folding one by one.

It's just because the life has gone out of the house so abruptly that I'm getting down. It's because the place is too big for one person, because Ceren hasn't got a phone, because I used to be content every night – that's why Ceyda's idea and Germany seem so enticing all of a sudden, Gül tells herself. And she forbids herself from giving it any more thought. What would she do in Germany?

Her father comes to see her almost every day now, and she pops over to Sibel's more than she used to. She chats to the neighbours, always walks on past Hayri's shop, and is happy to take a longer route with full nets of shopping, despite her weight.

She sits in the kitchen, cooks and eats to fight off something she's not sure is grief, boredom, emptiness, melancholy or fear. She sits in the kitchen again, and when her mouth isn't busy her hands are instead – either cooking, doing needlework or turning pages. She doesn't read satire now, and adversities no longer make her smile; she reads novels, foreign novels that tell of other cares and problems, books she doesn't see herself or her surroundings in, as she doesn't want that; she reads as though she's leaving the TV on.

In the year after Ceren's wedding, the blacksmith turns up to Gül's house with marks on his suit on more than one occasion.

'What happened?' Gül asks, the first time.

'What do you mean? Who says something's happened?' the blacksmith replies, a little too promptly.

'You've got marks on your suit,' Gül says, and begins brushing him down.

'Really? Hm, no idea where that's from.'

While she makes a rough job of brushing the dust from the blacksmith's jacket, Gül looks at his calloused, dry hands, which never quite come clean, not even when he uses that sandy soap paste. There are deep, red scratches on his palms.

'Did you fall over or something?'

'No,' Timur says, 'no, no. What gave you that idea?'

'I don't know,' Gül says, then she changes the subject.

Later, walking him to the door, she notices the scratches on the tank of his moped, and the battered pedals, and handlebars, which seem slightly bent.

It's the first time she's realised that her father's had a crash. There will be many more crashes in the years to come; some will go unnoticed, but others will be impossible to hide. Cars will be to blame – that or the state of the roads, or the bunglers at the garage – and no one will be able to persuade him to give up the moped. He'll never seriously injure himself and when he walks away with huge grazes, he'll shrug them off with a smile. Not because he wants to prove anything to anyone, but because he's never been one to feel sorry for himself.

My father will need someone to look after him soon, Gül thinks, pushing thoughts of Germany to the very back of her mind. Ceyda doesn't ask her about it on the phone either. And so the winter passes, accompanied by voices on television, dishes cooked on the gas hob, and the question of why emptiness can feel so heavy.

Gül travels to Erzurum for three weeks to visit the newlyweds. It's so cold there, a cold she's not used to in her home town, even though she can still remember the winter nights when she had to crack the ice in the bowl of water before she could have a drink. But here, a boiling hot glass of tea will be reduced to a clump of red ice if you head to the door, glass in hand, to smoke a cigarette. Gül thinks there's a good side to everything, including her extra pounds, which serve to protect her a little from the bitter cold.

Ceren is pregnant, and she only tells her mother once Mecnun has gone to bed. He's teaching primary school children, something he's not trained for.

"'I'll do my best to learn", he told me, "and if I manage it, then we'll probably be able to leave this province and I'll get to be a real German teacher. We're only here for two years, it'll fly by. This way, I get extra training, too. What have I got to complain about? And we've got our roots in this area: this is where my grandfather's father fought against the Russians".'

He had smiled and taken a sip of his rakı, Ceren says; he takes things on the chin, even though he seems so soft that life could pull him out of shape.

Sometimes, when she looks at Mecnun, Gül remembers Rafa and wonders what happened to him, that little Spanish boy who she played beştaş with in her first days in Germany. She will never find out that Rafa will study sociology in Marburg and move to Madrid after his studies, where he'll work at a press agency. She'll never find out that he sometimes thinks of her too, and that he wishes he could see her again, his friend who, in his memory, will forever be that neat young woman whose smile was so warm and kind, as if it could wrap around his whole body. He'll think of Gül almost every time he hears the word *abrazo*, though she rarely hugged him, and he'll wonder if other people have such enduring associations too.

Ceren is pregnant, my father's getting old, I'm not seeing my other grandchildren grow up, I want to be around for this child at least, Gül thinks, as she sits freezing on the coach on her way back from Erzurum.

Come spring, Gül decides to lose some weight. The extra pounds are a nuisance; it's hard to do the housework and she finds herself getting out of breath quicker. She starts a diet she's heard about from a neighbour. Every morning, she takes a tablespoon of vinegar on an empty stomach, to burn fat, and she eats two hard-boiled eggs twenty minutes before each meal. She takes sweetener instead of sugar in her tea, and there's no more baklava and no butter, no bread with meals, no snacks.

A week in and she can barely bring herself to look at another egg, but she bravely perseveres. Just as she's busy peeling off the shell, there's a knock at the door. Aysel is standing outside. The two women fall into each other's arms.

'I wanted to surprise you,' Aysel says, and Gül replies: 'Well, you managed it! Welcome, my love, come on in, what are you doing here?'

'Oh, don't ask, I had to come back here where I'm registered, for this divorce thing. I'm a bit scared really: they'll let him out in two years, then they'll probably dump him back here and he'll want to take his rage out on me. The rage that got him sent down in the first place.'

'First let me make us something to eat; you've got time, haven't you? You've got skinny in Istanbul – does life over there not agree with you?'

They go into the kitchen together, where Gül puts the peeled eggs in the fridge and starts slicing aubergines ready to fry.

'What can I say? It's Istanbul, it's a big city. It can eat you alive. But at least I've got work, even if it barely covers the rent and the minibus.'

'What kind of work?'

'Cleaning. A new place every day. I get up at six in the morning and I'm back home around seven or eight at night. We never worked like that, even in Germany. There's no piecework and no one hounding you, but I spend my life in rich people's houses. I can't recommend going to Istanbul, no matter how many Anatolians there are there. The traffic, the long journeys, all the people. You don't need anyone to keep you on your toes, because you're never off them. I would have loved to come to the wedding, but I just don't have enough time – you can't go taking leave just like that, your bosses will be straight out there looking for someone new if you're not up to it. Oh Gül, I just thank God that I've got work and I've enough to fill my belly every day.'

'Yes,' Gül says, 'we must be grateful. Even if you look like you're not getting enough to eat.'

The women spend the hours that follow talking about different things: novels Gül has read, series that Aysel watches as long as the master of the house isn't home, neighbourhood gossip, the children in Istanbul who sniff paint thinner, their days in Germany, how they could hardly speak a word of German and how they've already forgotten the little they did know. Gül tells her about Saniye and Yılmaz, and how Saniye's son suddenly turned up, and she'd love to know what the boy is doing now.

The long years of friendship shared in Germany mean less than blood ties in Turkey; once you're back, you lose sight of them. The years pass quickly as the two women fill the room with their chatter, floating in a cloud of melodies that binds them together.

Gül can't help but notice Aysel's sunken cheeks and the circles under her eyes; her friend looks tired, almost hunched, the smile on her face isn't enough to straighten her back.

She's going to rack and ruin, Gül thinks later once they've said their goodbyes. *She's wasting away in that city, day after day, and she's not been there long. Medet couldn't crush her, but it seems like Istanbul will finish what he started.*

How would Gül cope if she could no longer withdraw money from the bank every month? What security does she have? The couple of gold bracelets she owns and a few gold coins, that's all. How far would that get her? And who would she have to fall back on? Not her father or her daughters; not Melike, who she wouldn't want to rely on; not Nalan, who's busy raising her daughter on her own, gaining a questionable reputation; and not Emin, whose stinginess is the stuff of legend. Sibel. Sibel is the only one she can think of. Little Sibel, who was so sickly that they left her out of the bargain when looking for a new wife for her father after her mother died. Sibel, who has captured the past and hidden it in a stable. Sibel, who would take her in with open arms, Gül has no doubt about it. But she doesn't want to be a burden to anyone, she doesn't want to live her life at the expense of others. What did she hear her father say all those times? *I'd rather eat my own dick than go begging at the butcher's for a piece of meat. I wouldn't even take a bone if it was thrown my way. I've earned everything by the sweat of my brow, so I can walk with my back straight and my shoulders high.*

Gül turns the question over in her mind all spring long, losing pound after pound on her diet without ever feeling any lighter. This is the question that keeps her up at night; it's something she's discussed with no one, not even Sibel, though she's tried to ask her opinion about it a couple of times. This is the question that's so hard to ask, like coughing up stones.

'Actually, could you try and find out if there's a way to bring me back to Germany?'

Gül is hanging out the washing on the roof with Ceyda, and her question sounds as airy as if she were asking for a cigarette.

'Yes, sure,' says Ceyda, as though shaking one out of the pack. And as if patting her pockets for a lighter, she adds: 'I'll manage it.'

The two of them don't say another word about it for the rest of the summer.

'It seems like you don't want to come,' Gül says to Fuat. 'The best thing is for me to move back to Germany. Ceren's married and I'm just twiddling my thumbs all day; I'll find some kind of work, even if it's just cleaning.'

The words don't even require courage, though she needed it on the roof.

'How do you think that'll work?' Fuat asks, tanned on arrival for his holiday once again. 'You haven't got a passport or a residence permit; you took the return money. Everyone follows the rules in Germany, so how are you going to manage it? I don't see it working.'

'Ceyda says it will. You don't need to do anything,' Gül says.

'You won't fit in my flat, it's even smaller than our first place in Germany. Where will we put you?'

'It's not the only flat there is,' Gül says.

Fuat picks up the sports section of the newspaper, rather amazed by her determination, but still he doesn't seem to believe Gül will come to Germany; he just nods his approval and turns to an article about Galatasaray.

In the months to come, Fuat will curse himself for letting this moment pass so easily.

Ceyda pulls out all the stops so that her mother can return, and after a few initial difficulties, it looks like it's actually going to work out.

Fuat doesn't know what to say when she calls him on the phone: the flat's too small, far too small, he can't find a new place that quickly, no no, he doesn't want to turn his wife away, how could he? He just needs a bit more time.

He doesn't want her there, and that hurts Gül – how could it not? But what other option does she have? Move to Istanbul? File for divorce and hope for alimony? Count on Sibel? On God? Her daughters? In Germany, she won't starve and she won't be a burden on anyone.

The rejection is painful, whatever else has happened between the two of them over the years; every rejection is painful – but she's determined. She made her mind up at the end of the spring.

Her father is the first person she tells in Turkey. They're having lunch, baked aubergine served with rice and yogurt, and the blacksmith is bent over his plate, not noticing how nervous his daughter is.

'I've made a decision,' Gül says. 'I'm going back to Germany.'

She thinks of the lunch when her father cried: they were eating green beans and minced lamb, it was autumn, and Gül promised her father, still hurting from the past separation, that she'd be there for good.

The blacksmith goes on chewing without looking up from his plate, and Gül wonders whether he might not have heard her. Or whether he might be hiding tears. And how many times she has gone back on her word now.

'Do you remember that day,' he says quietly, 'when we had green beans…?'

Gül nods, and the blacksmith swallows, straightens up and leans back in his chair.

'I thought back then that we'd be separated again. Don't ask me why, I'm not a clairvoyant and I don't have intuitions, but that day I felt you weren't going to be here forever. And Fuat doesn't want to come back – I noticed that when he showed me this house.'

He smiles at his daughter. 'We've seen lots of each other for a few years, we should be glad of that.'

'Yes,' Gül nods with relief, 'yes. And this time I'll bring you over so you can see what it's like in Germany, so you don't have to talk to a voice from beyond on the telephone.'

How can I promise something so wholeheartedly? How can I promise something for his future if I can't even see mine clearly? she wonders. *Why did I say that?*

'You go on over and get settled in,' Timur says. 'Make yourself nice and cosy. Enjoy your grandchildren. And if God gives me enough time, I'll come and have a look at the place, that Germany. When are you leaving?'

'As soon as possible. Ceyda's taking care of the paperwork. It won't be on the spur of the moment, though, it'll take a few months.'

'And this house?'

'I don't know if Fuat will want to let it out again.'

'To someone who takes the doors with him when he moves out.' Gül is astounded that her father seems to be taking it so easily.

'I know now what's coming,' the blacksmith says. 'It's easier to bear pain you've had before.'

Gül has to write a letter to Ceren. It's not the first letter she's sent to her daughter since she moved to Erzurum, but it's the longest and hardest she's written. In it, she tries to explain why she'll be leaving Ceren behind in this country again.

And Ceren answers: *Mum, back then you asked if I wanted to come with you to Turkey, and I said yes, and if I didn't have a husband, I'd come with you again this time. I know you'll do the right thing. Don't worry about us. What could happen to me with a man like Mecnun by my side? He's so happy that he's going to be a father.*

Melike's first reaction when she hears the news on the phone is: 'That's good – you two will soon be earning more again.'

As if that were all that mattered, as if Gül had ever cared about that. Melike and Mert have bought a car: it doesn't impress the neighbours all that much but it's a car all the same, not a broken-down old banger.

Sibel, however, bursts into tears when she finds out her sister is moving away. She cries almost as heartrendingly as Ceren once did at the bottom of the stairs.

Gül hadn't expected so much emotion and she can't console Sibel; the sisters are locked in an embrace and even though it's not time yet, it looks like one of those scenes Fuat always calls *goodbyes with lots of snot*.

'We've only really got to know each other here,' Sibel says. 'The way we are as adults, not how we were as children. Everyday life tied us closer here, and now we have to trust in the shackles of the past again.'

Leaving isn't easy for Gül. It's not easy for her to leave everything behind again, without seeing her new-born granddaughter in Erzurum, to go to a man who claimed for months on end that he couldn't find a flat big enough for both of them. It's not easy, but what other choice does she have? She asks herself the same things over and over. *Where else could I have turned? Which other path could I have walked with my head held high?*

It's spring again by the time she steps off the plane in Hamburg. The city Saniye didn't like. She has a new passport in her bag. Her stomach cramps up as if she might never eat again, her heart seems to have slid up to her throat, she's sweating all over and she feels like she might burst into tears at any moment. How much stranger this country was to her the last time she came, and how much calmer she was back then.

Thank you:

A. H.

Seher Özdoğan, Tufan Özdoğan, Gülten Ertekin, Vedat Ertekin, Nermin Turan, Nesrin Demirhan, Maria Steenpass, Markus Martinovic, Tolga Özdoğan, Lutz Freise, Ayça Türkoğlu, Katy Derbyshire, Sabine Kaufmann, Angela Drescher, Marcel Vega.

The Translators (Would Like to) Note

I'd put this in quotation marks rather than italics, I think, because he's actually saying it out loud. Fuat is a great sayer-out-loud.

This sounds a bit hip for Fuat. 'Bring a child into the house?'

I don't understand this so I've kind of guessed it. Is she saying 'I had this idea and Fuat was mean about it', or is she saying 'Why did I have this bonkers idea?' or something else?
I think your second suggestion is correct, i.e. she's amazed at what a stupid thing she's gone and done. So I think you need to adjust the English accordingly. But only the first sentence.

Not sure about 'thickly hairy'. Perhaps 'all the way up to the thick hair on his chest'?

Katy Derbyshire: How can two people translate one book? By tearing it down the middle and taking half each? By one of them doing a rough draft and the other polishing it up? I didn't like either of those models. The first way, I suspect, wouldn't make for a consistent and convincing voice. And the second seems pointlessly hierarchical and equally unpromising for creating a well-rounded work of literature. So for the first book in the Anatolian Blues trilogy, *The Blacksmith's Daughter*, Ayça and I divided the novel into sections of three or four pages and translated alternating parts.

Nice one!!

I called it a chicken factory but I think it's fine to vary slightly, and it doesn't come up much.

Can this line start with a different word to avoid repeating the little para above?

Keep the German? Not sure, just a suggestion.

Heartbroken at this.
Yes!

Ayça Türkoğlu: We developed a shared style in the first few months of translating *The Blacksmith's Daughter*, so when it came to translating *52 Factory Lane*, we already had that under our belts. In this book, we get to hear more of the other characters' voices – Fuat, in particular, really comes into his own. I always love translating Fuat because he's so sharp-tongued. I know I can pull out all kinds of odd colloquialisms and rude turns of phrase and they'll suit Fuat down to the ground. There's much more humour in this book, I think, and it's a challenge to make sure it lands properly.

Ooh, nice.

Hahahahaha, hilarious and gross in equal measure.

Yeah, eff you, you perv.

Fab!

'off the books'? Or would she be all prim about it?
Maybe 'off the books' below?
Ha, I've slipped it in here!

KD: I suspect (or I hope) one of the reasons why the humour works in the translation is because we egged each other on in our comments, which we inserted as we edited each section immediately after translating. A bit like a running commentary while you're watching TV with a friend – or maybe like a Zoom chat section during a virtual event. Some of our comments were obviously about translation choices, but a good few were simply voicing our appreciation of the book. So there were lols and gasps and winces, extra jokes and shouts of encouragement to the characters, since both of us love them with a burning passion. And sometimes we shared childhood memories…

Tell me about it. Children who'd grown up in Turkey were always much smaller, spindlier than me. And my sister is basically an Amazon, so that blew their minds. You go into someone's home and get given guest slippers, and they'd inevitably be a size 2 or something, and you'd be hanging off the back of them.

I remember my nanna saying something similar when my cousin said she was getting picked on for having a Black boyfriend.

Happy to live in London and be free of the tiny tomato puree tube tyranny of my childhood.
Ha! I'm stuck with tubes. Do we want to make this tomato puree, by the way?

Just change this to 'she needs a permit' even though it's not what it means?
Yes, good thinking.

Is this to do with speed? I do not get the joke.

AT: Working together also meant an extra person to puzzle over parts of the text with. There are a fair number of instances where you're not quite sure what the author is trying to say, in a way that goes beyond comprehension of the words on the page. You might ask the author, but they might have already forgotten why they wrote what they did. Working together gave each of us that extra boost when it came to deciphering a slightly corny joke ('Squeaksqueaksqueak?' Come on), navigating cultural aspects that might otherwise be lost, and daring to move away from the meaning of the text on the page.

I always assume this is way cruder an expression than it seems to be. I can't decide if it's something Gül would actually say. Sounds crude to me! But then so does 'bugger'. Not sure…

I've had a bit of a look and I say we go with bloomers, but let's ask Selim too, just in case. I'm not as au fait with Black Sea lingerie as I'd like to be.

I might have gone overboard here. I think it's great but I thought at first it was Alper who was meant, so maybe change 'he' to 'it'?

Hmm, what do we do here about the difference in attitude towards children and fireworks between the UK and Germany? Almost everyone I know here gives kids fireworks on NYE. Lots of drunk men instructing kids on how to light rockets.

KD: In the case of this book, there are two cultures involved that Anglophone readers might not be familiar with – Turkish and German. And we wanted it to be clear to readers when the Turkish characters were doing things that seem perfectly normal in a German context – like casually allowing children to play with fireworks – and when they might stand out. While footnotes can be a thing of beauty, we never considered them for this book, so there were times when we made cautious additions. In the case of the fireworks we inserted a gentle 'like everyone else in the town' to the description of the family's New Year's Eve party.

This is just a placeholder for 'Arbeit ist Arbeit…'. What do you think – translate it literally (for a laugh), do something lame and explain-y (like this placeholder), or can you think of a corresponding English phrase?
Hmmm. 'Work comes first here'? 'You know what the Germans say: Work is work, schnapps is schnapps.'?

Ah so it's bread and butter!

I misread this as 'turns up after work'. Maybe 'after the morning bell' or something? Don't know if they'd have a bell, just thinking of that film 'We Want Sex/Made in Dagenham'.

This is hilarious and fab, but I wonder if custard just seems a bit out of place culturally. Not that we've been particularly fastidious about this kind of thing in the past. Up to you.

This needs work, but I'm sure this bit ('Es geht nicht nach dem Geldbeutel, es geht nach der Reihe') should rhyme in Turkish.

AT: In this book, as in *The Blacksmith's Daughter*, we put more Turkish back into the text. This included changes like recreating sayings that rhymed, as in the example above, and shifting terms of address into Turkish, where they might have been English in *The Blacksmith's Daughter*. Sometimes we aimed for specificity, at others, we were more relaxed. This free and easy approach felt right; we didn't get caught up in aiming for rigid consistency, but let ourselves be carried along and moved by the story, choosing what felt right at the time. I thought *The Blacksmith's Daughter* was my favourite book in the trilogy, but now I think it's this one, or perhaps the next…

It's 'Gott möge sie nicht bestrafen' but I feel like this has a similar vibe? Maybe? Like the way that old women try to pretend they're not being mean by saying things like 'She's not much to look at, bless her'.

Ürks! Is this awful?

Peak Fuat.

Not sure about this. He says Fremdenfeindlichkeit rather than racism, but would he say xenophobia? It's such a mouthful. The F-word was used much more a few decades ago; now it's more of a euphemism. What are your thoughts?
Yeah, that's tricky. I'd be inclined to go with 'racism', just because it's shorter and really means something. Xenophobia feels more like theory than real-life chat.

This is Gül, right?